INTO THE HEADWINDS
THE SECOND BOOK
TAKE TO THE SKY SERIES

By

Gregory Jonathan Scott

Copyright © 2016 Gregory Jonathan Scott LLC

All rights reserved.

ISBN: 0991467477
ISBN-13: 978-0-9914674-7-1

DEDICATION

To Scott, as always, I love you and will never hide that I do.
Take this flight with me again.

Faye Kennedy
Rebecca Peter
Tracy Shayler
Brenda Wright
Nichole Tran
Anne Lister
Kim Stone

Into The Headwinds – 2nd book / Take To The Sky Series

Copyright ©2016 Gregory Jonathan Scott

Cover Design by Greg J Meier
Cover art is for Illustrative purposes only and any person(s) depicted on the cover is strictly a model.

First edition April, 2016

Published by Gregory Jonathan Scott LLC

http://gregoryjonathanscott.com

https://plus.google.com/u/0/+GregoryJonathanScott/posts

https://www.facebook.com/gregoryjonathanscottauthor

https://twitter.com/GregoryJonScott

Edited by Diane Nelson

'Into The Headwinds' is a work of fiction. Names, characters, places and incidents either are the product of the authors imagination or are used fictitiously, and any resemblance to actual persons, living or dead, business establishments, events, or locales is entirely coincidental.

All rights reserved under the International Copyright Conventions. No part of this book may be reproduced or transmitted in any form or by any means, electronic or mechanical including photocopying, recording, or by any information storage and retrieval system, without permission in writing from the publisher, Gregory Jonathan Scott.

The unauthorized reproduction or distribution of this copyrighted work is illegal. Criminal copyright infringement, including infringement without monetary gain is investigated by the FBI and is punishable by up to five years in federal prison and a fine of $250.000 USD.

THIS BOOK CONTAINS material that includes graphic language and adult situations, which may be offensive to some readers.

Trademark Acknowledgements:
The author acknowledges the trademarked status and the owners of the following trademarks mentioned in this work of fiction: Google Maps & Google Earth, Casper the friendly ghost, Miami Dolphins, Samsung.

ACKNOWLEDGMENTS

The winged

To Diane Nelson, a brave spirit. Thank you for the many hours of wet noodle lashings, pointy fingers, and sneaky hugs. I'm grateful and loved every delightful one of them.

Prologue

There are millions and millions of different dreams. The boring ones. The messed-up ones. And the dreams that involve flying, which can be so amazing, that waking up would be a big downer.

Even though what had recently taken place seemed to be a fantasy to Neil, the experience with Kellan was no dream. It was as real as the stars in the sky.

It started in the urban village of Traverse City, Michigan, where biological and genetic manipulation of human and animal took place. The scientific tests were classified as top secret, and to the governments knowledge, the people on the inside were the only ones who knew about them. It was the place where unusual beings were created. Many. Some incredible, and some not so good at all. There was, however, one experiment in particular so magnificent that he was detained for years in order to keep the secret of his existence protected.

Experimentation and gene splicing of different species continually went on, each and every clinician committed to come up with a fighting machine that could outperform previous versions. It's happening in laboratories across the country. Secret ones. Most operated by the government, or agencies subsidized by them. All of them equipped with wrathful scientists trying to break the barriers of human strength, longevity and unheard of possibilities. It had been achieved by fusing human genes with animal RNA components.

Developments of many kinds were made in those labs and the good offspring were allowed the chance to live, some shorter than others, and the rejects were euthanized. Sadly, that was the way it was done to control the successful experiments, as well as minimizing the possibility of trial evidence getting outside the Traverse City Lab of Modern Science.

There were countless procedures in place that kept the outsiders out and the insiders in, and even with the military's meticulous measures of security at TC lab, there was always the chance that any of their creations under lockdown could break free. They knew that a small percentage of head-strong beings escaping and running free was statistically possible, however unlikely. Even with TC being secure as it was, the improbable eventually happened. Their most spectacular design of all times had fled one of the most secure facilities in the world, spread his wings, and flew away in the night.

That superior man was Kellan, the government's secret weapon with wings. The first of his kind.

The military's plan had always been to create an ominous fighting machine, and after several trials and errors through the years, they had produced Kellan, an angel with the perfect molecular structure of human and Avian. He was intelligent, strong, able to fly, and the unique warrior they had been working toward. He was an outstanding start to the program, and apart from being extraordinarily contrived, with wings, his chromosome arrangement was intentionally manipulated to steer his sexual desires toward the same sex. The intricate splicing of genetic material was done to prevent uncontrolled reproduction the natural way in the off chance Kellan's sperm was viable. It would allow continual improvements of new batches, and keep them along with his extracted DNA under their control. With a male-male mindset, hopefully Kellan wouldn't be enthralled with flying off to make babies. It seemed to be the perfect plan, but what no one anticipated was Kellan falling in love with Neil. That circumstance became a game-changer with implications ranging far beyond research and assets outside direct control of the government.

Could an angel's and a human's love for one another prompt unanticipated trouble for them, or be the strength they need to go on? They'd never know unless they took the chance.

Chapter 1

Outside of the lighthouse on Trout Island where Kellan and Neil found shelter, the wind whistled with boundless strength over the rooftop, tugging at the weakened shingles like every other one was being pulled away. The old lighthouse wasn't getting any stronger as the days passed and the hefty gusts made it feel as though the whole place was being pushed and pulled off balance from every side. It was the kind of shit-storm that could have blown the place down, with minimal effort.

After Kellan's escape from the Traverse City cell manipulation science Lab, and after the government flattened Neil's home in the battle to get Kellan back, the lighthouse secluded on the northern waters of Lake Michigan was Neil and Kellan's home, for the time being. Living in the rickety house was their only choice until they were able to find a place that would be able to keep them safe and hidden as well as that one had.

Outside, the dark lake waters were choppy as huge waves reached for the shoreline like rolling fists. Overhead, the cracks of thunder riled up Dylan, causing his furry ears to stand alert when he barked. The thunderous pops, along with a barking dog, startled Neil and wound Kellan up, too. To calm the rising tension in the room, Kellan ran one hand through the back of Neil's hair while simultaneously stroking Dylan's silky back, comforting the both of them as he cooled his own anxiety with controlled breathing.

While sporadic raindrops picked at the window, they watched shadows stretch across the floor as the sun hung in the sky behind fast moving clouds. As time passed, a few rumbles of thunder lingered in the distance, and the further the booms moved away, the more composed everything seemed to become.

God knew they needed tranquility.

While sitting next to Kellan on the worn sofa in the living room, Neil felt Kellan's gentle hand move from his hair, slowly glide over his shoulders, and then down his back where he latched onto one of the belt loops at his waist. Kellan did that a lot, and to Neil the grip Kellan had on him felt more like a security tether than anything else, making everything seem all right. He liked that about Kellan, how he continuously made him feel secure, no matter what predicament they were in.

Disturbances were far from over. Outside and in. One for sure was the laptop sitting beside them, pinned between the sofa arm and the cushion. It appeared to be vibrating, as if it were begging for them to open it up and have a look at the trouble inside.

Kellan squirmed. "You gonna open that thing or is it going to be me?"

Neil hesitated at first, peered at Kellan with a set of eyes that could have been looking through him, and eventually reached for the laptop to do the honors of flipping the cover back. He opened it and waited for the screen to flicker and come to life. It was slow, but finally took on a brighter existence from the blackened screen they were looking at.

A few bleeps and another flicker from the laptop caused Kellan's wings to recoil, all because he wasn't too thrilled with opening it again. He had ingested enough of what was on it and could honestly use a break.

Out of nowhere the hummingbird that had persistently

followed Kellan around was back, hovering outside the window looking in. Neither rain nor thunder seemed to keep that buggy bird away, which was odd. Birds and bugs don't typically care for storms.

What was that about and why was he following Kellan?

Unable to pull his gaze away, as if he was looking at a streetcar accident, Kellan stared back at the hummingbird and commented, "There's something about that bird that has me a little harried."

Seeing no bird on the monitor, Neil asked, "What bird?" He was confused.

"Out that window, there's a hummingbird that's been hanging around since I left the Lab. It's strange."

"Ah, yes. I've seen it before." Neil looked up.

"Why not let the bugger in. See what happens."

Rotating his head over his shoulder toward Kellan, Neil protested, "Are you crazy? It probably needs sugar water or something sweet to keep its wings flapping and thinks we are here to feed it. Plus, if you feed it, it'll surely stay."

"I wasn't actually going to do it, but you have a good idea. I'll go see if there's anything here that will satisfy its hunger pangs." Kellan grumbled as he stood, shaking his wings to let air at them. It felt the same way a morning stretch would when revitalizing tight muscles that had knotted up during the night.

Dylan quickly pranced over to the window and stared at the bird, sniffing, trying to gather its scent. He yipped once, looked back at Neil and then turned to the window at the instant the bird zipped away. Dylan hopped forward, barked again, and spun to face Neil and Kellan.

Startled by Dylan's second bark, Neil flinched. At that same moment, the laptop flashed and a sealed envelope floated across the screen. Neil baulked when he saw it. "It's up... It's up... And there's another message. Oh shit. What do we do?"

Kellan didn't go any further, turned back around and angled the laptop so they both could see what was there. He glanced at Neil and then at the screen. "Click it and get ready to read. This one isn't going to last any longer than the other one did."

"Aw shit, here goes nothing." Neil dragged the pointer

across the screen, chasing the flying envelope. Finally catching it, he clicked it open.

Within a few seconds, the email opened just long enough for the message to register, then closed and burst into a flash of flames and disappeared. Never to be seen again. Just like the first one.

Unlike the last message that told them to stay where they were, this one mentioned the lab had a classified secret as big as Kellan himself. It was a quick message, not really saying much and at the end it was signed by Buster.

"Holy shit, that was fast. Did you get it? And who's Buster?" Neil asked.

"He's brilliant."

"Who is?"

"Seth. I used to call him Buster, like... 'Hey, Buster... No cheating.' It was a nickname I used when he irritated me. This is good and looks to be a way for him to tell us he's the one on the other end of these messages." Kellan's heart rate went up and his body went hot.

Neil felt the heat emanating from Kellan's flesh and backed away a few inches. "What could be a bigger secret than you? And do you know what he meant when he mentioned 'time for child's play'?"

"I'm not sure, but he could be trying to tell us there's something in the files we loaded on this thing." Kellan took control, spun the laptop toward him completely and started opening one file after the other, hoping to find out what Seth had meant. It had to be code for something. But what? They could be there forever trying to figure out the child's play reference. Instead of wasting time, they went to the folder they saw earlier — the one that originally had shocked both of them — and scanned the contents. It had been their original intention anyway, but they'd become distracted by Seth's splash email.

Neil sat fidgeting, and out of sheer gusto, accidentally finger punched the screen when he saw a folder that caught his attention, and shouted, "Stop! Right there, that's it."

Startled by Neil's quick movement and finger poking, Kellan's wings instinctively snapped open. Once his nerves settled, he slowly brought them back in, wrapping one around

Neil to pull him closer to his side. "What was it that you said earlier? Here goes nothing?" Kellan clicked on the folder Neil had pointed out to open it.

While they picked through what was in that folder, they simultaneously mumbled, "Holy..."

Neil, however, added, "...fuck me in the ass."

Needless to say, Kellan was all for that. Even if he was under pressure.

Chapter 2

There it all was, the evidence that documented why Kellan existed, and why he was kept alive. The government experiments had succeeded with him, and they were planning to create improved versions that could defend the country in undetected ways. The file mentioned many samples of his DNA had been collected and were being stored, from hair follicles to feathers, skin grafts, saliva, and what seemed to be the most important— loads and loads of his semen. All of it was there, and probably many other things if they continued looking.

While they searched through the Kellan files, neither of them noticed the turmoil outside had settled down. The earth didn't seem to be growling anymore, and the only sound was the brush of wind up against the outside walls and the clicks of Neil's fingers tapping the mouse's advance button.

When Neil moved further along, there wasn't any indication as to what they did with Kellan's DNA, no solid information or anything else that either of them could find at the time.

"My Gawd! Could they be making more like me?" Kellan hadn't intended to blurt that out, but the idea of his DNA, and more importantly his sperm cells, being used with malicious intent in combination with other animal's gene sequences was more troubling than he cared to admit. There was a chance those nasty bat men were started by using parts of him. Why else would they extract so much of his DNA? He turned out to have everything the Traverse City Lab was looking for, except the one thing they needed during a war: the urge to kill.

Neil looked at Kellan, staying speechless at first, and then said, "I hadn't considered that until you mentioned it, yet now am hoping those bat men as derivative species isn't the case. But the possibility is all too believable because most of the records we'd come across so far had been true."

Usually Neil was the one turning ghost-white when hearing disturbing news, but it was Kellan's blood that ran cold that time, turning his skin paler than normal.

Kellan grumbled, "What if those Seekers are my brothers, or worse yet, my offspring. You think that's possible?" His pearly white wings drooped.

Not ruling that out since it was conceivable, Neil said, "Those things look nothing like you, and from what we've seen, they were engineered from bats and horrendous monsters from who knows what else. You, my love, are a God blessed angel and nothing that demonic could come from you."

Kellan held Neil's hand tightly, unintentionally squeezing the blood out of it, and pulled it to his mouth, kissing the back of it. His eyes were full of compassion even though everything was so confusing, unbelievably chaotic, and seemed hopeless. He refocused his attention before his thoughts on the matter worsened.

Both turned back to the laptop screen, looking for more.

Opening up another folder labeled 'Seekers', they found answers they were looking for, the main one confirming Kellan was not their father or their brother. That was good news to both of them, Kellan especially.

Although they thankfully couldn't find any documented information that linked Kellan to those flying monsters, what they located showed the science freaks at TC had used DNA from prisoners who had pulled off some of the most brutal crimes ever recorded. It appeared that was a trait looked for when making the beasts. The more horrific mind they could find, the better. The Seekers had no compassion in their souls or a single thought that cared about a life. They were purely engineered to kill, to take out anybody without giving it a second thought. The other parts of those Seekers were certainly from bat. Their hard black eyes, sharp dead features and leathery wings verified that without a doubt. Combining a night scavenger with a cold blooded killer, the result was a seven-foot winged monster.

Kellan backed away from the screen. "I'm relieved to see that bit of evidence."

"You and me both," Neil agreed.

Kellan hoped Neil remembered what the Seekers were capable of, how vicious they were with their ruthless strength, and trusted Neil was ready for them all over again. The bat men were coming, that was a given. TC was government operated and they were known to follow through with a plan to the end. That meant they wouldn't stop until Kellan was back in their custody and Neil was out of the picture—dead, chained to a tree, or caged.

The last time Kellan and Neil were at TC, they successfully carried out their plan at uploading the Angel's and Seeker's files, and destroying the data room after they got them. But how much damage could really have been done to a government-operated facility? The computer servers they obliterated were just a temporary delay, and with projects as critical to national security as Kellan was, backups were second nature.

Their situation wasn't looking good, and there didn't seem to be a way out.

Back when Kellan had fled TC, he'd been hoping for some kind of normalcy. He hadn't planned on hiding for the rest of his life like a hunted criminal or putting the man he'd fallen in love with in danger. Unless Kellan went back to TC, the hunt for them would never be over, and TC officials would be coming after them almost every day of their lives. In fact, the government probably had a good idea where they were and it was only waiting for the right time to strike, like they had done in the past. Choppers and Seekers would be all over them at any moment, dipping and diving at them, tearing up the place. That's how they worked.

Kellan laid a hand on Neil's thigh with an anxious pat and said, "We need to figure some shit out, and fast. Like what our next move should be. Should we stay or go? Any thoughts or ideas?"

"Right now I think we should stay put and keep clear of that Lab." Neil felt confident enough in his relationship to be able to speak frankly. "The best thing to do is to try figuring out what Seth meant by his message. It's gotta be a clue, hopefully a solution to our problem of having to live in no man's land. Why don't we just hold out for a while and wait for another message from him. Maybe he's got a plan already laid out. He's on our side, right?"

"I'm sure he is. Always has been." As much as Kellan wanted to believe in Seth, as much as he wanted to assure Neil it would all work out, the sad fact was he and Neil lived in different worlds. And though Kellan could only guess at what might be coming their way, one thing was certain—Neil had no clue what kind of nightmares might be coming their way. Military tornadoes were brewing, ready to touch down, and the way it seemed, there might be more than one.

Could Kellan live with that and put Neil in the middle of it all?

Chapter 3

About thirty minutes passed before Kellan mentioned they should probably shut down and think about something else for a while. Just as Neil agreed, another flash email appeared, although this time it—instead of disintegrating almost faster than they could read it—it remained on the screen. It was Buster... better known as Seth, their inside informant at TC.

Neil felt more at ease knowing Seth was on their side, even though the secret messages had him on edge each time they came through. They needed Seth, and maybe he would be able to assist with their survival on the outside, maybe he could reason with TC to let them live off site like a real family. Admittedly, that idea was a longshot, but they really needed some optimism, enough to give them reasons for moving forward.

Seth wrote: *Hello, Kellan and Neil. I hope this note finds you. If not, I'll figure another way to reach you. By now you know there are things I haven't shared with you. Obviously. I had no choice; it was the deal for being part of the team. What I need to tell you might be too dangerous in written form so we need to meet instead. Soon. But for now, as I mentioned earlier, stay where you are. Trust me on that. These people know everything and I'm detecting they aren't coming to get you right now or won't try for a few days. They're working at getting their shit together and fix what you busted. Hold tight till I tell you to move. 24-19-18-25-18-15-22-25-22-. Yours truly, Buster. (delete this)*

Before the message had a chance to purge itself, confident that was the way it was going to work, Kellan scrambled and stood, unintentionally hitting Neil in the back of the head with a wing. Spinning frantically, not getting anywhere, he bellowed, "Quick, get a pen, a pencil, anything. Something to write with."

Dylan barked at the commotion, trotting in a tight circle as he did.

Thinking fast, Kellan reached into the fireplace, grabbed a fire-blackened stick and wrote the numbers Seth gave them across the hearth.

Burying his head in his hands, Neil grumbled, "That was weird." He grimaced and stared up at Kellan. "This game of decoding is full of shit." It would be easier if Seth just came out and said what he needed to say.

Kellan was not about to disagree with Neil, but if Seth spelled it all out clearly, it could lead to disaster or death for all of them.

Seth was at risk, even more than they were. He was the one under direct scrutiny, the one who was leaking information and trying to undermine the government's efforts. Add to that, Seth was merely a human, fragile and bound to the earth. Remaining anonymous meant life for him, versus the alternative, which was probably death. The government facility he was involved with was all about foreign and homeland warfare. They knew how to take anybody out with a single needle prick to the neck. They were pros at that, knew what they were doing, and how to handle a leak, or anyone who got in the way. Seth had to do everything possible to stay clear of that pin-prick, but at the same time had to help his friends, Kellan and Neil survive their getaway.

Neil figured Seth would wait before sending another message. It was too risky otherwise. In the meantime, they'd have to be patient while waiting for the next puzzle piece to appear. For now, they'd digest and try to decipher the first one he sent, making sure they kept the codes in order.

Kellan read the first note from Seth one more time before dragging it to the trash bin at the bottom of the screen and deleted it for good. As he did that, Neil stood in front of the charcoal numbers scribed on the hearth, trying to figure out what they meant.

"What do you think he's trying to tell us?" Neil asked.

Kellan's brow looked like a screw had been twisted dead center, right between the eyes, he was thinking so hard. His eyes tracked Neil approaching but it was clear he was lost in his own thoughts.

Looking into Kellan's frosty blue eyes, Neil asked, "What is it?"

Kellan's memory shifted back to when he and Seth were younger. He remembered a game they used to play, one where only they knew what each other was writing. It was their very own secret code, but pen and pencil were normally required. A familiar twinge gripped Kellan's stomach. "I've got it."

Neil's pupils widened with excitement. "What ch-you got?"

Kellan whispered, "Child's play." His brows, darkly knotted with concern, smoothed over, leaving him with a look of curiosity. "We need to hunt for something to write with and on. There's gotta be something here under all this dust."

Neil reached for Kellan's arm, gripping him by the elbow. "The computer. Will that work? There has to be Word or Excel program on that thing."

"You're brilliant." Excitement caused Kellan to bring both wings to the floor with one hefty swoop and the down stroke lifted him from the floor and then lightly set him down.

"Whoa!" Neil squealed. "I don't think I'll ever get tired of seeing that."

Neither would Dylan, since he barked at the moment of lift off.

Kellan placed the laptop on the table in front of the sofa, opened it and then moved his hands to his thighs as if he had no clue where to go next. "Shit. This is not my thing. I need a pencil."

Neil stepped in, turned the laptop toward him. "Tell me what the plan is."

Kellan told him. "I need to run a column of letters beside a

16

column of numbers, vertically. Top to bottom, from A to Z and zero through twenty-six."

"Easy stuff. An Excel spreadsheet will be best, I believe," Neil suggested. He sifted through the programs until he found what he was looking for and opened it. Typing top to bottom, he entered A to Z, one letter in each cell. Alongside that, the same thing, only zero through twenty-six, but it ended being one number too many. "Are you sure we're supposed to add the zero?"

Kellan rubbed his chin then moved it to his forehead. "I think so. Let's try something. Type in the numbers he gave us vertically and then correspond them with the letters beside them."

The letters that appeared didn't make any sense. Forward, backward, up or down. Not even mixed up. "What is YTSZPWZW?" Neil asked.

"What the heck. I'm sure that's it." The screw twisted in the middle of Kellan's brow again, this time tighter than before. "Hang on. Let me think. It's been a while."

Neil took a guess. "Maybe we're supposed to add a vowel between each letter. Nope. That doesn't work."

"Get rid of the zero and try again," Kellan suggested.

"Nope. That doesn't make sense either."

Kellan snapped a finger. "Reverse the numbers, twenty-six to zero, starting from the top."

Neil did it and started entering the formula again. "Nada."

"What the hell?" Kellan went to the window and stared out of it. He was certain that was the game. They played it every chance they could get when they were children. He went back and glared at the computer screen.

While Neil played with letters and numbers, Kellan kept thinking. But it seemed like the more he thought, the further away from an answer he was getting. Kellan scratched his head. "Maybe we should quit for a few minutes, let my brain clear out. I know this is it, but I have to figure out how we played the game."

Neil leaned into Kellan. "I know a way to relax you." His hand went to Kellan's crotch where he gripped the familiar bulge, palming it with added pressure.

Kellan let out a muted groan as one corner of his mouth curled into a wicked grin. His chest swelled as he pulled oxygen into his lungs.

Neil moved his hand to the gutter of Kellan's abdomen and followed the line of dark blond hair upward to where it lightly fanned out across his chest. The newly growing hair had always been kept trimmed during his time at TC as a way of simplifying the medical exams that had been done to him, and now that he was no longer there, it was growing back. There in the short prickles, Neil laid his hand while moving in to softly kiss Kellan, soothing him, bringing his heart rate down.

Speaking into Neil's mouth in a warm whisper, Kellan said, "You know just how it's done, don't you?" Then he smiled, the corners curled in an uptick, and a slight tremble as the scrape of teeth graced Neil's lips.

Kellan inhaled deeply. "Keep it up, something's coming to me."

Neil softly spoke, "I have no problem with that."

Before another moment passed, Kellan reached for Neil's shoulders and moved him over to his side, cradling him under his wing.

"You got something?" Neil asked.

"Yeah... yeah." Kellan stared at the screen. "I was looking at the numbers laid out on the spreadsheet and noticed they appeared to be the numbered floors of a building. What do most high-rise buildings have in common?"

"No thirteenth floor?" Neil's voice rose along with one eyebrow.

"Right. Bad luck, remember?" Kellan leaned forward. "Delete number thirteen."

Neil tapped the keyboard, removing the number Kellan suggested, and then punched in the formula. "Okay. Sort of makes sense, but not quite. Do you know what he means by Chiblebe?"

"Hang on, there's more to this." Kellan thought back. "We also used to fool around with our vocabulary, adding the letter B after each syllable that made our words sound like the engine of a motor boat. We went on for hours laughing at how stupid we sounded and at how nobody knew what we were saying. We called it Ubangi-babble because it sounded like babble as our lips banged together when we did it."

"Okay, all good and fun, but how does that help us here?"

"Get rid of the babble B's."

"Okay. We get Chilee, but the country ends in one E or is he trying to give us a chunky soup?"

"The E doesn't belong, I'm sure it's just a pronunciation addition." Kellan brought up the secret child's play game. The thought that it could be used to communicate in real life was unexpected.

"Does this mean he's someplace in Chile? Or are we supposed to go there?" Neil turned frantic. "This isn't telling us anything."

"It'll be fine. This I'm sure is only part of the clue," Kellan said. "Let's just keep a close eye on the computer."

Unable to settle down, Neil got up and paced the floor. Kellan watched him, intermittently glancing from Neil to the computer screen.

The screen lit up, startling Kellan and pulling him back from his racing thoughts. It was another splash message from Seth. Kellan called, "Hey Neil, come quick."

They didn't waste any time opening the message. They were ready for it. It was another code to decipher. That time, they were letters.

Neil quickly typed ZXSXU into the spreadsheet as Kellan chanted them. Before they could catch their breath, the message disappeared like all the others, not leaving them a chance to double check the embedded code. "Shit. Hope I got it right," Neil said.

So far they had Chile 02725. They weren't certain if it was a postal code or part of an address in that country. They could only think it was a place they were supposed to go. What was Seth trying to tell them?

Neil wondered how much longer it was going to take Seth to pass on the next clue. It seemed like ten minutes, but was actually only two when the text came through, once more only letters. The screen lit up with VYQW, followed by the word OVER. Unfortunately Seth would have to sit tight and wait for a reply until they could figure out the clue he'd sent.

Kellan and Neil had the code: Chile 02725 4193 Over. What did that mean and what were they supposed to do with the information?

They both thought hard, racking the deepest part of their brains to figure out the coded text.

Sometimes games sucked. Secret codes – they sucked even worse.

"Let's try something." Neil opened up a search engine and logged into Google Maps. "Maybe it's where Seth is, or wants us to go."

Neil clicked on South America and then went straight to Chile. In the search field he typed the code, thinking it would populate a postal location somewhere in that country. It came up blank. There was nothing. Chile's postal codes were seven digits and they had five, four or nine, depending how they looked at what they were given.

"Dead end with that idea. What the hell is he trying to tell us?" Kellan leaned back as best he could without bending or crimping the bones in his wings.

"Let's just hang tight for a few. Maybe there's more to come," Neil said.

Chapter 4

Kellan had a new plan at the moment that didn't involve a computer or any major thinking that required using the technical part of their brains. "Why don't we take a breather, give our heads a break for a while. This has been a lot of information all at once, and I can't seem to think anymore."

Exhaling with a big-cheeked wisp, Neil immediately agreed.

When Dylan heard Neil puff, he popped his head off the floor where he lay, thinking the poof of air was going to be a misty sneeze. For some odd reason, Dylan became worked up by a sudden sneeze and always tried his darnedest to bark the noisy sneeze away. Nothing came of Neil's cheeky blow, so Dylan's head returned to its resting spot on the floor.

"Take off your shirt," Kellan begged.

"What's your plan? Why remove the shirt?"

"I want to take you away from here and you know how I prefer your bare skin against my chest." Kellan gave Neil a suggestive glance.

Giving Kellan a show, Neil gripped the bottom hem of his shirt and lifted it, sensuously slinking it up his rugged torso and over his head. "I'm ready, Love. Take me away." Neil cherished this part of his new-fangled life when he flew beneath his lover's wings, probably enjoying it as much as Kellan did. Flying was still a new pleasure for Neil, being airborne with the angel he loved. He valued every minute of it, mostly how it connected the two of them in a way that nobody would ever be able to understand. So high and so in love.

Once outside, Kellan stepped in front of Neil and faced him, moving in close. The heat of Kellan's breath streamed into Neil's ear when he whispered, "I'm so in love with you, Neil. I'm... so... in... love." Then he swept his warm lips across Neil's jaw, tracing the sharp angle until he reached his mouth. The tender kisses he received from Neil drove tremors up and down his spine that took him into the clouds without an actual liftoff. Mimicking a dance, Kellan took Neil by the hands. He gently locked one between their chests, covering Neil's with his and then placing the other behind his back at the base of his wings. Kellan lifted his wings up and then down in one smooth stroke. Gracefully he fanned them, one wing extended farther than the other, elevating them in a slow upward spin. If there had been an orchestra playing, it would have been a magical, passionately erotic moment.

As they rose to the sky, the world they left behind seemed peaceful, as if they were the only ones alive, and every bit of turmoil that followed them had diminished. For those few cherished moments, it was just them. In love and feeling free.

"Where are you taking me?" Neil purred, enjoying the breeze combing his hair and caressing his bare skin.

Letting the headwinds fill his wings, Kellan answered, "I'm not sure, just away from the chaos for a bit."

"But what about Dylan? Do you think it's safe to leave him alone?" Neil wondered.

"Seth mentioned the TC officials were going to lay off us for a while, so I think an hour or two should be okay. We need this, Neil—a few minutes alone—it'll do us some good." Kellan rolled over in midflight. Flying backward, wings down, putting Neil on top. They both looked back at the lighthouse as they flew, looking for any sign of danger. "You see, everything looks calm," Kellan said, and then pulled a wing in and they rolled back over, flying wings up.

It was the first time in a long time that Kellan flew in the light of day. It was risky, but flying low would help keep his winged secret between the two of them. Kellan's wingtips picked at the surface, lifting drops of water into the space around them. He gripped Neil tighter, pulling him against his chest, holding him there for the thrill ride he was planning next.

As if trying to break the sound barrier, Kellan pushed himself faster with robust beats of both wings. Below them, as he gained speed, the water turned to blurred streaks of blue and silver. He took them on a trackless rollercoaster ride, going up and then down, his wingtips lifting water on every upstroke. Adding excitement, he thrust them forward into an amplified twist, blanketing them in a spinning torrent of vapor as each wingtip graced the surface. Spiraling higher and then down again, he imagined the quick movements might be too much for Neil, so he slowed their flight and hovered in place, letting his wingtips lift vapor such that the sunlight would show through. The spectrum of color glistened in front of them, intermittently coming and going as the sporadic showers rose and fell.

As soon as the rainbow dissipated, they made their way around the island, Neil tightly gripping the forearms Kellan had firmly locked across his chest. Cool drops that felt like tiny bugs pecked at Neil's face, but the wind coming at them quickly scooped the water away, and what remained, dried almost immediately.

Not too far ahead of them was the north side of the island, opposite the lighthouse. Tall pine trees lined the beach, following the curve of the coast. Inland, the wooded forest gave the impression of going on forever, as far as the eye could see, penetrating the island like a wondrous blanket of blue spruce and white pines. The trees were fragrant, smelling of Christmas, and the magical scent channeled a spirit of joyous love through Kellan. To enjoy the aroma around them, Kellan slowed his flight to a more tranquil pace. The warmth of the holiday put the idea in his head of making love to Neil right there in the sky.

Yelling, Neil's words fought with the wind. "Is that an erection I'm feeling?"

Kellan's dick had indeed hardened, almost to the point of pain, and the warm holiday feeling of making love had quickly changed to a desire to just fuck. "When your favorite part of my body is so nicely tucked between your butt cheeks, it was only a matter of time before a hard-on happened. The fucker wants in."

"Unh... do you really think now is a good time for shoving a bone up my ass?"

"Unh... yeah... Anytime is a good time to shove my bone up your ass," Kellan mimicked Neil's tone.

"Then you better set me down and have at it."

More than excited to comply, Kellan veered to the left. "That looks like a good place to unwind." He tipped his forewings upward to slow their flight.

If pants hadn't been in the way at that lustful moment, they'd be screwing in the sky like they'd done before.

Positioning Neil gently, Kellan rotated his wings until he hovered, lowering them slowly to the ground, white sand pressing between his toes. Loosening the grip he had on Neil, Kellan spun him around, pushed the curly strands of hair away from his eyes and then kissed him with gentle passion.

Kellan walked Neil backward as they moved further away from the shoreline, pinning him against a massive oak tree. Kellan planted a few light kisses to Neil's lips, keeping them sweet while whispering he loved him. The tenderness was brief, and it quickly changed to crushing hunger. Unable to hold back, Kellan gave in to the desperate need to consume Neil, the anticipation of possession so powerful his belly clenched, throat tightening as though the jaws of death gripped his windpipe. It was an effort to breathe.

Captivated by Kellan's forceful advance, Neil's dick grew stiffer. There was no stopping the effect Kellan had on him. Unable to resist, Neil gripped Kellan by the waist with a hand on each hip and pulled him against his chest. Neil pecked at Kellan's lips, teasing nips interspersed with soft words of love, and edged with increasing passion until sensation nearly overwhelmed them both.

The fierceness of their kissing made Kellan's dick twitch. As it expanded, he leaked semen the way he always did when aroused, drenching the front of his jeans before he removed and tossed them aside.

Neil swiftly pushed his pants off, and then dropped to the cool ground at the root of the tree. Kellan moved with him, comfortably placing his body on top of Neil, kissing him, taking possession of his probing tongue.

Neil's legs spread open when Kellan slid into position between them, his angel's dick dropping perfectly into place for penetration.

Neil's entrance quivered greedily when he felt Kellan's erection brush against it, the semen seeping from Kellan's slit wetting the target it so desperately wanted to dip into.

They were in a private place, feeling natural and free the way a couple in love should.

Jumping at the chance to connect with Neil, Kellan tightened his abdomen, pushing his hips forward. The velvety crown of his cock broke Neil's tight seal, and as the bulbous head of his cock slowly eased into him, the sensation of Neil's ass channel felt like a furnace in there.

After adjusting to the welcoming pain that rapidly turned to exquisite pleasure, Neil murmured, "You feel incredible, Kellan." Then his jaw sprung open as Kellan's thickness pushed deeper, opening him wider. When he was able to speak again, he pleaded, "Give me everything you've got. Dig that dick deep the way you always do."

Inching in, Kellan filled Neil completely. He gazed down on Neil and noticed his eyes were intensely locked on his own, pupils blown, but lids heavy. "You feel amazing, too, Neil." Kellan moved his hips in small circles, watching Neil sweep his tongue across his lower lip at the same moment his eyes closed tight, brow scrunched.

At first, Kellan fixed his leaking erection inside Neil, holding it steady, letting the semen from his dick gloss the walls of his lover's convulsing channel. Then Kellan slowly slid his erection in and out of Neil with agonizingly slow strokes, making sure Neil felt every inch of his cock moving inside him.

Kellan felt Neil's channel clamp down on his dick, squeezing it tighter as if begging him not to pull out. Neil's body convulsed. His asshole flexed, sucking on Kellan, letting him know he needed to really fuck him, pound into him harder, drill him faster.

Enthralled with Neil's asshole eagerly pulling him in, Kellan gave in to what Neil wanted. He drilled his stiff cock into Neil, pumping in and out of him at a punishing pace. He would have slowed down, could have, but hearing Neil's grunts and groans of pleasure spurred him on. The harder Kellan fucked Neil, heard him whimper, the more he felt powerless to stop, and the urge to please Neil intensified. It seemed as if Neil's desire to get fucked was controlling Kellan's stone hard cock, instructing him not to rest until both were completely satisfied.

Kellan leaned against Neil's feet that were pressed into his shoulders. The position supported Kellan's weight such that it better helped him pummel Neil's semen slickened hole. Kellan eagerly ground his hips into Neil's ass, pushing his dick deeper as was ordered. In time with each forceful thrust, his wings flapped, assisting the powerful plunges in and out of Neil. When his dick pulled out, his wings came forward, followed by a swift backward sweep that shoved his cock back in. With that extra thrust, he hooked on hand over Neil's shoulder to keep from driving him head first into the tree. "You like the way that feels, don't you? You want me to ram you harder?"

A whole different experience doused Neil's entire body as he lay caught in an erotic wind tunnel. His hair snapped. His breath caught. "Yes... Kellan. Fucking fuck me. Shove your cock deep into my ass. I want to feel it coming out my throat. Jam it in. No mercy." Neil wildly shouted while raking his fingernails along Kellan's wingtips before tightly grabbing hold of them. It was a reaction that shrouded him from being under sensory overload, and all he could do was hang on.

From the pleasurable sting coursing through every plume when Neil tugged at his wings, Kellan roared, bearing teeth, "Aaaagh, fuck!" His eyes clamped shut and his head pivoted like he was angry. The bite of each stroke along his quills excited him more, causing his wings to break Neil's grip and snap toward the foliage above them. The sudden tug at his shoulder blades pushed his hips into Neil, forcing his cock to tunnel deeper still. "Damn! I think I just reached your chest."

Hearing Neil's deepened cries of passion caused Kellan's hips to instinctively pound into him harder. His wings roughly flapped, generating rushing gusts that nearly drowned out the erotic noises they were making, as well as the whistling wind cutting through the trees.

"You're gonna make me cum, Kellan. Keep fucking me. I'm almost there." Neil reached both hands around the back of Kellan's neck and locked them there, pining for another selfish kiss. He wanted to be pinioned at both ends by Kellan. One sweet tongue and one hard dick. Fucked hard as well as made love to. First one, and then the other, until he couldn't tell the difference.

Slowing his rhythm, Kellan's hand coolly traced every crevice and mound across Neil's chest, his warm touch forcing Neil to drag sharp breaths into his lungs. Kellan's gentle touch registered the swift rise and fall, relishing the smooth muscles under his fingertips.

Effortlessly rolling his hips, Kellan sunk himself further inside Neil. "I love you so much, Neil," he whispered.

Neil took every bit of Kellan, and the punishing pleasure made him whimper, but he was still able to say, "I love you too, Kellan—madly love you." He needed to tell him that. With his hands still fixed to the nape of Kellan's neck, Neil drew him down and kissed him. His legs spread wider as Kellan moved in.

Kellan's caresses and talented rhythm drove Neil nearly mad with desire, pushing him to that brink of spasmodic frenzy. Neil's entire body quaked and then tightened. An uncontrollable buzz raked over him, and he ejaculated before he wanted to. His throbbing cock let loose, squeezing pearly ribbons of semen between them.

Kellan felt the heat of Neil's eruption splash against his chest, and the pungent scent of semen made him immediately cum too, his throat thundering obscenities the entire time he ejaculated inside Neil. There was no holding back. Kellan went rigid, every muscle locked in a rictus of pleasure, and he soon collapsed on top of Neil, kissing him deeply.

Though Kellan breathlessly lay on top of Neil, his hips and pelvis refused to give up, continuing to drive his cock into Neil's flexing channel. Kellan's head dropped, face tucked into the well of Neil's neck where his warm breath streamed between their chests. Strenuous huffs broke free while Kellan's lurching body transferred everything he had inside the man he loved. Spurt after powerful spurt. Filling him completely. The intensity of the orgasm made his wings stand straight out. Each feather fluffed up and stood on end.

Kellan smirked with erratic gasps. "Holy hairy assholes, Neil. The clutch you have on my dick right now feels incredible. As it always does. If it's okay with you and your sweet, sweet ass, I'd like to stay inside you for a while."

Neil wrapped his legs around Kellan's waist and locked his ankles beneath his wings, not letting him go. He smiled softly, hugged Kellan tightly and kissed his earlobe. With a soft tone, Neil said, "I would love you to stay." Then he dropped his voice to a whisper, "Will you love me forever, Kellan?"

Kellan lifted his head away from Neil's pouty lips and peered down on him. Smiling back, he then kissed Neil so sweetly that the world seemed to stop spinning. "Yes, I will love you always."

Kellan could care less what he was about to do would seem corny. But he connected his forefinger and thumb to make a loop and slid it gently over Neil's engagement finger. "I love you, Neil, and with this ring, I make the promise to be yours—forever."

Neil accepted the bony ring on his finger, and kissed the man who placed it there.

Still embedded inside Neil, Kellan kissed him back, sealing the deal that made Neil his.

Neil squirmed, becoming aware again that Kellan's erection was still firmly tucked inside him. The connection he had with Kellan was more than physical. It went beyond how well he was linked by his well-penetrated dick just then. Trying not to spoil the moment, Neil sighed and then persuasively said, "Promise me you'll find a way to stay right where you are. Not for a short period of time, but longer than that. Endlessly. Wait... I mean... sure you'll need to pull out of me at some point, that's not really what I'm talking about. What I'm meaning to say is that I want you to stay with me. Forever. Like a family. You and me. Maybe try to make something more of our life together once we get through all the red tape with the military."

"I'll find a way to deliver on that, Neil. There's no way I could possibly live without you now. I've fallen in love with you, and I need to stay." Kellan's wings wavered when his hips slowly pushed into Neil, his erection sliding a little deeper to make sure Neil still felt him, to convince Neil he was there for the long haul.

Kellan spoke to Neil, his words heartfelt, his voice thick with emotion. "You are probably the only real family I have, other than Seth and perhaps my infamous creators, whoever they might be. I consider you my family, Neil, now more than ever after what we've been through so far. Other than putting that handmade commitment ring on your hand, don't forget about what we've already shared intimately because we love each other. Like the genuine kisses, the sincere hugs, and how we transferred, ingested and absorbed each other's essence in ways only two men in love would. Doing everything I had up until this very moment was because I wanted to share every part of me with you that I could. And I know I'm not wrong when I say, you did the same for me. I felt it. There's no denying that. I love you so much, Neil, and want you in my life in a very bad way. How I see it right now? You and I *are* Family, and there's no going back to the way things were."

Neil hugged Kellan tightly, feeling warmth emanating from the man he loved so much. The affection Neil felt from Kellan was truly from the heart: it was strong, and it flowed from deep inside, enveloping him completely.

Chapter 5

Naked, Kellan stood and held out a hand to Neil, steadying him as he rose, still shaky from the pummeling he'd been subjected to.

Together they brushed the sand from their bodies where it stuck. A good amount clung to Neil's back side and several bits adhered to Kellan's knees and palms.

Not flexible enough to remove all the sand himself, Neil turned away from Kellan and said, "Help me out here and give my backside a few bangs with your fist."

Stepping up behind Neil, Kellan snickered. "Well now. I didn't realize you were a power bottom. I'm definitely not one to judge, so if you're into that, I'm with you because I love you. But can we have a go at it later? I think I've done enough damage back there, and another thing, you've drained me completely, so I don't think I have any more to give."

"You know what I mean. Now start banging."

Kellan smirked but used a gentle hand, brushing and

blowing, instead of banging and pounding. "It might be easier if we rinsed off in the lake, don't you think?"

"Not good. What if somebody sees us... sees you... your wings?" Neil answered.

"I'll keep my wings tightly against my back. We flew here without a problem, so a quick dip couldn't hurt."

"Yeah, but..."

"But what?"

"Standing still is different than flying, like we're at a disadvantage on the ground. More defenseless."

Kellan faced Neil, pressed his naked body against him and said, "Look, I can fly fast, and if anything pops out of the bushes, I'll get us out of here. I won't let anything happen to you — or us."

Still uneasy about the whole idea, Neil skeptically agreed to a power dip in Lake Michigan, but only if they did it together and side by side.

They quickly rinsed in the lake, keeping it brief, and then hurried back beneath the pines before being seen by anybody or anything. Fast was the way it had to be. An angel being spotted frolicking along the beach would be disastrous for them and it would surely put Kellan back in a holding cell. If anybody other than the military got hold of him, he'd be prodded, poked at, and maybe taken apart to see how he worked. Scientists could be crazy like that.

For Neil, on the other hand, there was no telling what would happen to him. Possibly, they'd put him into a detention cell. Maybe experiment on him, see if he'd be useful to the program. In any case, being an outsider associated with an angel might give the researchers new ideas on how to produce the super beings they were after. Once the poking and prodding was complete, there was the chance of outright execution to get rid of the evidence. His guess was as good as any. So to be safe, the best thing both could do was lie low, stay hidden in the brush, then get back to the lighthouse and lock all the doors and windows.

While Kellan put his pants on, he gave thought to the number system Seth had sent. He scanned the beach with bleary eyes as if that would spark some kind of clue, which coincidentally it seemed to, because he had a bright idea just then. He turned to Neil and blurted out, "Oh, man. I think the numbers might be a Chilean phone number. What do you think?"

Neil looked at Kellan with his usual handsome smile and an expression in his eyes that showed interest. "That makes sense." His pace quickened while he finished putting his own pants on, tucking everything hanging here and there into place.

Kellan performed one of his spur-of-the-moment liftoffs, the one where he ran up behind Neil, grabbed him around the waist and took him to the sky before he had a chance to scream or gasp for air. That stunt was one of the things Neil should be getting used to, but he didn't seem to be, and probably never would. Surprise assaults always sucked in a major way, some more than others, but in any case, they all sucked the big wazoo. They'd both had their fair share of them recently and didn't need any more.

Beating his wings in timed rhythm, Kellan flew higher, his speed increasing as he followed the island's coastline that headed toward the lighthouse on the other side of the island. After being airborne for only a few minutes, he pulled a wing in, sharply turned to the right and put them out over the open water. Kellan flew for a few more minutes until they got closer to their dilapidated home. When the lighthouse was within sight, Kellan purposely flew lower, keeping an eye on the area around them.

Remaining cautious, Kellan reduced his speed dramatically before touching down in front of the lighthouse. There was no telling what could have happened during their time away, and staying alert would give them a head start if any Seeker was planning an attack.

When Dylan greeted Kellan and Neil with the familiar tongue-wagging smile on his face, it was the signal they were looking for, the one that said they could relax their guard, if only for a short time. As soon as they walked through the door, closed and locked it, Dylan ran off to grab a stuffed toy, brought it back and dropped it at their feet, gifting their return and coaxing them to stay and play. He pranced in circles a few times and barked to keep their attention on him, hopeful they weren't planning to leave again any time soon.

After Dylan finally settled down, Kellan flipped the computer on right as Neil sat in front of it. There they waited for it to come to life and when it did, they were hoping a new message from Seth would appear. When nothing showed on the screen, they looked at each other, disappointment clearly shown on their faces.

On a hunch, Neil tried the internet too, but no signal was coming in, and that disturbed him. His first thought was the TC officials had shut it down, which made him wonder if it was because they knew where they were.

Kellan sensed Neil's anxiety. "What is it?" he asked.

"The wireless connection seems to be offline. I can't get a signal." Neil cocked his head, looking up at Kellan, watching him as he gracefully lowered his wings, the tips dragging across the floor as he paced in a tight circle.

"We'll try again later. Maybe the router you were linked to is jammed." Kellan laid a hand on Neil's shoulder and squeezed. "In the meantime, let's find a phone so we can figure out if that number Seth gave us calls anybody. You wouldn't happen to have a cellular in that bag of yours would you?"

"Wish I did, but no."

"Where can we get one around here?"

"In town of course, but the best thing to do right now is to wait until the sun goes down. It's not a good idea to be dragging you through the streets in broad daylight," Neil said.

"I wouldn't go, but you could." Kellan didn't care for the idea of Neil going alone, but it was the way it had to be.

"Wait a minute," Neil sputtered. "I have a phone, left it at the lake house. I think."

"That place is toast. My guess would be there's no phone."

"But that storm shelter was built to withstand a nuclear bomb, and the last thing I remember was putting my cell on the pantry shelf to free my hands so I could grab shit. I never took the phone when we left."

"You certain?"

"We were being chased by black winged freaks, so making sure I had my phone wasn't on my mind. It has to be there, as long as nobody went in after we left the place."

"Are you sure we should go back there? It won't be pretty, I can guarantee that."

"I've seen it. Besides, I need the lockbox in there as well. It has all the important papers I need for the house, and a few other things I should probably keep close to me." Neil stood up, wrangled Dylan's ears as he did, then chest bumped Kellan as he leaned against him for a kiss.

Kellan's wings flexed and lightly fanned the room, then came around to wrap Neil in a hug. He spoke softly, "All right. We will go there, but promise me, I lead the way."

Neil looked into Kellan's sparkling blues and answered, "Deal."

ೞ   ಐ

By the time night fell, Kellan and Neil were nervous but prepared. Neil packed his messenger bag with a few survival items he found around the lighthouse: things like duct tape, a knife, matches and a couple of candles. Even though Kellan could see in the dark, he couldn't, so he added a flashlight that didn't work into the bag. Why? Just in case it was needed and because he knew there were supplies at the house, like a bulb and batteries. He'd replace them when they got to the shelter, and with any luck, there'd be light.

It was decided that they weren't taking Dylan with them, which meant someone had to take him outside for a few minutes to pee, poop and run if he needed to before they hit the friendly skies. While Neil ransacked the lighthouse, Kellan did the Dylan duties.

A sixth sense always told Dylan something was going on when he saw Neil packing bags or pacing the floors. He could feel it in his bones, and his tiny little brain told him he was being left home alone. The dog's face actually appeared to be thinking, *Dimmit, not again,* his eyes rolled in their sockets, following Neil wherever he went in the house.

On an impulse, when the door flew open, Dylan barged outdoors alongside Kellan, did his business within a matter of seconds, raced back up the stairs to the front door and stared back at Kellan to follow and let him back in. He wasn't taking the chance of mistakenly being left behind.

Dylan reached Neil before Kellan did, like there was a race going on between them. He stood in front of Neil, looking up at him, waiting for the invitation that told him he was going wherever they were.

Neil strapped the messenger bag over his shoulder, knelt down to Dylan's level and put a hand to each side of his head, kneading his ears and then stroking his jaw. "You need to stay here for a bit, Dylan. We'll be right back."

Dylan's face went long, ears laid back and his eyes drooped. The sadness on Dylan's face broke Neil's heart; it nearly killed him. This time, Neil had a bad feeling it wasn't just plain old separation anxiety, it felt too different. It was their current circumstances putting a bad spin on it, as if it were a final goodbye, like there was a possibility they'd never see each other again. It was an awful feeling, one that Neil couldn't dismiss and by the looks of it, neither could Dylan.

Making an effort to sound optimistic, Neil kept his voice cheerful when telling Dylan goodbye, not wanting him to detect that anything was out of the ordinary other than a typical gonna-go-away-for-a-few and I'll-see-you-later scenario.

Backing out the door, Neil kept an eye on Dylan the entire time, watching him sulk until the door latched into place. As Kellan and Neil made it down the steps and to the ground, they saw Dylan in the window, his feet propped on the ledge, looking out.

"We've got to make this quick," Neil said, looking at Dylan's sad eyes connect with his.

Kellan scooped Neil into his arms, thrust his wings downward with a single beat and took them up. Before flying to the mainland, Kellan circled back around to take one more look at Dylan who was still at the window with gloomy eyes and his sweet, sweet face.

Chapter 6

Six minutes after Kellan and Neil left the lighthouse, they were circling the house on the lake that looked to be nothing more than ash and soot. The home was nearly flattened. Yellow warning tape had been stretched along the property line, giving it a crime scene vibe, though in this case the intent was likely just a warning, not something that would actually deter busybodies. By the looks of things, it didn't seem to be working. All around the yard were flimsy strips that had broken loose on their own or possibly had been cut away. They were twisting and flapping over the ground with the breeze, appearing as thought they were waving for help.

The property where they were about to land was a sad sight to Neil after being such a good one for so many years. The saddest part of it was all his memories from childhood had been crushed within a matter of minutes. The idea of that got to Neil more than the house being so violently taken down.

Among the many acres of land Neil's grandparents still

owned, this particular parcel had been given to Neil along with the house that once stood on it. It was their gift to him for completing college and becoming a successful nurse. His grandparents had always supported his dreams, even if it meant he did not join the family business as a vintner. It was their financial and emotional support that allowed him to follow his passion: helping people.

The home given to him wasn't huge, as expected, for people with money, but instead, it was a simple three bedroom cape cod that overlooked Lake Michigan. Although the house was small, Neil loved it. It fit him to a tee. It had memories: his grandparents, him growing up, swimming in the lake. The government had destroyed more than just property, they'd ruined a link he had to all he cared about.

The only thing good about the place now, after all the destruction, was the way the bridge looked at nighttime in the distance. The suspension cables were lit as if it were always the holidays, reflecting a mirrored image against the calm water below it.

After enjoying the bridge and the year round holiday lights for a few brief moments, Kellan back-flapped his wings slowly to bring their feet gently to the ground. He landed close to the yellow tape on the inside of the property line at the back side of the house. Several feet in front of them was the shelter's entrance. By the looks of it, the tape circled the entire property, and every few feet were posted signs that stated, *Government Seized Property; Trespassers Will Face Imprisonment and Be Fined*. Closer to where the house lay broken, posted signs warned, *Keep Out*.

Neil stared straight ahead, couldn't believe what he was looking at, nothing registered the way he was seeing it. Recalling how the house originally looked, the image so clear in his mind's eye, it was as if time had stopped at a point just before the unimaginable had happened. He withdrew for a few minutes out of disbelief. It was beyond anything he could have ever imagined. To see his home in the state it was in, and to find it had been taken away by the government, split his heart in two. There didn't seem to be any hope of fixing either one, the home or his heart.

Kellan recognized Neil was having a moment that seemed personal. Instead of consoling him, Kellan stood quietly next to

Neil and waited for him to speak.

Neil reached for Kellan's hand and calmly said, "This just doesn't seem real, does it, Kellan." He glanced around the property, looking at everything. The huge maple tree he loved so much was there, however, it laid on its side… dying, taken down by the blast.

"To be honest, I've only seen this kind of thing on TV. Not a pleasant sight, that's for sure." Kellan brought his wings in, holding them high to keep them from touching the dirty ash-covered ground. He squeezed Neil's trembling hand and confessed, "This is my fault. I'm sorry, Neil."

Neil turned Kellan's face toward him with a gentle hand to his chin. "It wasn't your fault that the government blew my house into a million pieces. The way they took care of business had nothing to do with you."

"None of this would have happened if I hadn't shown up."

"Screw the house. Losing the house doesn't mean squat next to losing you, and I don't intend on giving you back. I can't and I won't. Now let's go find that phone." Neil kissed Kellan and lingered on the taste, savoring the sweet scent of desire before he said anything more.

The door to the shelter was still wide open and every few seconds the wind caught it and lifted it off the ground and back down again. The gentle bang hopefully kept the rodents, wildlife, and mean-spirited critters from setting up camp down below.

Taking the first step, Neil went for the entrance, but was quickly stopped when Kellan grabbed his arm and told him, "Let me go first. It's dark down there, and I can see what you can't." He pushed ahead of Neil, creeping one slow step at a time until he reached the bottom.

Like gum on a shoe, Neil stuck closely to Kellan's back, tiptoeing one step behind him between his wings. "I forgot how dark it gets down here. You see anything?"

Walking the dark dungeon-like hallway, Kellan answered, "Nothing but darkness."

"Maybe I should light a candle so I can see."

"Hold that thought, love. Wings with feathers, remember."

Once they made it beyond the dark hallway and inside the storm shelter, Neil lit a couple candles, handing one to Kellan for him to hold. "Not a thing out of place from what I can tell," Neil commented. "I find it strange that they hadn't come down here. You'd think the place would have been stripped."

"If you think about it, doing more damage to the place or taking a few cans of beans wouldn't have helped them find us. They already knew the place was practically uninhabitable, figured we wouldn't come back, so why pursue what isn't here. According to Seth, they know where we are anyway."

"Yeah, that's strange, too. I can't figure that out at all. Why not hog tie us already and take us back to the compound?"

"I don't know. But what I do know is we can't stay in one place for too long."

"Right. And speaking of that, let's move into the pantry and see about that phone."

That time, Neil led the way, holding the candle in front of him, looking at every shelf he visited the day they were chased out of there by bat-winged maniacs. Moving along, he then shrieked his favorite phrase, the one he always spewed when he was surprised or startled by shock or horror. "Holy fuck me in the ass. There it is." He reached for his phone, still in the same place he had left it, undisturbed, but deader than a struck opossum in the middle of the street. No life to it whatsoever.

"I don't believe it. Straight up gay luck is what I call that. Hope more of it comes our way, cuz we're gonna be needing it." Kellan leaned against Neil's back and kissed his ear before resting his chin on his shoulder to have a look at the phone. "Now all we need is a charger."

Neil turned his head, trying to return a kiss before stepping around Kellan and his big wings. "Keep those lucky gay fingers of yours crossed. I stashed batteries and chargers in a box on another shelf. Step aside my beautiful angel and allow me to get us some power."

Neil moved the candle to the end of the shelving unit and looked for the box labeled batteries and power strips. "Eureka." There it was. The carton he was looking for. He pulled it from the shelf and set it on the floor where he opened it and pulled the cell phone cables out. There were several different types, and one fit snuggly into the jack of his phone perfectly.

"I could fuck that brilliant ass of yours right now." Kellan smiled, staring at the cable in Neil's hand like it was a golden ticket to the chocolate factory.

Neil looked up at Kellan and grinned. "Are you being serious?"

"Your hunting skills by candle light is damn hot. Watching you sneak around in the dark with that warm glow on your face got me going. I'm hard as a rock just thinking about sliding my dick inside you, giving you the big one, blasting my load up that sweet ass of yours," Kellan confessed. Fucking Neil was always on Kellan's mind, night and day, like he was addicted to that fine tight hole now that he'd had it. Kellan felt whole when his cock was rooting deep inside his boyfriend, so closely connecting their bodies, making the man he loved feel as good as he did. It was easy with Neil, because he loved him so much.

Neil stood up and cupped the bulge in Kellan's jeans, feeling the flow of semen already getting his crotch and inner thigh wet. The man was incredibly self-equipped with his own lubricant that seeped from his throbbing dick whenever it was hard. That's the way TC made him, or at least the way he turned out. Mistake or no mistake, Neil liked that about Kellan, finding it a perk he could work with. They could fuck anytime, anywhere, at a moment's notice without having to scramble for a tube of lube. Kellan had all they needed to easily make their connection complete.

Neil's asshole twitched, knowing Kellan's hard cock was near and wanted in. Neil wanted Kellan to fuck him, but he also wanted to get the hell out of that dark storm shelter and back to a place where he felt more at ease. He whispered into Kellan's ear, telling him to save his erection for when they got back to the lighthouse, letting him know he appreciated his magnificent hard-on, but wasn't comfortable fucking with rodents and spiders watching on the sidelines.

"That's fine with me. I can wait to make love to the man I love. I have willpower." Kellan stepped away to take control of himself.

Neil grinned as he observed Kellan make an effort to adjust himself beneath his tented jeans, and patiently wait for that sexually frustrated erection to subside. It took a few minutes, but success eventually came.

Before they left the dark dungeon, they collected a few extra items they thought they might need: canned foods, extra batteries, and *the* important papers. Neil stuffed as much as he could into the messenger bag, and what didn't fit, was crammed into a pillowcase he had snatched from the musky bed.

Once outside, Kellan reached out a hand to Neil. "Come fly with me," he invited.

Chapter 7

Touchdown at the lighthouse was less than four minutes from when they left the lake house, two minutes faster than when they flew out there. The speedy flight back was all about Kellan's need to stick his stone-hard dick into Neil. He was having a tough time waiting, and needed to feel his man tightly wrapped around his cock.

Hearing footsteps outside and no longer having patience, Dylan rushed out onto the front porch before Kellan and Neil had a chance to get the door completely open. Anxiously, Dylan trotted by them and then spun around, muffled barks passed through the stuffed toy in his mouth. As quickly as he ran outside, he raced back in and stood in front of the cookie door, waiting. That was the ritual and he'd stand there until he got what he wanted.

While Neil plugged the phone in to get it charged, Kellan impatiently stepped up behind him, reached around his waist to undo his pants. He slipped one hand under the waistband of

Neil's briefs, curling his fingers round the hair above his hardening cock. His other hand traced the center of Neil's six-pack, stopping when he reached his chest. Softly, Kellan dragged his lips from Neil's shoulder to his ear, nipping his lobe. The heat of his breath made Neil's head fall back against Kellan's shoulder.

Neil trembled when he heard Kellan whisper, "I need my dick inside you, Neil. Let me in. Let me fuck that sweet hole from behind."

Kellan fully extended his wings to his sides, reaching twelve feet from tip to tip. It was impressive when he did that, and the reason for doing it, was to free up space for what would happen next. He pushed Neil's jeans only to his knees, hoping to restrain his legs from spreading too far apart, and keeping his ass cheeks nicely tight. Seeing Neil's bare ass in front of him put his sex glands on active duty, and his oversized seminal vesicle responded with plenty of semen to lubricate the hole he'd stick his dick into.

Kellan dropped his own pants to his ankles, semen oozing from the slit in his cock, soaking Neil's ass crack as the head of his dick pushed against him. Neil's whimpers were heard the second Kellan's velvet crown tapped his flexing star.

With anxious anticipation, Kellan pressed an open palm to the back of Neil's head, bending him forward over the back of the sofa to give him better access to his target. He lay against Neil's back and hummed with a deep rasp in his throat, "Get ready, Neil. I'm going to fuck your brains out, pummel your tight channel with force, and fill you with my burning spunk."

Kellan's virile commands turned Neil's dick to stone and his asshole into an enthusiastic sucking machine. Feverishly, Neil begged, "Shove it in, Kellan. Please. Just give me that big dick. Fuck my ass, good and hard." Neil's hole flexed, eager to feel Kellan's dick going in, wanting it badly. Unable to wait another second, Neil pushed back until he met Kellan's thighs, impaling his channel with every inch of his thick slippery erection.

Kellan watched his dick disappear like it was a magic trick, and without waiting, he started pounding into Neil's gripping ass like a fuck machine, pummeling him the way he had begged for it.

Neil groaned from the exquisite torture he was getting from having Kellan's cock plunging into him over and over again, punching his prostate, and keeping his dick stiff. His channel, lava hot, pulled Kellan in, sucking on his cock with mad love, savagely craving his sperm.

While reaming Neil's ass, Kellan gripped him firmly in both hands by the hips, pulling and pushing against every thrust. Their swinging balls and hardened thighs collided. He continued fucking, driving his dick in deep until the hair above it scrubbed against Neil's ass cheeks. Wanting Neil to feel more of him, he dropped prone against his back, sensually scraping his teeth over his shoulders while using his cock to tease his slickened asshole with quick jabs. He heard Neil whine, like he wanted more than just that, then witnessed him bite the cushion his face was forced into. Was it pleasure or pain?

From ceaseless excitement charging through Kellan, his wings came down abruptly, lifting his body off Neil and yanking his cock all the way out with a pop. He stood behind Neil, leaving his lover dazed by the sudden change and the cool draft skimming his vacant ass.

Kellan saw Neil had turned to face him with a weepy expression. He moved closer, curling his wingtips around Neil's chest and gently stroking his nipples. "You want more dick, Neil? Do you? I'll give it to you if you beg." Kellan pressed his stiff cock against Neil's flexing knot, circling it only with his bulbous crown.

The stroking feathers and teasing dick made Neil go wild. He whined. "Fuck my chute, Kellan. Stick me with your thick cock. Oh, Gawd, shove that fucker back inside me. Please." Sensing Kellan wasn't planning to give him what he needed, Neil waited no more and thrust backward, sinking Kellan's dick all the way in. He slid back and forth, gliding off it and then forcing it back in.

Close to the point of no coming back, Kellan reveled in the violent thrusts as Neil rode him with recklessness. His face contorted, and he forced himself to speak. "I'm about to cum, Neil. Keep riding my cock. Make me shoot all that I've got inside you."

As much as Neil wanted Kellan shooting semen into his ass right then, he made one of his snap decisions to end the joyride on his angel's cock. It was his turn to be the boss, to show Kellan how talented a bottom could really be. Impatiently, Neil pushed his ass into Kellan, bumping him backward so he could pull off his cock just as quickly.

Kellan's thick hard-as-stone dick suddenly felt cold. "Shit. What's happening?" His feathers twittered as his wings suddenly swept away from Neil's chest

Neil lifted himself off of the sofa and gripped Kellan's dick with a tightened fist, foiling the urge he had to cum. "You're gonna have to wait." Neil slowly stroked Kellan's erection, working him to the edge of cumming, and then taking that feeling away by intentionally stopping and starting. He felt Kellan's body tremble and his dick expand, tempting to cum in his hand. "No, no. Not yet. Save it in case I let you back inside me."

"Holy damn, Neil. I need to cum. Let me fuck you right now," Kellan wailed.

Neil squeezed Kellan's cock, antagonizing him. "I said, you need to wait." His mouth crashed into Kellan's chest, toying with each nipple, moving from one to the other, teasing and biting. Neil's teeth and tongue skated over Kellan's chest, up his neck and along his jaw. The torturous sensation made Kellan's wings tremor and stand erect toward the ceiling. Neil blew warm breath into Kellan's ear, repeating what had been told to him earlier. "You want more ass, Kellan? Do you? I'll give it to you if you beg." Neil slipped a semen soaked finger into Kellan's mouth, slowly moving it in and out, letting him taste his own release.

"Fuck this shit. Bend over that sofa and let me at that ass. It's time you felt the power of an amazing top." Kellan generated a strong gust when he brought his wings down from the ceiling, spun Neil around and pushed him over the back of the sofa where he'd come from. Without waiting to be invited, he crammed his cock into Neil's channel with one thrust, and the sudden intrusion forced the semen already inside Neil asshole, out. It ran down his inner thighs, dampening the jeans still around his knees.

Wholly satisfied with losing his lead, Neil cried out when Kellan rushed in, "That's it, beef my ass. Fuck me senseless, Kellan."

Obeying the commands, Kellan thrust every thick inch of his dick in and out of Neil, power driving his prostate to an intense orgasm. Kellan fought with his flapping wings as he dropped onto Neil's back, slip-sliding as he rocked, sweaty skin to sweaty skin. He growled as Neil squirmed under him. "Fuck, I'm getting close to cumming, Neil."

"I'm almost there, too." Neil gripped his own cock and stroked it.

Kellan felt Neil's ass channel squeeze his dick, and the sensation made the tidal wave of pleasure rise. Electric shockwaves strangled Kellan's spine and numbed his brain. He puckered his lips, clenched his teeth, and his neck strained as each nerve in his body fired. He grunted like a wild beast as his cock expanded and spit the cum deep into Neil's eager channel. Trembling from his intense orgasm, Kellan shook his head and warbled, "Holy fuck, I'm in love with your ass."

Those words were the final nudge Neil needed to push him into his own sperm shooting frenzy. It happened instantaneously, and there was no telling how much longer Neil would have been able to hold back from cumming anyway, he was too far gone. The assault on his prostate and ass channel had morphed into mind blowing pleasure the instant Kellan sank into him. All Neil's animalistic gyrating and guttural yelping made that clear.

While Kellan held his dick in place, Neil showered the back of the sofa with several spurts of semen. Groans erupted loud enough, his voice echoed off the walls and bounced back. The seat cushions his face was pressed into wouldn't have muffled those outbursts. He had even hollered at Kellan a few times, not out of anger, but in the way a bossy bottom would. Shouting out orders like: ride that ass... slow down... go faster... spank me... pinch my tits... and the best one, keep fucking until told to stop. Neil had not shown that side of himself to Kellan before, and because his orders were being followed without complaint, it made Neil believe Kellan was enjoying being told what to do.

All of a sudden, Neil's body stiffened, he let out a throaty howl, and semen started shooting from his dick. He jerked uncontrollably until the last spurt was ejected.

Neil's surges eventually ceased, and when he was able to stand without trembling, Kellan pulled his dick out and spun him around so they were face to face. They kissed, nostrils flaring, both laboring for air.

As soon as their heavy breathing settled and their heart rates returned to normal, Kellan drew Neil tighter against his bare chest and hugged him, holding on for a few minutes before letting him go.

Even though the pants around Neil's knees were wet with Kellan's semen, he still put them back on, finding it erotic to be wearing sperm soaked jeans.

Grinning at what Neil had done, Kellan removed his pants altogether and stayed naked. He felt freer that way, enjoyed how if felt when everything was dangling free. He rumbled, "That was one stupendous fuck." Then he heard Neil respond, "One I'll never fucking forget."

Chapter 8

Before checking the charge level on the phone, Neil wondered how much longer it would be until they could actually use it. The battery indicator was flashing, but the screen remained black. He didn't dare touch it, figuring if he did, he'd have to start all over again, and the wait to use it would be longer.

"Should we try the number?" Kellan asked.

"The phone is still charging. Maybe we should wait a while longer, just to be sure."

"As long as it's plugged in, I'm pretty sure it should be okay."

Neil gingerly reached for the phone. Everything became incredibly still, tension in the air so thick it seemed to have substance. For some odd reason, Neil lifted the cell phone to his ear and listened before entering the number across the keypad, first punching the three digit code that got them out of the country, then the nine numbers Seth had given them. "Oh shit, it's ringing."

Before the call made it to a human voice, Neil pressed 'end call.' He panicked, not sure what to do if he'd gotten through to somebody on the other end.

Stunned by Neil's actions, Kellan looked at him with wide eyes and a gaping hole for a mouth. "Oh… Well… Did you reach somebody?"

"No. I freaked out. Didn't know what I was going to say if someone answered." Neil set the phone back down on the counter top.

"Okay. At least we know it's a phone number and hopefully it gets us the information we need. Let's think for a minute. What time is it?" Kellan rambled, linking his fingers together and cradling the back of his skull in a thinking mode.

Neil picked up the phone again. "Why not just send a simple text to let Seth or whoever is on the opposite end of this line know we're here."

"Good plan. Do it." Kellan brought his hands back down from behind his head.

"What do I type?" Neil pushed the phone toward Kellan. "Here, you do it."

Kellan took it and typed, *Hello, Buster. Your move,* then tapped send. He kept it simple so if it was Seth that picked up, he'd be the only one who understood the message. If it was somebody else, they'd most likely ignore it and the game would start all over again.

It was late at night and they didn't expect to get a return message any time soon, in fact they hadn't expected to get anything until morning. But to their surprise, one came back immediately that said, *Good Job, guys. You figured it out. You rang too?*

Text messages went back and forth between them: *How've you been? You doing okay? Are we okay? Where are you now?*

It only took a few minutes for Seth to fill Kellan and Neil in by text that he was still at TC, and that he had opened the cell phone account in Chile to prevent the government's military officials from figuring out so easily what he was up to.

After being around Seth for so many years and keeping in mind the way his mind worked, Kellan had a good idea there was probably more hidden away in the guy's head than he let anybody know, a whole lot more. From what Kellan had understood so far, Seth seemed to have some sort of plan that would help him and Neil make a life together with limited interference by the government or TC. His guess was they'd live like a family in the witness protection program, hiding out someplace remote, like in the mountains or valleys in the Himalayas. Seth had always been the type of person who thought things through before acting on them, and with that, Kellan believed he wouldn't text any messages that could be incriminating to any of them through an unsecured data line. Instead, Kellan expected he'd choose a wiser plan, and that meant waiting for another child's play code, in the hopes that Seth would name a place for them to meet.

They ended their messaging session with the famous radio jargon. Seth was the first to text, *over and out,* and then Kellan replied, *roger that.* It wasn't the typical modern day text goodbye message, but it ended the conversation on a heightened note. Times ahead were going to get rocky, they all knew that. So a bit of stupid humor helped.

After the phone went dark, Neil's face showed signs of relief. "Finally some good news. Having an informant on the inside will hopefully help us out of the jam we're in."

"Trust me, he will. The guy knows how to fix my predicaments, he always has," Kellan answered. He shook his entire body, from head to wing to toe, the same way a dog does after a bath. Then Kellan lifted and laid his pearly wings over the back of the sofa before sitting down in front of the laptop. A small huff escaped him when he dropped in the seat, followed by rubbing his hands together that made him appear greedy.

Neil sat down next to Kellan, checking out his naked body from top to bottom. "You should probably cover up all that beauty or I'll be on that thing again in a snap."

Kellan raised his brow. "Nah. We'll be in bed soon, which means you should take yours off."

"Player."

Grinning, Kellan flipped the laptop screen open and then clicked at the desktop icon that expanded his child's play number system spreadsheet. Then he said, "And the game goes on."

Chapter 9

The night before exhausted Neil and made Kellan a little drowsy. It was the newly introduced gangster sex, the mind bending computer configurations, followed by more sex that tuckered them out. When the next morning arrived, they woke somewhat refreshed, evidence shown by the sword fighting that had taken place between their legs.

Morning erections and men go together like birds and their feathers do. A man can't seem to function in the morning without his woody in hand, the same way a bird can't fly without its wings in the wind.

Kellan and Neil predicted their day would be long because connecting with Seth wasn't going to take place until sometime after dark. They agreed to meet in a remote location just outside of TC, a place that made it easier for Seth to get to.

Waiting around for the time to pass was boring. They'd been in and out of the lighthouse several times, looking around the place, sticking their feet in the waves, walking and watching

Dylan play along the beach. They frequently tried the laptop for an internet connection, but bombed at that every time. They figured, by the fifth attempt, the service was blocked for good.

Throughout the day, Neil wondered about how he was going to deal with his ash-flattened home. Should he call it a lost cause, or dig into collecting his losses? Either way, their lives were definitely never going to be the same again, but the one itch picking at him was to get back what the government took away. Was it really worth fighting a conglomerate organization that would most likely win? Neil presumed the government had already put their spin on the downed-house situation, took control of it in their own authoritarian way. They did what they wanted, took what they wanted, and showed no remorse when they did it.

Insurance on the home was another concern Neil had, but since the circumstances weren't normal, calling in a friendly agent probably would no longer work.

Neil normally had a level head on his shoulders and knew what to do about many things, but it was one of those times where he seemed to need advice. Because he was on the fence about what to do, he confronted Kellan, wondering what his thoughts for the next step should be. The logical answer Kellan gave him was to wait, and in the meantime, suggested not to contact anybody other than Seth unless he planned on adding unwanted attention to their predicament.

With Kellan's sensible reasoning, and not giving further thought, Neil mentioned the time to meet Seth was getting close, and unlike the last trip, Dylan was going on the tour as well.

They packed Dylan in the overnight bag, strapped everybody together and took off into the wind.

It was a perfect night for flying. The air was warm without being too humid. The stars were out, twinkling like diamonds behind the floating clouds, and the moon was bright enough to light the way.

Kellan flew low, but high enough to keep the bag Dylan was in from skimming across the water below them. In the distance were the lights along the Michigan mainland, outlining the waterway into Traverse Bay. Scattered around in the bay were anchored boats that apparently had plans to spend the night on the lake. Lights on board the boats flickered as they rocked and bobbed like floating corks.

Neil looked up at Kellan's chin as he dangled beneath him and asked, "We can trust Seth, right?"

"Yes. Of course. Why do you ask that now?" Kellan pulled in a shoulder and they dipped to the left. Dylan's bag swung to the right before coming back and veering to the left.

"He does work for the place you ran from. I just want to be sure he has no ulterior motive and this entire plan is to put you back there."

"I can't imagine him doing that to me. Trust me when I tell you this. He's here to help."

They flew southbound over Grand Traverse Bay toward Old Mission Point where they told Seth they would meet him. A clue they were almost there was when they passed over the old lighthouse situated at the northern-most point of the peninsula. Michigan had many lighthouses, most seemed to be built at every turn along the coastline. If there was a rock in the water, it sported a rotating beacon.

Neil had been to Old Mission Point before, and it was as he remembered it. Practically unchanged, with much of it still left to the wildlife, it was in a quiet part of Michigan that was mostly bogs, vacant fields, and miles and miles of trees that kept the point hidden from humankind. The only way to the point by land was along sporadically placed dirt roadways that weaved in and out of the trees, many trails only wide enough for a motorbike or a two wheeled cycle.

As they waited for Seth, Kellan stood behind Neil, tightly holding him against his chest, rocking from side to side. His wings flexed open, catching the crisp air coming at them off the water. It funneled down the curve of his fore feathers, covering them with a cool breeze.

While they stood locked together watching Dylan romp in front of them, jumping small waves rolling toward his furry feet, a set of headlights moved in behind them and swept across the bay. Spinning around, neither Kellan nor Neil knew for sure if it was Seth driving in, but as they observed the car moving closer, a few flashes of the headlights made them believe it was.

Dylan's head popped up and growled, but when

commanded by Neil, he stood still.

When the car stopped, they noticed it was a small vehicle that looked to be a motorized golf cart. From what they could tell, that two passenger car made perfect sense given the terrain.

It was a relief when Seth stepped out of the small car and walked up to them.

"It's good to see you, Seth." Kellan hugged him, hugged him hard.

Seth observed Kellan. "You look good, even with the hair growing on your chest. It sort of suits you. What's up with that?"

Kellan rubbed his chest with one hand and clasped Neil's hand with the other. "Neil likes it, so I plan on leaving it."

They quickly exchanged good-natured remarks while Neil stood quietly, seeming hesitant still with Seth, having little to no evidence he can or will live up to the faith Kellan has in him.

Kellan jokingly asked, "We were wondering how you were going to get here with no pavement leading the way. We thought you'd be riding across the water on a hippocampus?"

Seth laughed, "That myth is ridiculous. There's no such thing as a hippocampus."

"I wouldn't be so sure about that. The shit that's come out of that lab has yet to convince me otherwise. Look at me." Kellan fluttered his wings.

"Ya got me." Seth checked his watch, noticing the time had flown. He lowered his tone and spoke seriously. "Let me quickly tell you what I know about TC, and then I've got to get out of here. It could be dangerous for all of us if they found out I'm with you. For all I know, they could be hiding in the woods, watching."

Kellan and Neil both clamped their mouths shut, startled that their fears might actually be based on reality. It was one thing to guess about potential dangers and quite another to have it confirmed. Both of them knew Seth had been employed by the government all along, still was, but what real proof did either of them have that he was completely on their side?

Neil, who had only encountered Seth a few times, had doubts about him. Unless Neil was able to get into Seth's mind and know what he was thinking, putting total trust in the man didn't seem to be a good idea. Although Kellan seemed convinced of Seth's good intentions, Neil had reservations, but without evidence one way or the other, he was forced to accept what Seth was saying at face value, at the same time keeping a watchful eye on the man. It wasn't the best of all possible scenarios but that was all he had to work with.

Another question Neil pondered was: why hadn't the government jumped all over them by now? That struck an odd chord with him, and he wondered if Seth knew something more than what he was telling them. From the information he and Kellan had already collected from Seth, it seemed the military knew where they were. It was almost as though Seth was the one orchestrating their next move. Neil wanted to trust Seth, but gaps in what he was willing to share with them smelled fishy, and the odor wasn't coming from Lake Michigan.

Seth broke the heavy silence by saying, "TC is coming down, Kellan. After you and Neil crashed the data room, most of the west wing was destroyed by fire and water, so it's unusable. The place is moving and I'm going with it. As a matter of fact, it's happening as we speak, and the building will be deserted within the next day or two. When necessary, the government works fast."

Kellan looked shocked. "Is that why you mentioned we have a couple of days to sit tight?"

"Yes, two at the most," Seth confirmed.

Kellan felt his stomach shift. He'd felt strangely liberated for the past few days, getting used to his winged freedom, but suddenly—given Seth's news—Kellan could almost feel TC coming for him, as if they were already out there lurking in the bushes. He'd almost forgotten he was a fugitive on the run. He needed to keep moving, not stay in one place for too long. If he did, there'd be bat men and government officials on his back all over again. "Where do we go from here? Any ideas?" Kellan's voice cracked as he spoke directly to Seth, desperate to get moving.

Seth laid a hand on Kellan's shoulder. "I've been thinking about it for quite a while, figuring there'd come a time when the Lab may no longer have use for you once they took what they needed. I'm like your older brother, so my job is to take care of you and the ones you love." He glanced at Neil, who had a mystified look on his face.

Seth then sincerely added, "I'm not sure if you had noticed, because I had hidden it well, but I've always had a difficult time seeing you confined, Kellan. Couldn't bear it. Now that you're out of that place, I swore to myself to do whatever's necessary to make sure you don't go back to the way things were."

After realizing how much pain his friend had gone through over the years, Kellan slouched, his wings drooping as his shoulders dropped. "I had no idea, Seth. I've really made a mess of everything. Maybe I never should have left."

"Don't be nuts. You needed to move on, be freer than what you were. You have wings, and you need to spread them and fly. Have faith in me, Kellan. I've got you covered."

While Neil still had reservations about Seth, hearing the man's heartfelt confession went a long way toward alleviating some of his concerns. He asked, "What are you planning, Seth?"

Seth inhaled deeply. "You already know the government will get you back one way or another, right? Instead of them using force and tranquilizers as they had done before, I've convinced them that it was best if you came to AZ willingly."

"What? Are you mad?" Kellan growled, keeping his tone low.

"Just hear me out. Getting you to AZ is the best plan, Kellan. This way you won't be on the run for the rest of your life."

Kellan's hands went to his hips as he bit down on his lips and paced in circles while looking to the sky. "So now I'm going to be locked up again? How does that play out as being best?"

"It's not going to be like that this time. Let me explain."

"How can we believe what you're telling us?"

"Because they aren't done with you yet. You were engineered with hopes of someday protecting this country, and they are working on improved versions of your kind every day. You were their first real success. They need you, if for no other reason than to be the benchmark for whatever their next steps will be.

"Why not use what the Seekers are able to offer? Aren't those improvements?"

"Not exactly. They are designs that went differently than expected, and are now being considered killing machines if the country were to be put at an extremely higher risk. They still want to learn from you, Kellan. Study you. They need to know why you think logically before you attack. The Seekers don't have that rational side."

Angered by what he was hearing, Kellan's wings went up and came back down harshly. The sudden shift in the air lifted him off the ground and back down again with a thud. When he landed, he looked at Neil who was standing tensely with Dylan tightly at his side.

Once again, Seth inhaled deeply. "The only condition they had was if you flew to AZ, there would be back up choppers nearby for safety reasons and in case you tried to flee. I told them that would be fine as long as they offered assurances you would live without being caged."

"This is so fucking insane."

Seth then told him, "If it would ease your mind, they actually suggested putting you guys someplace in Colorado. It has lots of private spots where you could live peacefully."

Kellan's wings fluttered when he heard peaceful living.

"Maybe you and Neil could live like a normal family there with..." Seth stopped speaking.

"I can't believe I'm thinking of agreeing with all this. But with... what?" Kellan caught Seth's slip of the tongue. "But with what?" he asked again, noticing Seth's facial expression revealed he had more to tell but for some reason was holding back.

"What I have to show you next might convince you to agree quicker. It's the real reason I came out here in the first place. Follow me to the car, I've got something extremely secret I'd like you to know," Seth said.

Kellan gripped Neil's hand and side-stepped Seth on the way to the car, trying not to show concern that what he might tell them could be bad.

Seth opened the door, reached for a purple folder and an electronic tablet he had sitting on the passenger seat. He left the door open to let the light from inside flood the pages he was about to show Kellan.

Neil's heart sped up when he saw there was a tablet as well. He wasn't sure he was ready for what was on it, and whatever was, he truly hoped it was going to change his thoughts about Seth being trust worthy, and show the man had integrity.

So far, everything that Neil witnessed coming out that lab,

with the exception of Kellan, had been a downright nightmare, and much of it shouldn't even exist. TC was enormously fucked up and the people there didn't seem to realize they were about to turn the world upside down with the shit they were creating inside that place.

"What I'm going to show you, Kellan, will be a bit of a shock. So I need you to keep it together and not get hysterical," Seth said.

At that moment, Neil huffed and so did Kellan. Neither wanted any bad news, and what they were about to be shown better be convincing enough to consider going along with Seth's plan.

Seth chose to let Kellan see for himself instead of telling him. Seeing was believing, and pictures told a thousand words. Seth tapped the tablet screen, and it quickly lit up. He then clicked open a video feed and stood silent to let the feed run.

They viewed the screen that showed what looked to be an examination bed in a tiny room, like the ones Kellan was familiar with at TC. On it was a small form, all alone in a darkened room but with just enough ambient light coming from somewhere they could make out a few details. It was a little person who appeared to be no more than nine or maybe ten years old. Given the few features visible they were able to see, it was a boy. He lay snuggling a stuffed bunny while stroking the long lazy ears dangling down the sides of its head.

Neil lost his ability to breathe, afraid of what he might see next.

Kellan's heart thumped so hard, it caused pain in his chest. He strained to get a better look at the kid but couldn't see much. The tiny form was clutching the toy bunny so tightly that only a small part of his face was visible. It appeared that he was keeping it hidden, like he was crying, or ashamed to show his face. A morbid thought crossed Kellan's mind that made his heart ache, making him believe the kid was disfigured in some way or he was one of those experiments that had gone horribly wrong. From what he'd been familiar with during his time at TC, that was a continual occurrence until the maniacs got it right. Kellan hoped for the best, flushing away the hideous thoughts that there could be something seriously wrong with the kid.

Both Neil and Kellan must have been thinking the same thing — why was Seth showing them the video feed?

Then the pain in Kellan's chest grew bigger when the small boy let go of the bunny and sat up, legs stretched out in front of him over the center of the bed, his little feet knocking together like he was keeping rhythm to a song he might be singing. There was no sound accompanying the video clip so they could only guess.

What they saw was far from what Neil and Kellan were expecting to see, catching them totally off guard.

"Oh dear God," Kellan hummed. He couldn't believe what he was seeing. The cutest image ever. Kellan knew he himself was gorgeous, a magical wonder, but what he saw sitting on that bed was spectacular, even to him. He was looking at a small version of himself, a little angel and that angel looked just like him.

Neil cupped both hands over his nose and mouth, feeling winded. He gasped, "Sweet Jesus, could it be? Bless that gorgeous little angel."

Completely enthralled by what had to be the most beautiful creature on earth, both Kellan and Neil gave in to a wash of emotions riveting them to the scene playing out on the small screen.

That was when Seth opened the purple folder and handed the documents in it to Kellan. They mentioned that Kellan's DNA was used to conceive another life form. There were tests documenting that, giving clear evidence there was a child. A boy child. One with wings.

Neil was captivated by what he was experiencing, had never expected Seth to tell them a smaller angel existed, or even, an enhanced version of Kellan. It was almost unbelievable. Then to be told the boy was a cloned version from Kellan's DNA was what really astounded them, gave them good reason to follow Seth's plan to the end. They eventually emerged from their trance-like state and gave into reality. Kellan first, followed by Neil.

Kellan was mostly concerned as to where the little angel could be. There had never been any sign of another like him at the Lab all the years he was there. Surely he'd have seen something or at least heard about it, outright or discretely.

Kellan reeled as the consequences hit him hard, bringing with it sadness to the point of numbness. It wasn't because he hadn't been given the chance to know the tiny angel, presumably his son if the documents were valid, but because Kellan was all too familiar with being locked in a tiny room all his life, not knowing the people who might truly love him or ever given the space he needed to really fly. Kellan looked at the little angel and wondered if the boy ever thought the same thing.

Kellan continued watching him, observing the way he moved and maneuvered his wings.

As the tiny angel sat there in the small room on the edge of the bed, Kellan saw himself, the family resemblance irrefutable. He knew the boy was his. His hair, his eyes, and the pearly white wings told him so. Kellan couldn't look away and instantly fell in love with him, the boy he never knew. His beautiful son with wings.

Glancing over at Neil, Kellan saw tears forming in his eyes. Not those that surfaced from sadness, but jubilant ones, the type of tears that come without notice when the heart becomes overwhelmed by pure happiness.

Kellan, wrestling with his emotions, turned to Seth and asked, "How long have you known about him?"

Seth confessed, "Truthfully, I just found out about him after you left. I had no idea he existed, and I don't think anybody at TC wanted me to know about him, like he was more top secret than you were."

Doing everything he could to keep from going hysterical, Kellan asked another question, "Who's been taking care of him if it hasn't been you?"

"The files show a signature on every document—all the same—but I can't make out who it belongs to."

Neil was pacing, making tracks in the dirt. "Does this mean he's not at TC?"

Seth flipped through a few more papers, showing them there was no mention of a location. "I don't think so."

Kellan's chest puffed up like he was getting ready for battle; his wings flexed, too. "Tell me where he is, Seth. I need get him out of that fucked up place."

"I would if I could, but I'm still working at figuring out his location. All I know is that he was born at TC, held there for a while, and then moved. Where to, I don't exactly know yet." Seth reached the last page and then closed the folder.

Neil suggested, "If he isn't at the lab, why would the files be kept there? Wouldn't they be wherever he's at?"

"Good point," Kellan added.

Seth pressed the file to his chest and folded his arms over it. "Not necessarily. All files are kept wherever the creation had been. Digital and paper form. We keep duplicates on everything. Since Kaleb was born at TC, there were duplicate files kept there too."

Kellan's eyes snapped open and he looked up. "Hold on. Is his name Kaleb?"

"All the files are labeled Kaleb, so I am calling him that." Seth sounded certain.

Neil smiled at that. He liked his name.

Kellan put a hand to his jaw. "I can't believe I might be a father. We need to get to him, Seth. Help us, would you please?"

Nodding agreement, Seth said, "The moment I have something, I'll send you a text. Stay close to that phone."

Reluctant to get going, especially when they were still trying to come to terms with news that changed everything, the men realized they had little choice. Time wasn't something on their side anymore.

The sound of a boat engine was enough to remind them they needed to get moving.

Seth flinched, glanced out across the water and made a comment that he should be going and they needed to get out of there too, back to the island where it was safer. "One more thing," — he reached inside the car and pulled out a small case — "I don't know if you need these, but they belong to you." Seth, gave them both a quick hug, hopped in the car and drove away with the lights off.

Putting an end to the risk of being exposed as they were, Kellan rushed Dylan into the satchel, scooped Neil into his arms and took to the sky. It was dark and balmy, and their flight back home was a quiet one.

Chapter 10

Before Kellan brought them to the ground, he circled the island, looking for anything that might be out of the ordinary. He paid close attention to any signs that a Seeker might be ready to pounce as soon as they touched down. There was no noise from Dylan, so it seemed the coast was clear.

Neil finally spoke after their noiseless flight home. "That child of yours is gorgeous, Kellan. He has your eyes, nose, and mouth. It was amazing."

Kellan lifted his head. "Yeah, I noticed that too, but I'm not sure I'm cut out to be a father."

"Why would you say that? Look how you've taken care of me since we've met. You'd make a terrific dad." Neil took Kellan's hand and walked with him into the lighthouse.

Dylan crazily ran between them to the cookie door like nothing had changed, and there he waited, smiling with a lapping tongue.

"Kaleb is ten years old and I've never been around a single

child. I have zippo experience in that area," Kellan confessed, squeezing Neil's hand with laced fingers.

"I do and would love nothing more than to help you raise that kid." Neil stepped in front of Kellan and kissed him gently on the lips.

Kellan registered all the confusing emotions in his heart, most being different scenarios of his concern for Kaleb. He was having a tough time dismissing that his young child might be locked up someplace, probably miserable, or worse, suffering. He was only one person, but assuming Neil would be with him, there was a possibility he could work through any doubts he had about being dad-material. Even with his uncertain thoughts, he was determined to bring that angel home to meet his dads.

As much as Kellan wanted to act on impulse, there were still other considerations, other issues to address. If there was any hope that he could live a normal life with Neil, Kaleb and Dylan, he needed to wait to hear what Seth had in store. Hearing there was a place in Colorado where they could live seemed promising, but how could they do that if Kellan was still tethered to the government?

Kellan followed Neil into the kitchen, gave Dylan the cookie he had been waiting for before taking a seat next to Neil, who had already found a spot on the rickety sofa.

When Kellan sat, Neil tipped into him and said, "For now, let's try not to think about any of this, and wait for any ideas Seth has. Until then, I'm sure Kaleb will be okay. They didn't hurt you, so it doesn't seem likely they'd do anything to harm him."

"I can't get little Kaleb out of my mind. I keep seeing him alone in that room, and it's ripping me apart."

"I know it's difficult to see him like that. It is for me too, but he's safe where he is and we can't do anything about it right now. He'll be okay." As positive as Neil tried to sound, his face revealed his reservations.

Breaking the tension, Dylan stood in front of them, snapping his teeth like he was still chewing.

Kellan looked at him and said, "What's wrong with him?"

"The cookie is stuck in his jaw." Neil massaged each side of Dylan's face, helping him transfer the cookie piece between his teeth so he could finish eating it.

A weak smile made it to Kellan's face when Dylan grabbed a stuffed toy and put it on the sofa between them. Having Dylan there with his quirky ways helped keep his mind off Kaleb. "What did you do with that portable case Seth gave us?"

"I wasn't thinking when we came in and don't remember what I did with it. It's probably by the door." Neil got up and found it where he thought it was, placed it in Kellan's lap and told him to open it up.

"What could this possibly be?" Kellan wondered.

"Maybe there's something to eat or a few pairs of your pants in there. Open it and see."

Kellan snapped the latches back and flipped the lid open. His eyes popped and so did Neil's. "What the—?" was all Kellan muttered.

Neil chuckled, he couldn't help it. "What on earth made him think to send those?"

"How do I know, but I'm glad he included a few pairs of jeans."

"Well… These could be fun." Neil reached into the case and pulled out a twelve inch double ended dildo, wiggled it a few times, and then reached back in and took out a different one that had a set of balls and a vibrator switch, and said, "Now, this one I'd like."

"Put those down." Embarrassed, Kellan plucked the dildos from Neil's hand and tossed them back in the case next to the biggest bottle of oil Neil had ever seen.

Neil leaned into Kellan. "They aren't the first ones I've seen or used myself, so there's no need for you to be shy about having them. I'm sure Seth thought they would help the both of us keep a sane disposition through all that's happened and what might take place."

"Yeah, the guy is always thinking." Kellan inhaled and rolled his eyes.

"Listen, why don't you take Dylan outside for a quick walk, and I'll have a nice surprise waiting for you when you get back."

"That doesn't sound good. What's on that twisted mind of yours?" Kellan squinted at Neil, one eye closed further than the other.

"Don't worry about it. Just take Dylan outside and let me

worry about working the tension out of those wings of yours. That's my job now."

Kellan shook his wings as he pushed himself from the arm of the sofa, ruffling them vigorously to let in a little air. Doing that always helped him relax a little and was a clue Neil recently picked up on that indicated Kellan was truly tense.

ରୋ ୨୦

After Kellan left the lighthouse with Dylan, Neil disrobed quickly. He stood naked in the living room, anticipating a one-on-one fuck with Kellan. His dick was harder than a rock already and there was clear semen oozing from the crown. Neil swiped a finger through the drippy glaze, brought it to his mouth and sucked it from his fingertip.

Neil reached for the vibrating dildo and bottle of lubricant and prepared himself for entry by plunging wet fingers into his own tight hole. Neil got even harder as he fantasized about Kellan getting off in his mouth and coating his tongue with his hot spicy cum. He had never mentioned to Kellan how much he enjoyed swallowing his semen, but he was sure Kellan could tell he did by the way Neil sucked him dry after dumping his load down his throat.

Excited to get started, Neil slathered the dildo with oil and then worked his asshole a little more with a few slippery fingers. He then lay back on the floor and waited for Kellan to return to watch him in action, letting him get a taste of what Neil already had the pleasure of seeing him do on the laptop.

After what seemed like an interminable amount of time, Kellan returned to find Neil completely naked on the living room floor, spread eagle, ready to shove one of the dildos Seth had delivered up his slippery asshole.

"Damn nice. Seeing you like that makes me want to take a vibrating dildo up my own ass while fucking you at the same time," Kellan greedily said. His wings started rising, like they were getting an erection, too.

Looking up with a grin, Neil noticed Kellan's dick was visibly stiffening and his jeans were getting wet with semen.

"It's your turn to watch, Kellan. There will be no more hang-ups about me seeing you fuck yourself with a rubber dick. This way we'll be even." Neil put his legs in the air and spread them far enough apart so he could ease the vibrating pleasure rod effortlessly into his flexing pucker. Just the thought of it going in caused Neil's rock hard boner to start twitching. His meaty cock popped upward and then fell against his stomach with a thud, nestling in the hair at the base of his dick, oozing pre-cum that dampened his six-pack. His legs instinctively spread further apart when he circled his lubricated knot with the head of the dildo and popped it in. The urge to make it go deeper grew stronger. He pulled it out, and then pushed it back in a little further. He trembled each time the buzzing dildo head moved over the magic spot inside him, and before the orgasmic sensation peaked, Neil stopped the motion to catch his breath.

At that breathless moment, Neil caught a glimpse of Kellan in front of him, getting ready to sit down on one of the other dildos. Neil followed Kellan's lead and did the same, shifting to his knees and perfectly centering the lubricated dildo with his slick entrance, all the while making believe it was Kellan's dick he was about to impale himself with. Neil then pleaded, "Let's go all the way down on these fat cocks, Kellan. Let's make them disappear, together."

As their harmonized torsos lowered to complete penetration, guttural groans echoed in the small room. Their eyes locked on one another's, turning smoky with lust.

Neil watched Kellan move, noticing the pleasure he was getting from a dildo sliding in and out of his body. That magical sight almost made Neil cum without even gripping his own cock and stroking it. Imitating Kellan, Neil rocked his hips in a way that moved the dildo deeper inside him.

Neil became intensely aroused as he observed Kellan take the dildo to its maximum depth, leaving hardly any space between his ass and the floor. Neil's attention stayed pinned on Kellan while he watched him brutally rock his hips back and forth, driving the dildo repeatedly against his prostate to increase the pleasure of getting fucked. Each time Kellan swiftly gyrated on the dildo, his wingtips slapped Neil's cheeks before snapping back and doing it all over again. It was like a method of pleasure by torture.

Becoming enthused by Kellan's muscled torso crunching and flexing as he moved, Neil's eyelids dropped to thin slits and his mouth sprang open. Unable to drown it out, soft moans of desire increased to a throaty roar when he turned the dial on the vibrator to a higher setting. His body buckled, and he started quaking.

Teetering on the edge, they shared an erotic moment without touching each other. They bounced up and down together, rocking in unison, the dildos assaulting their prostates, pushing their sensual moans to a level neither one could control.

Neil locked his eyes on Kellan's, wanting him to come over and take him. As if connected to Neil's thoughts, Kellan uncoiled his wings, swished them forward into Neil's space but didn't touch him. The electricity his wingtips created while skating above Neil's inner thighs caused the tiny hairs to stand and follow the floating feathers. The space between them and the sexual pull was almost too much to bear.

The anxiety of it all amplified Neil's sexual drive. He leaned back on his hands and spread his legs, giving Kellan a better look at the dildo moving in and out of him. By the way Kellan so quickly snapped his wings behind his back and bent forward with the eyes of a wild animal, the idea of opening himself up seemed to have worked.

"Hot damn, Neil. Seeing you like this makes me want to pull that dildo out of you, replace it with my dick, and screw your brains out."

Neil's desire was mutual, but at the moment he only wanted Kellan to gaze at him stroking his cock. Tease him a bit more. Push the man's need to copulate into overdrive. Introducing thoughts of actually getting fucked by Kellan made Neil's body squirm. The fantasy excited him, took his mind on a trip. Eager to give Kellan a better show, Neil licked his fingers and pinched his nipples. His back arched when he did that, forcing the dildo further into himself.

Kellan groaned, "Oh, Gawd, Neil. If you keep that up, I'm going to sperm-coat your chest right now." His wings fluttered at his sides.

Neil gasped behind a slanted grin, but continued to pleasure himself while Kellan watched. He kept the dildo in place while making sure Kellan could still see, managing circular movements of his hips to hit every desired spot deep within himself. The vibrating dildo felt amazing the deeper inside his tight hole it went, and he whimpered as the orgasmic sensation kept building. More semen dripped from Neil's dick as he slid the dildo in and out of his slippery channel with one hand. Shuttering from the intense pleasure, he rolled back at the foot of the sofa and pushed the dildo even deeper. His legs opened wider as he pulled the vibrating device out and then shoved it back in. He labored for air as he drew the entire dildo out again. Slowly circling his expanded sphincter with the head of the dildo, Neil then plunged it back in without mercy. "Fuck, that's good," he rumbled, and then repeated the motion again and again, pulling it out completely and pushing it back in. His back arched from unbound pleasure and his moaning hit an octave he never figured he was capable of reaching.

Clear semen milked from Neil's flexing prostate ran down the full length of his dick, settling into the hair at the base of his shaft. Being attracted to his own semen, Neil selfishly transferred it to his tongue.

After being lost in his own butt fucking session, Neil suddenly noticed Kellan had changed positions and was propped face down over the arm of the sofa while plowing himself from behind with the rubber dildo. Kellan's face was full of pleasure as he slid the dildo in and out with one hand and the other pinched his nipples. Semen spilled from him and the pleasure made his wings flex toward the ceiling.

Wanting to mimic Kellan, Neil urgently shifted onto his hands and knees and held the dildo in place by backing his ass against the base of the sofa behind him. He rocked back and forth on his hands and knees, sliding the slippery dildo in and out of his slick back door. He closed his eyes and let his imagination soar. "Fuck me, Kellan, fuck that ass," Neil growled while prodding his prostate into a fiery frenzy with the girth of the dildo.

At that moment, Kellan whimpered and so did Neil, both treasuring the vibrating dildos that were reaming their greedy assholes. If their rock hard, throbbing dicks were any indication, being a bottom was no hardship for either of them.

Kellan vocalizing his need, his pleasure, was enough to send Neil into orbit. Almost out of his mind, and so turned on he was barely aware of anything but the winged angel and his own desperation, he felt the freight train coming, totally out of control and hell bent on taking him on a one-way trip to paradise.

Then he heard Kellan growl, "Oh fuck, I'm gonna cum."

Kellan stood, turned and sat on the edge of the sofa's arm with the dildo still inside his body. Pushing back, the dildo went in further, mercilessly massaging his prostate into what had to be a mind-blowing frenzy. His abdomen went tight and he twitched with guttural roars.

Neil propped himself up to do the same, holding the vibrating dildo up his ass while sitting on the floor. He reached for his rock hard cock and stroked it. Neil mumbled while imagining Kellan was the one pummeling his ass, shoving his thick dick in and out of him. He muttered to himself, not caring that Kellan could hear him. "Keep fucking me, Kellan. Drill my tight hole. Make me cum."

By the time Kellan reached for his own thick dick, he was already spitting cum across the floor in front of him, one hefty shot after another flew from his dick. His face went screwy and then soft, giving away his undeniable pleasure from getting fucked in the ass. He twisted his nipples between finger and thumb, adding heightened pleasure to his already powerful release.

Extremely aroused after watching Kellan cum, Neil rolled back, lying on the floor and gave his cock a single stroke. His throat roared as pasty white semen blasted from his cock at gunshot speed. Several ropes of cum laced his chest and pelted the roof of his open mouth, giving him no choice but to swallow. Neil enjoyed the taste of himself — loved his cum. He stroked his cock again and another hot ribbon of semen shot high, whipping his cheek and ear with a saucy splat. Neil jerked forward and wailed until the last spurt let loose, splashing his chest and stomach again. Gasping with synchronized tremors, he pulled his knees to his chest, letting the vibrating dildo shoot from his ass. As the rubber dick slipped out of him, Neil glanced at Kellan who was sucking his own cum from his dripping fingers.

Seeing that turned Neil on. He dove for more of his own,

scooping semen from his wet chest into his hand and letting what he collected pour onto his tongue and down his throat. Greedily he swallowed while imagining Kellan's spurting dick in his mouth.

Kellan lifted off the arm of the sofa, and when he stood, the dildo dropped from his slippery chute to the floor as his dick still dripped semen over the edge of his hand. "Holy fuck, Neil. Doing that live with you was intense and a whole new fantastic-fucking experience. So much better than being alone, that's for sure. You surprised me with that little stunt, but it was worth stumbling into. Next time I want you to use your dick on me in place of the dildo."

"That can be arranged, but a little later. At this second, I don't think I have any more cum to give you." Neil grinned, still lying on his back covered in cum and the head of the dildo pointed at his asshole as if it had a plan to go back in.

"My ass will be ready whenever that dick of yours is."

愁 愂

Kellan had fantasized many times about having Neil fuck "him" instead of the other way around—Neil on top, Kellan on the bottom. He wasn't sure how they were going to pull that off with wings on his back, but he was certainly going to find a way to make it work.

Being a hot bottom doesn't always mean back to the ground and legs up. There's crab straddling a cock that works great for a bottom. Face down, getting cock-plowed from behind does too. Even taking a boner in the ass as a sidewinder can be a satisfying position for a bottom. As long as the asshole gets the cock, a bottom man that does make.

Kellan had never been fucked in the ass by a man's stiff dick before, only the dildos he'd come into possession of at TC. Even without the experience of ever having a man's cock sliding inside him, Kellan was convinced that it was going to prove much better than a tubular shaped slab of rubber. The whole process of fucking himself took too much of his own energy to maneuver a dildo in and out of his sex chute, and most of the time, cramped his wrist. Having Neil use his asshole to get his rocks off would make fucking more exhilarating, and knowing he'd be pleasing Neil by letting him inside was as thrilling to Kellan as it was to get fucked by him.

"I've never seen your eyes sparkle like that before. What are you thinking about?" Neil asked.

Kellan flexed his wings and gave them a gentle beat as he lowered himself to his knees at Neil's side. He laid a hand to Neil's chest and caressed it, circling his thumbs around each nub the way he knew Neil liked. After releasing a slow breath of air, he answered, "I was imagining how good it would feel having that perfect dick of yours sliding in and out of me, injecting me with a part of you that would make us closer. You know, mark me so it's known that I belong to you. I'd like that very much." Then he kissed Neil quickly on the lips as if trying to mask an awkward moment.

Neil quickly lip pecked Kellan back and said, "You make it sound so animalistic. But I will say I like where this is going."

"When I've seen how you've reacted when I've fucked you, how much you liked it, I wasn't sure you'd want to trade places. That's why I hadn't mentioned flip flopping before."

Neil raised himself from the floor, placed a hand to the nape of Kellan's neck and kissed him gently, with meaning. When he pulled away he said, "I never encouraged switching roles because I was waiting for you to decide when the time was good for you. I'm not the type of person that takes what is not offered first."

Kellan scooted closer to Neil, and whispered in his ear, "I love you, Neil. Any time would have been good for me. You've seen how I get with those dildos. Tonight you've witnessed it up close and personal. Now I want a real man to show me what it's like so I don't have to do all the work on my own. It can be rough on the wrist and these wings keep getting in my way."

"Say no more, I've got you covered." Neil grinned, and gave Kellan a quick peck on the neck that made him chuckle and twitter his wings.

Then Kellan said, "Awesome. I can't wait to get started. Let's give making a family a try."

C8 BO

Neil's spine stiffened from what Kellan had said about starting a family. What came to mind was so off the wall, it blindsided him. Until that moment, he'd always known when two men butt-fucked, it was about increasing the pleasure between them and intensifying each other's orgasm. But considering where Kellan had come from, Neil's fertilization belief seemed likely — the idea of starting a family wasn't something he'd ever considered, yet when Neil had seen Kellan's son, it seemed the most natural thing in the world. But that wasn't the only way to jump on the family bandwagon.

Feeling stupid, Neil blurted, "You don't lay eggs, do you? I mean... My sperm... you know." He blushed furiously.

It took Kellan a few moments to get what Neil was asking and when he did he burst out laughing. "What is it, change of heart? You no wan' to fuck me?"

"No. Not that at all. I want to. Really I do. I was just thinking if I left a deposit up inside you, would there be any chance of producing an egg or a child?"

Kellan chuckled. "You make it sound so automated. I hadn't given that any thought, but it's funny that scenario popped into your head. To ease your wandering mind, there's no chance of any eggs or fowl-like babies dropping into a nest because you fucked me. I hadn't been equipped with any lady bits, thank the heavens for that. I couldn't imagine having to deal with *that* issue."

Neil sniggered, followed by a sense of relief. "You've said it before, you wouldn't be surprised by the shit that comes out of that lab, so what was I to think? I don't know the risks your asshole holds. For all I know, I could fertilize whatever's up there."

Then Kellan let out an abdominal crunch-busting laugh. "Fertilize me as much as you want. There's no need to worry about becoming an expectant parent. Not gonna happen by way of my asshole."

"That's good to know, and I'm glad you found a humorous side to our conversation."

Kellan lay on his side next to Neil, propping himself on one elbow. He ran the back of his other hand down Neil's chest, dragging cum with it and stopping when his nails met the hair above his dick. He circled his fingers through the warm fur before wrapping a good grip around Neil's shaft that quickly hardened from his touch.

Neil lay on his back and propped a bent arm under his head to lift it from the floor. He watched Kellan stroke his cock, slowly and softly, making his dick feel good and aroused all over again. "What are you up to now, stud?"

"Nothing. Just playing. You feel good in my hand, and I'm relaxed when I hold you like this." Kellan's grip made Neil's erection twitch.

Neil reached up and fanned his fingers over Kellan's chest, feeling the new hair that was growing. His hairy chest felt good against his palm and he knew Kellan liked the way his petting hand felt.

Neil then noticed Kellan's facial expression change, a look that showed he was thinking deeply and it was no longer about having sex. Neil was so tuned into his lover, it was chilling how he knew when something was troubling him. "You're thinking about Kaleb aren't you?"

Kellan rolled his eyes until he was looking straight into Neil's and said, "You can sense my thoughts already. Now that's impressive and must mean our auras have aligned. I only hope Seth will be able to find out where he's at without any problems. Now that I know Kaleb is out there somewhere, I'd really like to see that kid. The sooner the better."

Neil sighed. "Who would have thought that yesterday we'd be talking about a child of yours today, let alone starting a family? Makes you really think how quickly your life can change, doesn't it?"

Kellan tucked the arm he was holding himself up with under Neil's head, and then laid a cheek on Neil's shoulder. The traces of semen still coating Neil's chest found a way to his nose, and its musky scent obviously made him harden. His wings extended full length behind him, sprawling flat out across the floor. He sighed, inhaled a couple times and then kissed Neil's chest goodnight.

Chapter 12

Even though Kellan woke with a stone stiff erection, it didn't stop him from asking Neil about his. "Are you going to tell me about the dream you had last night that gave you such a rock hard boner this morning?"

Neil stretched his entire body with a gritty groan. "Since you're asking. I dreamt my dick was buried inside you the entire night and your ass wouldn't let go once my bone found its way in."

"Excellent dream. Wish I was there with you," Kellan grumbled. Hearing what Neil just said made his own dick start leaking the renowned Kellan lubricant.

"There's still time to bring the dream to life." Neil watched Kellan's reaction, hoping what they talked about the night before still stood as an option.

Kellan couldn't wait another second to have at Neil's cock, take it for a ride, straddle it like a bronco riding cowboy. Ever since they spoke of flip flopping, he wanted it badly; in fact, he had a hell of a time sleeping through the night because his asshole wouldn't relax. Kellan decided there wasn't going to be any more holding back.

The excitement of what was about to take place had Kellan's seminal vesicle already producing a hefty amount of semen as though he was prematurely ejaculating before they even got started. But like all the other times, Kellan's self-made lube would ease the butt-fucking entry. Kellan furrowed his wings upward behind him at the same time he flipped the covers down around their feet.

Neil lay on his back, face up, all his rock hard goodness exposed.

"Holy fuck, you look good. Every fucking bit of you." Kellan was heating up and wasted no time making his move. He was so hot and bothered, ready to cum, and all it took for that was to just look at Neil's naked form. Kellan feverishly straddled Neil's thighs, making sure the semen that was flowing from his dick poured over Neil's cock, wetting it for penetration.

As Kellan's slippery sap glazed over Neil's cock, it didn't take a mind reader to see how eager Neil was. The upright cock, growing stiffer and harder by the second was a dead giveaway. Taking advantage of the opportunity, Kellan moved forward, sat on the cum soaked pole and sank down on it, taking every bit of it in, deep into his guts, all at once.

After only a few bronco bull rides up and down on Neil's erection, the sensation that Kellan felt inside and out was too great. Everything about getting fucked by Neil was driving him wild, from the dick jammed inside him to the warm hair at the base of Neil's shaft that scrubbed against his taint and ball sack when total penetration was made. Sexual craving spread through Kellan, exceeding any he'd experienced before or could have imagined. Uncontrolled cries echoed as the promise of an ultimate climax seized his body and threatened to drive him over the edge so far he'd end up numb and wiped out.

The slurping sound heard with every up stroke was what finally pushed Kellan over the edge. At the final stroke, when he pulled off Neil's erection and sank down on it again, the intense orgasm within him forced ribbons of semen from his dick to splash over Neil's chest and face. Even after watching Neil cum, seeing the flush of pleasure bathe his face and body, it still came as a shock to experience the out-of-control sensations of nerves detonating, releasing him with a roar of pleasure as his body quaked and gyrated ahead of each blast. His eyes clamped shut and his brain felt like it had blown wide open.

At the same moment Kellan sat back onto Neil's lap, taking his cock back in, Neil lost all control. His hips violently thrust into Kellan, and with each plunge, Neil spewed a fiery load far into Kellan's semen slicked chute. Spurt after spurt, Neil grunted while filling his man.

Breathless, Kellan collapsed against Neil and waited for the final twitches dominating his body to finish. While Kellan pumped the last of what he had from his dick into the gutters of Neil's abdomen, his slick chute sucked Neil's dick off until every drop of cum found a cozy place inside him.

Neil's body jerked a few more times, spitting the remaining spunk from his dick into Kellan.

"Hot Damn!" Kellan's lungs heaved as he lay pressed against Neil's wet chest. "I'm sorry, Neil. I didn't mean to cum so quickly. But your cock felt so fucking good."

"Wow! That was intensely hot. There was no holding back for me either. The second you sat down and clamped your ass around my dick, I was dumping my load up your hole like I had no control." Neil exhaled, letting go of his dirty desires.

Kellan regrettably slipped himself off of Neil's cock and sat beside him, crossing his legs the way an Indian would if sitting on the ground in front of a fire pit. "Dimmit! I didn't want the first time you fucked me to be like that. I've been so horny since last night's talk about trading places in bed that I couldn't wait another minute to feel you stick your dick into me. We'll take it easy for sure next time and make slow passionate love the way it should've been done. I really want that."

Neil sat up and faced Kellan, cum from Kellan dripping down his face and chest. "As difficult as it may be, we can overlook this one. Make believe it never took place."

"Impossible, but I'll give it a try. I'll bottom for you later on." Kellan adoringly kissed Neil, tasting the sweetness of his own spunk that had found its way to Neil's mouth. He licked his lips, swallowed and went back for more.

Interrupting their tender moment, the hummingbird that had been hanging around hovered at the window, tapping the pane with its beak a few times.

Neil noticed it first, and then Kellan turned in time to catch it zipping away.

"All right. That's it. There is something weird about that bird. It seems as though it's trying to warn us about something." Kellan stood up, tucked in his wings at his back and went to the window to look out.

Just then, there was a knock at the door that made Dylan scramble to his feet and grumble a low bark, like he was gnawing on a piece of leather and making sounds while doing it. It was a warning growl that meant the intruder would get it full blast if they stepped through the door without being invited.

Neil's heart synchronized with each desperate knock. He took after Dylan to calm him down, shushing and consoling him by stroking his back.

Startled too, Kellan spun from the window and crept across the floor with his dick held securely in one hand. He peeked as best he could out the window next to the door, and with a gritty whisper, he said, "Who the hell could that be?"

Neil whispered back, "I don't know. We're not expecting anybody."

"Stay where you are and don't answer it. Whoever it is could be dangerous for both of us." Kellan put a shushing finger to his lips as he looked over at Neil who was crouched down on the floor with Dylan.

Neil shook his head. His face was creased with worry.

Then another knock, one that was more like a gentle tap.

"Fuck!" Kellan's throat sounded horse and breathy. "Sshh. Keep quiet. And get ready to fly out the back if we need to."

A few seconds later a breathy voice came from the other side of the door, calling, "Kellan... Neil... Are you in there?"

Kellan stood erect and relaxed his wings. The sound of Seth's voice pulled him out of battle mode. He turned toward Neil and nodded, letting him know everything should be okay. Providing Seth was alone.

Neil was already standing, struggling to cover his own dick with both hands. Dark silky hair sprouted around and between his fingers, and the cum he forgot about dripped down his chest and found refuge in the gutters of his six-pack.

Dylan stood quietly by Neil's side, watching the door as Kellan stepped up to it. Hesitating a second, Kellan leaned against the doorjamb and asked, "Seth. Is that you and are you alone?"

Seth stood on his toes trying to look through the window at the top of the door and answered, "Yes. I'm here alone. Can I come in?"

"You can, but hold on, we're not dressed."

"No big deal, Kellan. I've seen you in all your glory before," Seth confirmed.

"But it's different this time. Neil isn't dressed either."

Seth replied in a low grumble, "Kellan, I'm a nurse. What either of you have swinging between your legs will not shock me."

Neil looked down at his dripping torso, then up again at Kellan and winced. Seconds after that, he shrugged. His right lip tilted up as if he was trying to convince himself he didn't care if Seth saw him in his current condition.

"All right then. But no judging what you see." Kellan clicked the lock.

Finally the door creaked open. Seth was standing outside on the stoop, alone like he said. In his hand he carried more folders and the electronic tablet he had the night before. Aside from that, he had a smile on his face that looked like he was pleased to find them. Then all at once he went serious, the way he always did when something seemed to be wrong.

Kellan invited Seth into the house and didn't care that he saw them completely naked, or that Neil was cum drenched and glowing from early morning lust. Seth's expression when he saw Neil doused in spunk made Kellan smirk. Kellan had always been a big producer of semen at a single discharge, and it would have surprised him if Seth hadn't realized most of what was dripping down Neil's chest had come from him.

Seth awkwardly said, "Hello," followed by a hand to the forehead salute.

Kellan saluted back, losing the grip he had on his dick. It swung free and hit him with a wet smack against his inner thigh.

As Seth moved further into the room, heading toward Neil,

Kellan recognized he was filtering air through his nose and must have been able to identify the pungent traces of freshly ejaculated semen. The man on man mating ritual and the masculine touches they gave one another was nobody's business. At that point, there was no way to hide what they'd been doing anyway, so Kellan didn't give a rat's ass what he thought about that either.

Kellan went to the sofa and pulled a cushion from it, putting it in front of Neil to conceal all he had. "What brings you to this island, Seth, and how did you get here?"

"A watercraft comes in handy when there's water involved. As soon as you put some pants on, I'll tell you more about it. Get dressed because I need to show you this." Seth waived the folders in front of him.

"I'm fine like this. Show me what you've got," Kellan said.

"Not happening. I don't care if I'd seen you with all your junk dangling before, go put some pants on," Seth ordered. "I'm not going to stand here with your hairy nuts and floppy dick swinging all over my papers."

Neil laughed.

Seth turned to Neil and politely asked for his help, "Would you mind getting this lumpy lug dressed, or at least into a pair of shorts?"

Spinning Kellan by the arm, Neil took him away and told him to cover up his precious parts.

As they walked away, Kellan fanned his wings, pushing air into Seth, making the folders in his grasp flap in the breeze.

Seth held his papers tightly, keeping them from blowing away. "There he is. The child I know."

The keyword Kellan heard loud and clear was child. "You got something on Kaleb?" he asked, hopping back toward Seth on one foot while snaking the other one into one of the pant legs. His wings flapped, attempting to keep him balanced.

Neil zipped the pants he had put on and then wiped Kellan's cum from his chest with the shirt he picked up from the floor.

Seth laid the folders open on the countertop in the kitchen. Starting with page fifty-two, he pointed out the place where he thought Kaleb was being kept. It appeared he was still in a government facility, which was located in Arizona.

"There's another one of those labs in Arizona?" Kellan questioned.

"AZ and TC are far from being the only two. Those are the two big ones I know about. Trust me, Kellan, there are many more like them hidden in this country alone. I can guarantee that."

"Amazing. Who would have thunk? Why would they keep us so far apart?"

"It worked in their favor. You here, him there. That way you'd never see each other and would have no reason to attempt making contact with each other. They wanted you two to think you each were the only one."

"Are there others?" Kellan seemed shocked.

"I don't think so, but I'm not positive. I haven't found any evidence of any more. But I could do some additional searching when they place me there."

"You're moving to Arizona?" Kellan squawked.

"That's the other thing I wanted to tell you and why I came here today. Sorry for the short notice. My few bags are already packed, and I'm scheduled to fly out of here tomorrow morning."

Kellan paced the floor, and because his nerves were getting to him, his feathers flickered and filled with air. "How are we going to find Kaleb with you out of the picture? You're our inside source. We can't leave him in a storage room. He needs to fly. And now that I know he exists, I have to be with him."

"Imagine that. You understand now why they kept him from you?" Seth organized the papers in front of him and closed the folder. "This could be good news, Kellan. With me in Arizona, it might make it easier for us. I'll be on site, hopefully closer to Kaleb. I can find out more about him, maybe be his caretaker, and when I do, we can figure out what to do when we locate him."

Neil agreed. "That seems to be the best way to find Kaleb and give him a life with a family environment." Then told Seth directly, "Depending on what the government has in store for the kid, there might be a chance you could somehow be convincing with what you have planned."

Kellan trusted Seth to have made good decisions. "All right. You've got a point, and by the sounds of things, plans of you moving aren't going to change."

"Right now they're not. TC is done and there's no place else for me to go. Have faith in me, Kellan."

Seth stroked Kellan's wing feathers like he used to do when they were together at TC. Kellan automatically reacted to the soothing gesture, similar to therapy when his life spiraled out of control. Like now when so much was up in the air.

"Can you write down all the information as to where you'll be? I'm not letting you walk away and only leaving us with a phone number for texting."

"You'll have all you need. I'm leaving you with everything I brought out here today. These are paper copies and I won't need the tablet anymore. I can download anything I want you to see directly onto that thing, so keep it with you. If you get locked out of it, I've written the login and password on the folder's inside cover."

Neil interrupted and asked, "I'm sorry Seth for not asking you if you wanted anything to drink when you got here. Can I get you something now or will you be leaving soon?"

"Thanks, Neil. I'll take water. Do you guys mind if I hang out with you for the day? I have nothing at home but a couple of suitcases to look at."

Kellan spoke before Neil answered. "Of course, stay all night if you'd like. We aren't going anywhere and Dylan can share his spot on the floor with you."

Seth smiled, finally relaxing, his expression so relieved it seemed he hadn't done that in months.

Neil brought back three glasses of water locked together in his grasp and gave one to Seth and another to Kellan, keeping the third for himself. "We can go out on the porch if you'd like, there's nobody around here who can see us, and there's plenty of room where you won't get struck by a wing," Neil said.

"I could use a little sun and stretch my legs," Seth answered.

After they made it to the porch, Neil and Seth took a couple of chairs and Kellan sat on the rail, letting his wings dangle behind him over the side.

"You guys found a good place for hiding out. That water view is nice and tranquil, and I bet the suspension bridge looks grand from here at night," Seth said.

"It's no vacation home, but it's working out fine," Kellan answered.

Peace and quiet settled around them, yet Neil felt antsy and out of sorts. He needed to feel Kellan's touch, if he didn't, he felt empty or even lost. Neil left his chair, walked across the decking and stood between Kellan's legs and leaned against him, his bare back cradled by Kellan's chest. Kellan wrapped his arm to the front of Neil, locking his fingers around his waist.

"Is there a reason you're watching us so closely, Seth?" Kellan glanced at him, over top of Neil's shoulder.

Seth answered, "It's strange to see so you so much in love, with Neil. And you know how amazing I think you are, so I enjoy looking at you whenever I have the chance."

Kellan blushed.

Then Seth added, "The hair on your chest is a little different. I'm not used to seeing it. It does give you a rougher edge though."

Neil raised his right hand over his left shoulder and caressed the hair on Kellan's chest with the back of his knuckles. He noticed at that moment that the prickle was starting to feel softer. "I like it and hope he keeps it. But only if he wants."

"Anything for you, Hun." Kellan kissed Neil behind the ear, and then whispered, "Because I love you."

"I hope you don't mind all the new lovey-dovey crap, Seth. However difficult, we'll try to keep our cool," Kellan said.

"No biggie. Carry on."

Neil went back to his own seat and sat down. "How'd you find us, Seth?"

"Simple. TC knows you're here and they have the location documented. I had an idea they did, so I just pilfered through a few files at TC to find what I needed. When I came across your position, that's when I found Kaleb's documents. If I hadn't been looking for you, I never would have found your kid."

Neil recognized that although Kellan trusted Seth, he had mentioned he didn't trust TC, and with all the assurances they'd been given, it was unsettling to think the government could pluck them out of the sky anytime they wanted, if they had a mind to.

Kellan down beat his wings that carried him above the decking and back down again. He back flapped to keep himself in place and his feet off the ground. "Seriously! Are we safe here?"

Neil stood because he didn't know what else to do.

"You're fine for a few days, Kellan. They don't have the need to come after you right now. I've convinced them of that and there's too much to be done with moving TC to AZ."

"I trust you on that, Seth. Don't let us down," Kellan puffed.

Seth looked up. "Since you've mentioned down, why don't you get out of the sky and join us."

Kellan dropped a few feet but didn't land. He snapped his wings open and gave them a few strong beats that took him straight up in a rocket-like spin. When he reached what looked to be a hundred feet above ground, he tucked his wings against his back and freefell, spinning downward, head first.

Watching Kellan bomb-drop, Neil gasped, nerves stinging, even though he knew Kellan would save himself in time.

Kellan stretched both wings to their farthest point and then pulled one in, taking him on a sharp turn before spinning upward and climbing again. Quickly drawing both wings to his sides, he dived toward earth, plummeting downward like a falling rock. Just before striking the ground, he arched his back and brought his head up, snapping his wings out wide to catch wind like a raptor backpedaling to land feet first on a branch. At that instant, he back flapped, changing his beating wings to a smoother wave. Gently he floated until his feet touched the ground.

Seth's mouth dropped as he took every bit of Kellan in. "Damn, I had forgotten how maddeningly gorgeous that was. Never, ever, EVER will I get tired of seeing you do that."

Holding a hand over his heart, Neil grinned. "That there is my angel."

Chapter 13

"I see you hiding behind the curtain again. Come over here and sit down like a good boy, and remember to keep your wings folded behind your back so you don't keep knocking things over."

Kaleb first peeked with one eye around the edge of the drape before jumping out from behind it like it was a big surprise he was ever there. When there was no reaction from the teacher speaking to him, he said, "Yes, Mister Trobsky." Unable to keep his wings under control the way he was asked to because he had the attention span of a puppy, Kaleb fluttered them, which took down a set of books from a shelf he passed. He screamed when the books hit the floor, which then turned into hysterical laughter while he hopped on one foot to the school desk where he should have already been.

"Must have patience," was all the teacher thought. "Aaand Kaleb, my name is Mister Trotsky with a T. There is no B in my name. Look at the spelling on my name plate and say it correctly." He tapped the top of the metal plate with his pencil to draw

Kaleb's attention to it.

Appearing shy, Kaleb ground his toe in small circles against the floor behind the heel of his other foot. He crookedly pursed his lips to one side and said, "Yes, Mister TROT-skeee," trailing the teacher's name as his voice faded.

"Much better, Kaleb." Trotsky forced a smile.

Trying the teacher's patience seemed to be Kaleb's goal. If the boy didn't make an effort every day to make the river flow backward, Trotsky would be convinced there might be something wrong with the kid. If Trotsky told Kaleb to write with a pencil, he'd reach for a crayon instead. If Kaleb was told to sit, he'd make an effort to stand. The angel thrived on pushing his limits with Trotsky. It went on like that almost every day of Kaleb's life. All ten years of it.

The challenges between the two practically began the day Kaleb was introduced to Mister Devon Trotsky, a few days after Kaleb was born and moved from TC to AZ. At that time, and even before Kaleb arrived at AZ, Devon knew little about raising kids, especially one like Kaleb, a rambunctious boy with wings. But as the years went by, Trotsky managed to find ways to get the child under control as any parent would. Everything about bringing up a kid was a learning experience, there was no handbook. Trotsky found there was as much to learn from Kaleb as there was to teach him. Kaleb clearly wasn't an average child. In order for him to learn, it took a lot of patience and a huge curve for learning by everybody involved. Seth was someone who could attest to that. He'd managed a similar task for twenty-eight years, however not quite as laborious. Kellan was a bit softer than Kaleb, more angelic like he was supposed to be. Kaleb... meh... he was bursting with more zest than his dad. It didn't seem possible at times that Kaleb had come from Kellan's gene pool.

The nurturing years went by quickly and when Kaleb turned ten in February, his little mind figured it had learned all it needed. Just like most children, an education seemed foolish and a waste of time. Kids, as they saw it, were meant to play, grow, and in Kaleb's case—fly. He was a boy, young and full of unmanageable energy, and he became more mischievous with each passing birthday, as if each added candle was his free token to charmed naughtiness. Kaleb didn't want to sit at a desk and learn, or keep his energy bottled up. He wanted to run, explore. He needed to put his wings to use and fly.

Kaleb was intrepid for being an angel who stood only four feet tall, give or take an inch or two, but double the height when his wings were extended above his head. On occasion, when he felt like it, tucking his wings neatly against his back showed he was a small boy; however, he had a form that was solid like his dad. The little squirt had more muscle tone than somebody ten years older than him and definitely not like anyone his own age. He was bred with a thick chest, which gave him the support he needed for flapping a six-foot wingspan. In many instances, Kaleb flexed his wings in the classroom, purposely testing the teacher's tolerance level. He was naughty like that, and thought it was funny when he did it.

Pumping his wings a couple times, Kaleb climbed onto the stool at the opposite side of the table where Trotsky was already sitting. Like an antsy child, Kaleb irritably sat there waiting to get started while dangling his feet loosely toward the floor. Impatiently snorting, Kaleb folded his arms on the tabletop, dropped his chin down onto the back of his hands and stared at the teacher. Behind heavy lids, his cerulean blue eyes looked up. While he held his gaze, his wings fanned softly behind his back, overturning papers that were tacked to the walls at either side of him. He looked impish sitting there, a spitting image of his father. It was Kellan all over again.

Kaleb huffed and finally spoke. "Um... Mister Um... Mister Trobsky. I mean Trotskeeeee. When do I get to fly again?"

"As soon as we're finished with today's lesson, Kaleb, I'll take you to the park so you can fly," Trotsky replied.

Kaleb inhaled and then let out a throaty roar, making a sound that showed he was having trouble containing his excitement for flying. He liked flying, even if it was at the fabricated country park constructed within a massive birdcage on the grounds of AZ. Flying was bred into him, and the chance to do it again made his wings waver from exhilaration. Even being a small boy, the power in those wings could move furniture across the floor with a single beat.

Turning his head over his shoulder to watch the destruction he just conjured, Kaleb giggled at everything he made move around the room.

Once again the doctor thought, *"Must have patience,"* then told Kaleb, "Bring them in, Kaleb, and let's get started."

Chapter 14

Kellan made sure his wings were tucked against his back before walking from one side of the living room to the other where Seth and Neil were sitting. They were powering up the tablet again to have another look at Kellan's son, Kaleb.

They came across several video feeds where Kaleb was in that holding cell. There was no telling where it was, and what they saw was disturbing because nobody should be held in lock down like that if they didn't deserve to be there. Especially a defenseless little boy.

The room Kaleb was in appeared to be institutional, like it was an examination room at a doctor's office. If the camera had only panned around the room, they might have been able to tell what that room was.

Kaleb walked around the room, skipped a few times with twittering wings, moving in and out of the camera's view as he did. He might have been singing, but without volume, they couldn't tell for sure. There didn't seem to be anybody else in the room with him, so they were fairly sure he wasn't speaking to anyone.

Several minutes passed where they hadn't seen Kaleb in the room, which told them he might have been taken somewhere else. Coming across that gave them the idea he wasn't in that room for long periods of time.

They closed that video stream and moved on to another one. To their surprise, Kaleb was smiling and playing a video game on a large television screen. He was maneuvering a plane across the sky, dodging trees, mountains and lightning bolts. He looked like he was pretty good at it, and when he turned left or right, his wings followed the planes tilt. If there had been space in the room, he'd be airborne. It appeared that he was operating a training tool of some kind, possibly being taught to fly, taking on treacherous terrain that he might encounter when he got older.

Kellan intently watched Kaleb, remembering his own training days and how different they were from what he saw the way Kaleb was being taught. There were no electronics included in Kellan's growing years. He flew the skies live, with jet fighters chasing him off course, pushing his limits in and out of the clouds. Those were the good days where education and training were hands on.

While Neil watched Kaleb play the fancy computer game in a homier setting, he mentioned the place looked much better than the cold gray room he was in a minute ago on the other video feed.

The video stream on the tablet they were viewing gave the impression of the space being a home, brightly lit by natural light, and the room he was in appeared to be a main living area. Beside the television screen that was hanging on the wall was a doorway that looked like a bathroom in a hallway. Not a public room, but one that would be seen in a family home. On the other side of the TV was a window, and outside there was a wooded parcel. They couldn't tell how deep it was, just that it was there.

Kellan was a bit happier with what he saw, knowing Kaleb wasn't always being treated like a gerbil in a box the way he thought he had been, left only to be visited at feeding time.

They could see Kaleb a little better in that new room. They could see his bright blue eyes, his blond wispy hair, fair skin, and mannerisms that were as if they were watching a younger version of Kellan.

"Are you sure this isn't Kellan, Seth?" Neil asked, amazed at the resemblance.

Seth chuckled. "I know, right? The kid is a spitting image of his dad." He looked at Kellan and smiled.

"There's no doubt in my mind that kid is mine. This is incredible." Kellan tried to keep his heart whole, not let it break, but seeing a tiny image of himself on the tablet brought tears to his eyes. Happy ones, yet sad at the same time because he wasn't with him, holding him and teaching him things a dad would.

Neil reached for Kellan's hand and held it.

As they watched Kaleb, they could see a difference in his actions from when they saw him in the barren room. Maybe it was because he was happier, felt freer? Regardless, there was a sure sign the kid was in a better place and it seemed to show in his mood.

There were several video feeds found on the tablet, with one in particular that stood out to them. It was the only one that showed evidence of any adults and that one was of Kaleb in a classroom. There were no other children, odd creatures, or any other angels. Just him. Alone.

Other than the classroom video, none of them seemed to show doctors or teachers. By what they saw on that feed, it seemed that the adult had the camera fastened to the lapel of his white lab coat, only recording the subjects in front of him. Every now and then a hand would come into view, appearing to be male by the watch he wore and the visible hair on his wrists and knuckles.

They watched a few more feeds before they shut the tablet down. All seemed the same, with the exception of room variations and what seemed like quick wardrobe changes. Like Kellan, little Kaleb was always shirtless—the reason being there weren't many articles of clothing that fit comfortably over a set of wings. It was easier and less confining to go without.

As soon as the screen on the tablet shut down, Kellan's heart rate sped up and the heat that escaped his body was felt by Neil. With Kellan, body heat always followed a fast heartbeat. That's the way his body worked and because he had the RNA components of an avian.

Tension ratcheted in the wake of Kellan's speeding heart rate, all because he was getting anxious, feeling a vital need to find Kaleb. Kellan found himself wishing he was with Kaleb, hugging him, and holding him in his arms, the way a good father pined to do with a child he loved. Kellan hadn't known the strength of parental affection before, nor had he ever met Kaleb, but seeing him, knowing Kaleb was his, turned his heart inside out and he needed to get to him.

Neil sensed Kellan's tension rising higher, though holding his hand seemed to help a little.

Kellan quietly turned to Seth and begged, "We need to find him, Seth."

Seth tried to hide his doubts while at the same time offering Kellan some assurances. He said, "I promise to do everything I can. When I get to the AZ facility, I'll find a way to watch out for Kaleb while I work on getting you three together permanently."

Neil tried to be encouraging by pointing out, "He looks good, Kellan. Safe and happy. He has a home that seems nice and by the looks of things, he's being taken care of just fine. He's being looked after as well as you were when you lived at TC." He glanced at Seth.

There was a glint of hope that lit Kellan's eyes when he thought about seeing little Kaleb in person. He hung on to his faith and trusted Seth's plan would happen without a doubt.

Chapter 15

With help from a few glasses of wine, Kellan was able to come down from the anxiety of knowing Kaleb was lost in the world somewhere. He struggled, but he was eventually able to exclude Kaleb from his mind, and until he knew where his son was and how to get to him, it didn't do any good thinking about the shoulda-coulda-woulda's right then. It would only sour his evening, making it a bad one, and knowing Kaleb was okay, he looked to Neil instead.

Neil's sexy bare chest, rippling abs, and deep pelvic V that drew an arrow to his dick were always a prized distraction for Kellan. Whenever he saw Neil without a shirt on, Kellan seemed to lose control of his mind, and all he could literally think about was fucking Neil on the spot, even if someone else was in the room. He didn't care. Seth or no Seth. While at TC, Seth had seen him at his best many times — completely nude and carrying out sexual activities that were so hot coal nuggets would turn into diamonds. After that, whatever Kellan opted to do to Neil shouldn't faze Seth in the least.

Without further qualms about who knew, and who saw, Kellan fantasized about sticking his dick inside Neil, sliding his erection in and out of his favorite man. That beautiful thought was a certain distraction. Kellan embraced it, allowing the unrest and worry to slide away, even if only temporarily. He needed to be in a better place. Neil was that place, so he grasped that and went with it.

Once he made the decision, Neil was all Kellan could think about. Whenever Neil was close, Kellan's dick sprang to life. As if angry, his growing erection pressed vigorously against the zipper of his jeans, persistently seeking Neil's asshole, eagerly wanting in. Neil's hot tight hole was like a siren song, something he couldn't ignore, nor did he want to. He was totally obsessed and under Neil's spell, and the same would probably happen to any guy if they knew how good his channel felt. Kellan, the lucky one, had the pleasure of feeling Neil again and again, marking him sexually, making him totally his.

Standing with his back against Kellan's chest, Neil heard whispering in his ear when Seth wasn't looking. "I'm so fucking hard for you right now, Neil. You want my dick inside you?" He pinched Neil's nipple, making him shudder. He knew how much a tweak turned Neil on and shamelessly tortured him.

Neil answered with a nod, because saying yes out loud would have embarrassed him if Seth had overheard. Neil was a private person when it came to sex, not a person who was very thrilled about being an exhibitionist.

Kellan ran his hands up and down Neil's abdomen, his fingers lightly following the gutter in the center, and hesitating at every horizontal crease.

Seth wasn't blind to his surroundings and was aware that newfound lovers were always looking for every chance to hump each other. "For the love of Pete, do you two want me to leave?" Seth saw the lovers on the verge of mating.

"Come on now, Seth. You've seen all this and what I can do with it. You don't have to go," Kellan said, flashing a sneaky grin.

"Yeah, but when I saw you in all your glory, that was scientific bullshit, and on film. This here is the real thing, and you're my brother for crimony-sakes. I can't watch you two going at it two feet away from me. Can you at least wait until I'm sleeping?"

"Deal," Kellan immediately agreed.

"What?" Neil coughed.

Kellan held Neil tighter from behind and put a cupped hand over his mouth. "Just go with it darling. You might like it."

"I need more wine. Please, more wine." Seth set his glass on the table in front of him and let Neil fill it, and then he stepped outside for a moment to get some fresh air.

As soon as Seth left the room, Kellan spun Neil around to face him. "You've done it again Neil. You got me hard and wet." He pulled his dripping dick from his pants and added, "Quick, Neil, get down and suck the semen from my dick. I want to see it glaze your tongue."

Neil hurriedly looked over his shoulder to make sure Seth was out of the picture and hopefully not coming back anytime soon. Then he dropped to his knees and took Kellan's dick into his mouth. He sucked on the head like it was a bottle, taking as much of Kellan's semen down his throat as he could before pulling his lover's dick out so he could breathe. While gasping, Neil smacked the side of his face a few times with the full length of Kellan's dick, making thick ropes of cum streak his cheek. Wanting more, he circled his lips with the crown of Kellan's dick before shoving it back into his mouth to feed on what was still oozing from the slit. Kellan's delightful semen was too good to waste.

When Kellan jammed his cock back down Neil's throat, its bulbous head banged against his tonsils and it made him cough. Totally engrossed in sucking Kellan's cock, Neil hadn't realized he was choking on it.

"Oh shit. Get up." Kellan quickly pulled his cock out of Neil's throat when he heard the front door opening. He spun around while uncomfortably forcing his semi-hard dick against the inner thigh of his pant leg and waited for the swelling to go down.

Neil hastily stood, licked his fingers and wiped his face, the hot flush of embarrassment completing the process.

Kellan straddled the arm of the sofa, flicking his wings down the outer side, feather tips touching the floor. To conceal the wet spot his dick made at the front of his pants and the erection that was still there, he pulled Neil against him so he could take a seat between his legs.

Acting casual after he entered the lighthouse, Seth reached for his wine glass and took a good sized gulp, almost drinking it as if it were water. He looked at the ceiling mostly, trying not to notice Neil's flushed face and his chest spotted with semen. It was obvious Kellan had been fucking Neil's mouth while Seth was outside counting stars.

Without further thought, calling it a day seemed to be the unmistakable choice. Plus, Kellan could privately exchange body fluids with Neil like he so badly was aching to do, and hopefully Seth would slip into a deep sleep he seemed to desperately need. Before anybody moved, Kellan noticed Seth's eyes slowly looking around the room, and then lock on him and Neil. He wondered if Seth was thinking the same thing he was—like everything about the two of them looked wholesome, and how they'd literally become inseparable over the past few days. The hold Kellan had on Neil made that clear.

The lovey-dovey moment continued when Kellan moved a hand to Neil's hair and combed curled fingers down the back of his head. Kellan's comforting touch made Neil's head tilt forward, and his eyelids drop. Even though Kellan's fingers were in Neil's hair, the gentle stroking seemed to hypnotize and soothe Seth as well.

A little past eleven, Seth swiveled on the sofa, swinging his legs horizontally so he could lay back, shut down, and go to sleep.

Kellan lowered his voice against Neil's ear. "Get your ass to bed and prepare for a massive intrusion."

Neil shook his head and pointed at Seth.

Kellan silently shrugged his shoulders, gesturing that he didn't care.

Even with Neil's doubts about Kellan having sex with him while Seth lay next to them in the dark, there was still an erotic thrill that went along with being caught with a dick up his ass. Fear and excitement rolled into one gave Neil an adrenaline-charged rush, and in the back of his mind, he wanted it to happen. There was a first time for everything, and getting fucked by Kellan with a possible set of eyes on them was a risk he didn't mind taking. He was too horny to push Kellan away.

Kellan lay down behind Neil, and as soon as he did, Kellan's cock went right into Neil's rear end. It sucked him in completely, full hilt, no mercy, until the hair on Kellan's pelvis scrubbed Neil's hind end.

Neil was normally a screamer while getting fucked in the ass and practically bawled until the ceiling came down when he let his load go. Kellan knew all about that. He was always there and was the one who made it happen.

Each time Kellan dug his dick in, he had to cup a hand over Neil's mouth to keep him from groaning too loudly. He couldn't do much about Neil's nostril forced whimpers either. He needed to breathe, and with that came the erotic moans Kellan was trying to keep a secret. As long as Kellan's dick continued sliding in and out of Neil, the shushing attempts couldn't possibly work. It was as though Neil's pleasured prostate was linked to his vocal chords.

Aside from being sexually aroused from having his raging erection going to town on Neil's asshole, Kellan was tormented by stints of laughter. It had nothing to do with the incredible sensation teasing his dick, but how Neil was reacting to a dick induced prostate massage and trying to keep quiet about it. To add abuse to the destruction, Kellan reached around Neil and grabbed hold of his dick, matching stroke for stroke with each thrust to his ass.

Between whimpers, Neil quietly gasped. "Fuck, I'm about to cum."

Holding Neil from behind, Kellan whispered in return, "Get ready. Me too."

က ဿ

While Kellan and Neil were going at it in the dark, there was movement out of Seth a few times, like he might have been drifting in and out of slumber because of the noises being made. Kellan had been aware Seth never had issues with two men being together, but those moments that woke him might have something to do with one man actually sticking his dick into another's willing orifice right there next to him. The timing for doing that might have been a bit off, but Kellan was so damned horny at the time, he urgently needed Neil's help at getting his rocks off.

During the night, one of the few times Kellan had gotten up to step outside for a bit of fresh air, Seth had followed him. While they sat on the front porch, Kellan noticed Seth drifted into deep thought as though he had something to say.

"What are you doing up at this time of night?" Kellan asked.

Kellan listened as Seth talked. "I've been thinking about what I'll be doing once I get to AZ. I was never fully briefed or given a roster of any kind, and I don't quite have answers for some of the things they'd mentioned to me. Most of them are troubling because I don't have a clear idea of what I'm about to face. It's a new location, with a lot of variables, and none of them add up in a way that makes sense. Of course I know my core responsibilities are to be a nurse when I get there, but the most perplexing part is who or what I'm going to be taking care of. That still remains a mystery until I walk through those doors. I have a sneaky suspicion I'll be babysitting Seeker's or my worst concern—having to euthanize the bad ones."

"If I were you, don't worry 'till you get there. You might be pleasantly surprised."

"I hope you're right," Seth agreed. "I suppose the best thing to do is try to focus more on my personal agenda regarding Kaleb. Where he's being held, who has been taking care of him, who his doctor was, and anything that would help me locate him. Considering Kaleb might be a part of you makes the kid important to me."

"You're a good guy, Seth, and it means a lot to me that you're doing this."

"It's that strong family tie. I look out for you, remember?"

Kellan lifted and shook his wings, like he was stretching them after a night's rest. "Why don't we get back in and get some sleep. I can tell it's needed. You look exhausted."

Seth stood. "You know me well."

After everybody was back in bed, Kellan whispered in Neil's ear to see if he was ready for another round. His erection that had already found Kellan's hand was probably a yes, and the soft moaning out of Neil might have been all Kellan needed to bury the boner.

Neil squeezed a whisper between his moaning, "What do you think Seth is thinking about two guys fucking beside him?"

"He probably has a boner." Kellan surprised Neil with that answer.

"Damn them. Couldn't they wait one day? And why the fuck do I have a hard on?" Seth grumbled into the pillow.

For the most part, Kellan didn't care what Seth thought of them screwing around. The idea of having an onlooker was erotic to Kellan. He'd been observed all his life, in more compromising positions than the one he was in at the moment, and knowing that Seth had seen what he'd done in private, there didn't seem to be any reason for Seth to look away.

Neil had some reservations about voyeurism. He didn't feel it was creepy being watched, he just wasn't used to it and having Kellan's dick hammering his ass was an act he considered private. Now that he was with Kellan, it was highly likely he'd have to get used to observing eyes. With that, he wasn't about to let a sneaky peek from across the room get in the way of a mind blowing ream job from his boyfriend.

Not that Neil was willing to give up his scruples and reservations, but for at least one night, he was willing to overlook them.

Chapter 16

Neil rolled over to reach an arm out for Kellan and surprisingly learned his angel wasn't there. Shaken when he found himself lying alone in bed, Neil quickly sat up to look around the room for his absent boyfriend. It was the middle of the night by the way the moon still shone in the sky outside the window. The position of it made Neil think it could be two or maybe three in the morning.

Tangled in the bed sheet, Neil scrambled on all fours to the edge of the mattress to see if the pants Kellan had on were still lying in the same place he'd left them. Leaning forward, Neil's silken hair fell in long wisps in front of his eyes. He saw Kellan's pants were on the floor, but there was no sign of him. He sat back on the heels of his feet, slumped his shoulders forward at the same time he dropped his hands into his lap. Consumed by sadness, Neil continued looking around for Kellan, glancing into the kitchen and at the entry door that was left ajar. He vigorously combed his tousled hair back and propelled his feet over the side of the bed.

Neil tiptoed quickly to the door, passing Seth who was still sleeping soundly on the sofa, snoring like he was struggling to breathe. Neil thankfully saw Kellan sitting on the beach with his knees pulled tightly to his chest, and his wings open at his sides. The breeze graced every feather, lifting and dropping them as if some celestial pianist was tapping on the keys.

Light from the moon penetrated the clouds here and there, picking at the tiny waves that reflected blue sparks back into the dark sky. If the moonbeam's beauty could make music, it would have been then.

Neil stood peacefully in the open doorway, watching Kellan slowly rocking back and forth while the fist-like waves came to shore and circled his feet.

Neil quietly strolled across the beach, knelt down and lifted Kellan's chin from his knees until their eyes met. When he looked at Kellan, Neil could see there was an emotional change that hadn't been there earlier, and when he hugged him, Kellan sighed. The heartbreak Neil was witnessing brought tears to his eyes, and a single drop fell between Kellan's wings, finding refuge in the sandy beach behind him. A small wave rolled in and took the tear away.

That's when Kellan softly spoke, "Don't they know he's just a kid and the best thing for him is to be with his dad?"

There wasn't much of an honest answer Neil could give Kellan other than telling him what he thought. "Right now, I'm sure Kaleb is doing fine, and he'll be okay until we can get to him."

Kellan looked at Neil earnestly and said, "Every time I try to get him out of my mind, he pops right back in it. I keep seeing his sweet face in that dirty room, and I remember what I went through. Now that I know he's out there somewhere, I can't seem to sit still and wait."

"We'll find him, Kellan. Together. With Seth's help." Neil was determined to be optimistic, it was the best way to help Kellan cope.

The more Kellan thought about Kaleb sitting by himself in a cold cell, the more his despair turned to loathing. He didn't mean for his thoughts to go in that direction, but his disgust for what they were doing at the Lab made his temper rise. "Why are they doing this? They aren't God. They can't just create a person and then put them away, only to bring them out to prod and run tests on them to see what they're capable of. I can't believe there are people who would do that. It's like giving birth to a child and then throwing them in a dumpster. Who would, or could, do that? It's something that's simply not done if anybody has even an ounce of conscience."

From what Neil had heard, he understood that Kellan was talking about himself and what he'd gone through at TC, believing the same was being done to Kaleb. While there was no knowing for sure—and Neil certainly understood that—the fact remained Kellan could still be right, at least to some extent. The video feeds they'd seen were mild, nothing that showed any kind of abuse or mishandling, however those were only a few of probably thousands of hours on file. With so little to go on, Neil had to rely on his own intuition, as well as the fact that Seth offered calm assurances. There was a good chance Kaleb was ultimately being taken care of very well. What the government had with Kellan was a good thing, and Kaleb was most likely an improved version of him. Why would TC create another such being only to torture or hurt it? That just didn't make any sense. Not to Neil. "Kellan, keeping Kaleb protected, safe and well would be an act in AZ's favor. I can't see them causing him any pain or harm. They didn't hurt you, did they?"

"No, they didn't. But what if they decided to start?" Kellan pulled his wings in when he felt it sprinkle rain, making a canopy with them over his and Neil's head.

Neil looked up, watching the tips of Kellan's wings come together above them. He then dropped his gaze back to Kellan's eyes and kissed him. "Listen to me."—He looked deeper into Kellan's tortured expression—"Seth isn't irrational, and he knows more about what takes place on the inside than we do. He raised you perfectly, so I'm sure he feels whoever is teaching Kaleb is doing the same. I could almost promise you Kaleb is, and will be, fine."

"We should be flying to AZ to find my kid right now."

"We will soon, but after Seth gets there first." Neil fanned his fingers over Kellan's chest in a soothing manner, letting him know that everything would turn out okay. "Try not to think about it."

Interrupting their conversation with a massive blast that seemed fit for a finale, thunder exploded like dynamite and lightning blew up the sky. The clouds rolled in like billowing smoke, and the rain turned into a deluge.

Neil reached out and tugged Kellan by the hands, lifting him from the ground. They walked side by side back to the light house while the pouring rain pummeled them from above.

Reaching the porch, Neil pressed his lips to Kellan's.

Kellan kissed back. "I'm glad you're here."

Chapter 17

The next afternoon Seth landed at Sky Harbor International airport in Phoenix, Arizona. While waiting for his luggage to travel the carousel, he sent Neil a text message letting him know he had arrived.

Seth wasn't one hundred percent on board with uprooting from his home in Suttons Bay and making a big change in such a short time frame, but considering TC was soon to be stripped to the bare walls, he didn't have much of a choice. Seth moved right into TC out of college, and because he was educated by the government the way they wanted him to be, there didn't seem to be many places for him in the real world.

Seth hailed a cab outside the airport, and it took him to his residence in Phoenix that had been arranged and paid for by the government. It wasn't anything he had expected, and walking into a two bedroom, two bath, ranch style floor plan, was a pleasant surprise. It felt homier than a studio apartment where a full spin in the middle of the room completed the grand tour.

Everything was already in its place, and he had nothing much to do except put the clothing he brought with him away and wait for his alarm to ring in the new day.

Seth was the type of person who was always on time, so as instructed, he made it to AZ Monday morning. It seemed to be one of the hottest days of summer, and as the sun rose, the heat index continued to rise to an unbearable temperature.

The place reminded him a lot of the Adler Planetarium in Chicago, but built in the middle of nowhere. There appeared to be nothing around it for miles except dust and tumbleweeds.

On his way across the parking lot, Seth glanced at every part of the hexagonal building in front of him. The single level structure, however tall, was concrete on all sides, with no windows, and a domed rooftop that was probably meant for star gazing at one time. The entire building didn't look that large from the outside, but Seth was pretty sure it went underground several stories. He was never given any specifics on the place or where he would be stationed inside, only told to be ready to get started first thing in the morning. So that he did.

Upon entering the ten foot doors, he was immediately greeted and ushered through a metal detector by one of the biggest men he'd ever seen. The guy had a body like a champion wrestler, thick and brawny, with shoulders three times wider than his ass. The place was old with unfinished cement walls on the inside too. It smelled musty and ancient, but the shiny marble floors made it look clean.

When the huge guard reached for Seth's satchel, his meaty hand opened up like a massive baseball glove. Seth's shoulder bag fit in one hand like it was a small lunch box. "Careful, that's my lunch," Seth said.

The man grumbled something under his breath as he shoved the satchel through the x-ray scanner and head gestured for Seth to walk through the archway for a full body scan.

After Seth successfully passed through the metal detector without incident, he was escorted to a secluded room to be fingerprinted, have his photo snapped, and given a gateway badge that would allow him access to certain areas within the building. The man who took care of that was as burly as the wrestler at the metal machine. Were these creatures made in the lab or were they trueborn human beings? The size of them made Seth believe they were manufactured machines.

It took about an hour to wrap up the initial orientation on the main floor before Seth was led to the elevator that would take him down below ground where every other part of the facility existed. There was a beast of a man inside the elevator who operated the lift to the fifth floor where they apparently wanted him stationed. When he exited, Seth wasn't surprised to find another husky man waiting to take him someplace else.

Walking beside the knuckle dragger, Seth looked at everything he passed by. Other than being windowless, there were similarities all around that made him think of TC. He felt more at home than he thought he would, and hoped other clinicians from TC would be part of his team. Having them there with him would simplify his plan to bring Kellan and Kaleb together because he'd be able to manipulate familiar workmates.

Fifteen minutes after leaving the orientation office upstairs, Seth finally reached the lab where he would be working. As he walked in, there were three technicians in the room already at work, Seth would make four. Nobody spoke a word, which was typical. Seth hoped he'd know the people, but obviously didn't. None of their faces were recognizable. They checked him out, giving him a cautious once over, but whether or not they'd been filled in about what Seth had been doing the last twenty-eight years wasn't apparent. For himself, he'd been given no information about his new co-workers but it wouldn't take long to find out what he'd need to know.

Instead of guiding Seth to a work station or lab table, he was taken to an office in the back of the room, one behind a wall of glass that had two desks pushed together in the center of the room. Only a few short moments after Seth had stepped through the doorway, a tall skinny man followed. Seth recognized him from TC the second he saw him. They hadn't worked together, but Seth knew of him, and if he remembered correctly, his name was Oliver. Seth was happy and relieved he was going to share office space with someone he knew, at least by reputation. Oliver was considered a brilliant engineer of genetic splicing.

Oliver was a strikingly ugly man with a long narrow nose, bulging eyes circled by deep shadowy rings, and prominent ears that looked like handles on a kettle. His overly long face seemed as though it had been put together with spare parts, much like Frankenstein, none of which seemed to match. Despite his looks, when Oliver spoke, his voice was unexpectedly deep, with a sweet musical quality that was very appealing.

Over the years, Seth had proven himself to be one of the finest specialists at TC. He probably understood innovative creature development better than anybody else had at the GMO facility. He knew what he was capable of, and being closely observed by the governing military, figured that was the reason he had been placed at AZ. From what he knew, AZ was where leading engineers and doctors had been stationed, and because he had been moved there, he assumed he was one, too. He didn't know too much about Oliver, only that he was an engineer with years of service at TC. Rather than guessing, Seth asked if he knew what the reason for them being there was, if it would be a continuation of where they left off at TC or something completely different.

Oliver told him he wasn't sure about the assignment but he was willing to share the little he did know. "There's a lot planned for AZ, and from the documentation I've been allowed to see, we are key people for the success of new species. Some had already been started at TC and transferred here. You must have known some of it?"

Seth said, "Honestly, I was sure there was more going on than what they let me see, but had no idea exactly what they were up to. A large part of me didn't really want to know. I took care of Kellan and was happy with just that. What part of all this did you handle at TC?"

"I was lead genetic engineer, managing most of the gene modification and splicing. I was the one who made sure the good embryos didn't expire."

"Okay, that makes some sort of sense why they put us together. You'll lead the technical part of fertilization, and as soon as the embryos hatch, that's where I come in."

Oliver walked around to Seth's side of the table and leaned a hip against it. "I've heard you were a major part of raising Kellan, and to my understanding, you're one of the best at growth and development."

"I'll admit to that. Kellan turned out to be one of the finest."

Oliver added, "I'll say. He's the reason AZ is continuing the research and improvement program of angels. The government is looking to expand on creating more like him, however, they want those they can control. I'm expected to tone down their ability to make decisions, and I presume you will make sure they don't learn to think too much on their own."

"Like robots?"

"More or less," Oliver agreed. "The TC embryos that were brought to AZ had been engineered to be more than just flying machines. The military wanted them to be advanced versions of the mean-spirited Seeker's that already exist, only with additional genetic structures extracted from sharks. Until recently, my team hadn't been able to hinder the gene that produced a set of gills. At this point, it's either gills or lungs, we can't do both. The fetuses never made it to the final stages of incubation and had to be terminated. After months of trial and error, the life forms were finally showing positive signs of developing as planned. There was visible movement seen through the incubator walls, and the monitors connected to them showed their internal organs were functioning properly. Everything is currently moving along as planned. New life forms mean new possibilities. Now it's up to you and me to follow through with whatever they want us to do."

"You mean like raising Seekers?"

"If that's what they will be called, then yes, that's what I'm being told."

"I prefer to keep my distance from the newer versions because I've seen what those creatures can do the way they are now." Seth had been educated to be a pediatric nurse, but at that moment was far from an ordinary RN. He understood he'd be taking on challenges along a path he was familiar with, like raising angels. To be told he'd be introduced to Seekers and rearing them made the whole idea of moving to AZ nauseating. How would he adapt, and if he didn't, would the government just let him go? As a witness to certain things that took place at the facilities, simply walking away from AZ might no longer be an option for him.

Seth was determined to overlook the displeasure of what might take place for him at AZ, and play the hand of cards he'd been dealt. His own quandary wasn't what really mattered, but what he knew was best for Kellan. He wanted him to feel he was no different than anybody else, to live like a normal human being. If babysitting Seekers was what it took to make that happen, then so be it.

After talking briefly with Oliver, Seth took a seat behind the desk meant for him, the one that faced Oliver's. He bumped the PC mouse to activate the computer screen, bringing it out of hibernation. Seth typed the secured password they gave him at his orientation, and he spent most of the morning organizing his files.

Shortly after noontime, Oliver made it a point to take Seth on a tour of the Lab and showed him the areas he'd have access to. On the way, he introduced Seth to the clinic staff and the Seekers he'd be helping raise someday soon.

Just then, reality hit Seth like a sucker punch to the gut that left him speechless. He wasn't prepared for what he was looking at, never expected it to be so foul. He'd never been that close to a Seeker's unborn fetus before and he found them to be hideous. The entire time he looked upon the creatures in their incubation containers, he wanted to choke on his own rising vomit. What he saw wasn't the only thing that made him sick to his stomach. Knowing he'd take part in raising possible killers was what churned the acid most.

"You okay?" Oliver asked, his face showing concern. Seth forced a smile and turned away, annoyed he'd revealed his feelings so easily.

After leaving the incubation chamber, Oliver pointed out each lab room they passed and their function, ending the tour at the Data room where all the back up and hard copies of everything were kept.

That's when Seth's face lit up, and the reason he really wanted to be at AZ. He was there to do a job he was educated for, but also to surreptitiously gather details about how it would get him closer to Kaleb.

Chapter 18

Still at the lighthouse, Neil mentioned to Kellan he received a text from Seth letting them know he safely made it to Arizona. Neil's reply to the text was, 'good to hear and talk soon.' He kept it short.

Kellan was getting anxious sitting at the lighthouse doing nothing. "Can you send Seth another text to find out when we can fly out of here?"

Neil said, "I could, but he just got there so we should be patient."

"Maybe we should check the tablet. He might have sent something to it we need to see." Kellan pushed his wings downward and the force lifted him off the floor a few inches and over to the sofa where they left the tablet. When he turned it on, nothing from Seth was there.

"Give him some time, Kellan." Just when Neil pointed that out, they heard a loud thump above their heads, as if something heavy hit the roof.

Panic stricken, Neil hollered, "What was that?"

Kellan spun to face Neil, his wings brushing the walls as he did. His nasal septum was sensitive enough to alert him it was a Seeker outside. Those beasts always smelled like hot iron and dirty blood.

Dylan whimpered when he heard the noise, clueless as to what it was or why it was there. He sniffed at the air in front of him, trying to get hold of the scent that Kellan had already picked up. He growled because he knew something uninvited was out there.

The terrorist on the rooftop arrived so quickly, they hadn't had time to make a run for it or fly away. If they had stayed alert, even after Seth's claim that the government wouldn't bother them, the intruder might not have caught them with their guard down. The screeching they heard outside let them know there was at least one Seeker, but if there were more than that, they weren't able to tell.

Trying to figure that out, Kellan lifted a finger to his lips, urging Neil to stay quiet, while the entire time he was glancing up at the ceiling to get a fix on where the Seeker was. He corralled Neil and Dylan into a corner, putting them safely behind him before whispering, "It sounds to be only one. You two stay here while I get rid of it." Those bastards always seemed to travel in pairs, so hearing just one Seeker had Kellan wondering what was going on.

Behind Kellan's open wings, Neil lowered himself to the floor and held Dylan at this side. They sat quietly and watched Kellan creep out the door. Neil had expected a government invasion, but figured it wouldn't be so soon. Their last encounter with Seekers was still fresh in his memory, especially the sickening sound of their screams and a smell that made his stomach churn.

Once outside, Kellan extended his wings, shaking them until every feather turned black to match the dark sky. Before any Seeker had a chance to spot him, or take him out, he quickly beat his wings to get off the ground. As he corkscrewed higher, he saw the ugly beast leave the roof, powering to a high altitude and heading in a downward dive straight at him.

In midflight, the Seeker swooped under Kellan and latched

onto his chest, its stringy drool flapping from its jagged teeth as it screeched in Kellan's face.

Kellan huffed when the Seeker hit him, its weight shifting him off balance. Spiraling, wings tangling with each other's, they dropped toward earth.

Kellan wrapped his strong hands around the Seeker's throat. It let out a grunt and threw its head back, and for a moment, seemed unable to growl. Still attached, they hit the ground, and the force of the crash broke them apart. They cartwheeled along the line of trees at the back of the lighthouse, head over heels across the ground, dirt and stones tumbling with them.

Anger consumed Kellan, and his heart thundered within his chest as he aggressively crawled across the ground and then stood, fists clenched at his sides, ready for battle. Snapping his wings straight back and quickly dropping them, he lunged at the Seeker.

Watching Kellan closing in, the Seeker clawed at the ground to get up, pushed off and hit the sky, its leathery wings beating hard to get away.

Determined to break the Seeker's flight, Kellan kicked off the ground and flew in behind it.

Dodging Kellan, the Seeker forced its wings toward its feet, propelling itself forward. At that moment, it hit a pocket of turbulent air, bucked and dipped, and went into a nose-dive. As it dropped, the Seeker back flapped and hit the ground running. Bending its wings, the thing twisted and skipped backward to face Kellan, its clawed feet ejecting gravel and dirt in all directions. The Seeker lost its balance during the spin, launching it into an earth-churning spill. Its heavy wings slapped the ground over and over as it log-rolled sideways.

Coming in behind the Seeker, Kellan skidded to a stop, sweeping his wings in front of his face to shield himself from the stony tornado the Seeker had created.

Breaking the roll, the Seeker managed to extend its wings and lift itself upright. It stood as if it had never gone down, shook its gnarly head and then stared straight at Kellan. The thing held its hands in tightened fists, palms dripping blood where its own fingernails dug in.

As the dusty haze receded, Kellan found himself caught in the gaze of large dark eyes that never seemed to blink. Panic caught him. He groaned inwardly as the urge to kill came crashing down on him like storm waves on a rocky shore. He started to curse, but swallowed down the words while keeping his eyes fastened on the beast. His body clenched. His heartbeat sped up. When the Seeker charged him, he kicked up dirt, and brought his wings forward in unison to force what he lifted into the Seeker's face. He jumped, heading straight up with a plan to swoop behind the Seeker and knock it out cold.

The Seeker howled when the gritty dirt bombarded its eyes, the desperate sound echoed off the distant hills like thunder. Angered, its featherless wings immediately lifted, tips touching far above its head and then down again. The force catapulted it after Kellan. While airborne, it reached up and firmly gripped Kellan by the foot.

Kellan twisted in its grasp. His wings flapped downward against the Seeker's upbeat, turning the air currents around them into turbulent gusts, upsetting their maneuverability.

The Seeker lost its grip and dropped away. But as quickly as it fell back, regained speed and reconnected with Kellan face to face. Its stench grew in the small space between them. Their hands and feet locked the same way two eagles' talons connect in mid-flight.

Bound together during their rapid flight straight up, they spiraled higher above the trees in a beastly rage. The Seeker screamed and Kellan roared as they leveled off in a wide arc that put them over the lake.

As they fought, their powerful wings collided harshly, tips striking tips with punishing force. Bone on fragile bone, the impact echoed like rifle shots, the sound reverberating over the water. Fighting to stay airborne, the Seeker's wings crunched as Kellan's strong grasp bent and twisted them. The leathery flesh ripped, mimicking the sound of the Seeker screeching.

After a lengthy brawl above the lake, Kellan cracked his skull into the Seeker's nose, shattering the brittle bone, spewing blood that spread to its eyes. The sudden blow broke the Seeker's grip, giving Kellan a moment to drop backward into a rolling dive to restore lost strength. With powerful wing beats, Kellan flew into the Seeker as its leathery wings hit the upbeat. He scooped and pinned them together with a locked arm embrace. Bones cracked as Kellan straddled its back in flight and squeezed.

Trying to break loose, the Seeker frantically jerked and kicked. It howled as they dropped, spinning downward toward the lake.

In less than a minute they hit the water, the abrupt collision torturing their bones even more. Kellan tumbled forward over the Seekers head, rolling awkwardly onto his back. Water arched over him, pelting his face with what felt like needles. A few seconds was all Kellan had before he sank, or worse, as the Seeker landed on top of him and pushed him under. Kellan quickly rolled and dove beneath the surface, then pushed his wings back toward his feet to help propel him up and out of the water. Spinning as he lifted, water sprayed like a waterfall shower from his wings.

Before Kellan got too far, the Seeker reached up and grabbed him by the ankles, pulling him back into the lake. The battle started again. They bobbed fiercely in and out of the water, pounding one another with balled fists. Cascades of waves engulfed them as their swinging limbs skimmed the surface.

With all his strength, Kellan forced the Seeker's head below water, trying to take away its ability to breathe. The Seeker's size and swiftness was not easily restrained as it channeled its rage to its core. It was able to make it to the surface by powerful wing beats propelling it. As the Seeker rose, it ejected Kellan backwards onto his back, putting him at a disadvantage. Coming out of the water high enough, the Seeker used the momentum to arc over and land on Kellan, driving him beneath the surface.

Needing oxygen, Kellan thrashed his wings to propel himself out of the Seeker's reach and upward until his head was above water. He gasped deeply, sucking in air. Another thrust of his wings lifted him higher. He fought with the Seeker, half of their bodies above the surface and the other half still kicking beneath it.

Kellan coiled a left hook, jamming a bloody fist into the Seeker's chin, with skull numbing force, plowing into it with horrendous power and shattering the few teeth the creature had. That sent the Seeker reeling into a feet-over-head somersault, throwing it backward into the dark water with an enormous whack. Its wings enveloped it on impact, joints popping as they bent.

Kellan went after the Seeker again, holding it under him with all his strength. He wanted to kill it, but couldn't. Death by his hands of any creature, human or not, was never anything he wanted to live with. Catching his breath, Kellan eased back, letting the Seeker's head slowly rise above the frothy surface. It choked on and spit water as its head popped in and out of the ripples while the rest of its body wavered beneath the surface. The hazy glower in the Seeker's eyes seemed darker than usual, showing a clear sign of weakening. Kellan also sensed the Seeker had stopped fighting back, indicating to him that he'd managed to put an end to its determination at taking him out.

Feeling the Seeker getting weaker, Kellan let it go, climbed on its chest and jumped into the sky, leaving it floating face up and wheezing to get its air back. If someone had asked Kellan why he'd leave an enemy alive when it was clear the battle was far from over, he'd say to keep his conscience clear. No deaths by his hand, if he could help it. If the beast had succumbed to the water and drowned, then that was on fate's hands, not his.

Without waiting for the Seeker to fly free or sink, Kellan flew to the beach. When he landed, he found Dylan and Neil standing on the deck, watching. Before meeting them, Kellan turned in time to see the Seeker clumsily lift off and fly away, its flight path erratic. Where the Seeker was going, Kellan didn't know, but he had a good idea it would be coming back soon.

As soon as he felt comfortable that the Seeker was headed away from them, Kellan flew to the deck of the lighthouse where Neil and Dylan waited anxiously.

Still shaken by what just happened, Neil looked Kellan over and then asked, "Why'd you let that beast go? Wouldn't it have been better for all of us if you killed that thing?"

"I know. I had my chance, but I just couldn't do it." Kellan turned toward the retreating assailant, his expression resolute. "I couldn't live with myself if I had. Call me crazy for letting it go, but something within me has a hard time killing anything. You saw what I did with that spider in the kitchen? I carried it outside so it had a chance at life."

"You're a good man, Kellan. I knew that the first time I met you." Neil reached for Kellan's chin and turned his gaze back toward him.

Kellan looked intently into Neil's eyes and asked how he and Dylan were holding up after seeing what just took place.

"We're good." Neil lifted the tranquilizer guns he was holding in each hand until they were level at either side of his shoulders. "I had these ready, and thankful I didn't have to use them."

"I forgot about those." Kellan shook more water from his wings as he moved to Neil's side and looked out over the lake to make sure the Seeker was definitely gone.

"My plan was to be ready for those bastards if any more came to town." Neil lowered the guns to his sides, nervously tapping the barrels against his thighs.

Kellan looked to the sky one more time, and then insisted they leave that evening with or without a departure message from Seth. Their well-being depended on it after what had just happened between him and the Seeker.

Neil followed Kellan's line of vision, searching for any spots in the sky that might start getting bigger. "Do you think that thing is gone?"

"I'm pretty sure we won't be seeing that one for a while. I busted him up pretty badly, might have cracked a few bones. Walking or flying might not be on its schedule for at least a day or two."

"What's the plan if others show up? Didn't you say those things rarely travel alone?" Neil asked.

"That's what I find odd. That one seemed to be here on its own, even though those monsters have been trained to fly in groups — never by themselves. If there were more, we would have run into them by now because they don't hide out and wait for the perfect moment to swoop in on their target. They just travel from point A and attack object B."

"Maybe if I send a text to Seth, we can find out if he has anything on this one possibly getting loose, or maybe he knows if AZ sent it." Neil went through the door to find his phone.

"You could, but I don't think AZ would have sent a Seeker on an eighteen hundred mile trip to pluck me from the sky." Kellan followed Neil into the house, tripping over Dylan who fought to be first inside behind Neil.

"Unless…" Neil started to say.

"Unless, what?"

Neil faced Kellan. "I wonder if all those Seekers were moved out of TC, or could a few still be there?"

"That could be."

"Or perhaps, that one had gotten away without their knowledge."

"Unlikely. The military is too organized for that to happen."

"Unh… you flew the coop, didn't you?"

"Good point."

After sending a text to Seth, Neil packed a satchel with items he figured they'd need, preparing so they could leave at a moment's notice.

Dylan was next. His bag was set open next to the satchel, ready and waiting to load him in it.

Neil rechecked everything he had packed, including the messenger bag where he stashed the pistols and tranquilizer drugs. "This looks like too much crap for you to carry," he said to Kellan. "Maybe you should fly, and Dylan and I take a plane?"

"Absolutely not. We're not separating. If I lose you, I'd die," Kellan argued, placing a hand on Neil's shoulder and squeezing it. "All I need is the pants and sandals I have on. That's it. Don't worry about packing anything for me. I'm a minimalist survivor."

Neil added, "I don't need much either. I'll dump a few things. How far are we going?"

Not too sure, Kellan answered, "We'll just head toward AZ and stop only when we need to. I can fly pretty far rather quickly, so we'll probably be there within a day."

"That fast, huh?"

"Yep. You know how I fly," Kellan said. "Did Seth reply?"

Neil looked at the phone. "Not yet."

"Send him another text. Let him know we're leaving town and headed his way because sticking around here would be foolish."

Neil's hands shook while punching letters across the phone's keypad, backing up several times to correct the errors his misguided fingers made.

Noticing that Neil was trembling while he typed the

message, Kellan took him in his arms and hugged him from behind. His lips swept across Neil's ear when he whispered, "Everything is going to be fine, just like you said."

Chapter 19

On the other side of the country from where Kellan and Neil were, Seth read the text messages that Neil had sent him. Before answering any of them, he made sure he was alone. He couldn't risk getting caught in a game of espionage with an outsider by anybody who might be in the room with him. It would be his head on a stick in the desert if discovered. After viewing the messages from Neil, Seth tucked the phone into his shirt pocket and went about his business, keeping a low profile for the time being until he could figure a way to work out the details.

While Seth sat at his desk, he was able to access some of the internal files that showed who came and left the building, where they went on the inside, what they were there for, and who they had come to see. He also had access to the Seeker files as well as other folders outlining creations he'd be working with. That was a huge plus. Having access was a blessing because he'd soon need information stored there to find out more about Kaleb and that character named Trotsky.

When he looked through the digital registry, he couldn't find evidence that any Seekers had been sent out of the building to find Kellan, or that any had gotten loose. The facility had trackers on all of them and those tracking devices were linked to a digital display of the entire world, none of which pinpointed a Seeker outside the AZ building.

What Seth couldn't figure out at the time was where had the Seeker that Neil mentioned come from. All Seekers appeared to be accounted for and brought to a secured area at AZ. It didn't seem plausible for the government to end a search of this kind so quickly. The Seeker was too valuable, and the military couldn't take the chance of just anybody stumbling across a creature such as that. They would have drained the entire lake to find the body, dead or alive. Records documented all of that, and also mentioned divers had performed a thorough sweep of the lake and found no evidence that any had been located or were still missing. If what Neil had stated about a recent Seeker attack was true, it could mean that one might have survived the battle under the bridge with Kellan at the time of *his* TC escape, and the government was covering it up.

After running the assumed scenarios in his head, what Seth had found next told him they hadn't stopped looking. One fact he had established was an unmanned submachine still roaming the bottom of the lake in search of the Seeker, recording everything it passed.

Not seeing any concrete proof in the documentation, Seth speculated a Seeker had survived Kellan's thorough beating and found a secluded place in northern Michigan to hide for a while until well enough to fly. If that was the case, it meant the Seeker might be evolving, which could be cause for alarm.

If every Seeker was implanted with a tracking chip, why weren't they able to trace that one any further than where it went down in the lake? The Seeker might have located the chip and ripped it from its own body. Or another reason could be that Kellan busted it up so badly, the chip was dislodged or damaged. During the fight, he had banged the back of its skull against the cement barrier under Mackinac Bridge numerous times, so that seemed most logical.

At that point, Seth's brain was on borderline overload and

close to a meltdown, but before his mind had a chance to shut off, he documented his own notes about the recent battle Kellan had in Michigan with the one Seeker the military was looking for. With presumed evidence that the Seeker was alive and lurking led to a more dangerous situation for Kellan. After all, Kellan was who they were planning to send out in the field to summon the monster out of hiding.

Setting the Seeker records aside, Seth moved on to the Kaleb files. Sometimes changing his thought pattern helped him think more clearly when he returned to the subject he was struggling with.

Looking through the Kaleb files he had access to, Seth didn't see much of anything he hadn't already come across or already knew about. The only missing part to the puzzle was where on this green and blue earth was that boy. Seth wasn't certain how he was going to locate Kaleb, but finding him was his number one priority.

Seth's major plan was to get the government to agree with allowing Kellan to live independently. That seemed like a tough sell being that he's a multi-million-dollar project who can't simply walk the streets. An asset like him needed constant government surveillance, and would never be left completely unobserved.

In order for him to handle the matters on so many fronts — the rogue Seeker, the danger to Kellan and Neil, the issues of convincing the government to let Kellan live out his life semi-independently — all required him to multitask, motivating him relentlessly. After what seemed to be a long afternoon of probing through material, Seth still managed to spend a good part of the day flipping through files to help him figure out where Kaleb could be.

Needing a break, Seth placed his computer on hibernate and made a trip to the restroom. On his way down the corridor, Seth passed a white-coat who came out of the same bathroom he was about to enter. Seth nodded a polite greeting to the man, slowed his pace, which allowed him to read the security tag pinned to the man's lapel. He thought, *"Holy shit! That's him."*

Without going all ape-shit and attacking the man with questions he hadn't been prepared to ask, Seth stayed on course for the bathroom. He needed to regain his composure after recognizing the name across the man's chest. Seth stood in front of the mirror with his knuckles pressing down onto the countertop, staring at his reflection for what seemed like five minutes. He couldn't shake off how close he had come to the one man he knew for sure was linked to Kaleb, and how quickly they crossed paths. The entire time he stood thinking about Mister Trotsky, he stared directly into his own eyes looking back at him, almost as if he was waiting for his image to influence his next move. The thought circulating in Seth's head was that the search for Kaleb just became less challenging. All he needed to do now was figure a way to approach Trotsky and start asking questions. Discretely.

Was he actually getting close? Already? That fast? On the first day?

Seth shook his head to snap out of the daze he was in, coming up with ways he could inconspicuously meet Trotsky. For starters, he memorized the time of day it was right then, as possibly being a daily bathroom break for Trotsky. He was an instructor after all, so perhaps it was a short recess for Kaleb that took place daily, which would allow him to get away again at the same time every day. If that wouldn't work, Seth would try to get his schedule, find out what he did, where and when he did it. Maybe he'd figure a way to stumble into the man at lunch break. That idea might be best. It'd give Seth plenty of time to have a good chat in a more relaxed setting and squeeze in a few questions without seeming obvious.

Before leaving the bathroom, Seth fished the cell phone from his shirt pocket and swiped the screen until Neil's number appeared, and instead of placing a call, he sent a text message to let him know he'd call later that evening. That's when he'd fill them in on what he knew about the Seeker still in Michigan, and if he had anything more on Trotsky and Kaleb, he'd tell them that, too.

Seth splashed his face with water and patted it dry with a stiff piece of paper towel. He figured a quick rinse might help him reorganize thoughts that seemed to have gotten out of whack. He had a suspicion he was sharing a floor with Kaleb and Mister Trotsky, maybe just down the corridor. That certainly would make everything a whole lot easier.

When Seth returned to the office, Oliver was leaning back in his chair, arms propped behind his head, watching from the corner of his eye, looking wary. Oliver never said anything, just stared as Seth walked into the room.

"Aw fuck, he knows," Seth thought. He sat down behind his monitor and logged into the system, glancing over the screen at Oliver a few times, trying to figure out what was on his mind. The way it appeared, Oliver was there to keep tabs on him, report what he saw, like some kind of informant. Seth's guilty conscience was making him paranoid, and he was convinced Oliver was there to do more than just handle data entry. Eventually Seth broke the tension and asked, "Where do I find whom handles whose files around here?"

Oliver looked up. "Why would you need to know that?"

To reduce suspicion, Seth said, "I'd like to know where Kellan is." He tried to make it sound like a legitimate request. "Have you heard anything?"

Oliver leaned into the desk on his elbows, forming a steeple with pointy fingers in front of his lips. "The last I heard, he was still on the outside, in Michigan, on an Island with a guy named Neil and a dog named Dylan."

Surprised how much Oliver knew about, Kellan, Neil and Dylan, Seth raised his brow and took a stab at asking Oliver if he knew anything about the Seeker that was still missing. Oliver's response wasn't much more than what Seth already knew. He mentioned the military had lost contact with it several days back, and they had organized a taskforce to locate it before the thing was spotted walking the streets, or flying the skies for that matter. Four days from the day Kellan pulverized that Seeker under the bridge was plenty of time for it to pull itself together and start showing its ugly face in broad daylight.

Seth almost stopped breathing when Oliver said the search party was also going to bring Kellan and his boyfriend to AZ, saying it was way too big of a risk for them to continue flying freely. He swallowed his anxiety before Oliver noticed anything odd, and then came up with a plan he hadn't thought of earlier. A new plan he'd bring up to Kellan and Neil when he spoke to them later in the evening. What he was thinking could work.

Chapter 20

Dusk shadowed the lake, and as luck would have it, the Seeker hadn't come around the lighthouse at all that day. Taking advantage of being left alone, Neil and Kellan were able to somewhat collect their bearings before heading west to AZ across the skies of America.

The Seeker's assault made them think twice about sticking around the island any longer. Were they ready? No. But they had known the time to leave would be soon, just not right that minute.

Neil had been pacing the floors all afternoon and into the evening, waiting for the sun to go down so they could get moving. Kellan watched the windows and doors while Dylan kept an eye on both of them.

Neil looked at the phone, and whispered, "Seth should be calling soon, don't you think?"

"If AZ's anything like TC, he won't be calling until late tonight, maybe around ten or even eleven o'clock. That's the time the place should slow down, and he'll have a moment to himself,"

Kellan speculated.

"That late?" The thought of having to delay just to get that phone call wasn't sitting well with Neil. "Please tell me we're leaving before he calls. I've had just about enough of this place."

"Of course. Yeah. That'll be best." Kellan turned away from the window, the tip of a wing brushing across Dylan's back.

"Good. I need to get out of here."

"If you're edgy about that Seeker making another move on us, I'm pretty sure you can relax. It looked to me like I'd done some serious damage judging by how it was flying. It was having a tough time staying in the sky so I don't think it'll be paying us a visit anytime soon. Nevertheless, we need to get out of here before it has a chance to prove me wrong."

After carrying what he'd packed out the front door and onto the deck, Neil sadly said, "I guess this is it. Time to fly." It was like leaving the first home they'd made together. Although most of the memories were ugly ones, it was still like theirs.

As soon as they got outside, Neil strapped Dylan's empty bag around his waist to avoid having to carry him in his arms the entire way.

Once again the hummingbird flew in. It zipped around like a wild bumblebee, a busy one, clearly trying to get their attention. That buggy bird was acting out of character as if it was another manufactured creature.

With a *what the fuck* expression on his face, Kellan glanced at Neil who returned the look and asked, "What are we supposed to think of that thing?"

"I'm not sure. Perhaps we should follow it and see where it takes us," Kellan replied.

After that remark, Neil's face puckered with skepticism. To him, relying on a hummingbird to be their guide didn't seem like a good plan at all. He was okay with it following them, but letting it lead the way was a big no-no.

"This is it then. Strap up." Kellan reached for Dylan's bag and made sure it was secured around Neil's waist, weaving his belt over and under the strap. After finishing that, he gave Neil one of the longest and deepest kisses he'd ever given him, one that would last a lifetime if he needed it to. Backing away slowly, Kellan whispered, "I love you so much, Neil, it hurts."

Neil smiled at Kellan and told him the same thing. He knew exactly what Kellan meant by so much love being painful—the heart hurts when there's a chance it could get broken. Neil leaned in to lightly kiss Kellan's lips one more time before spinning around and backing into his chest. "All right, mine angel. Strap me up."

Kellan used the bed sheet they'd brought out, tied it over their shoulders and down across their hips, turning it into a full-body hammock for Neil to be cradled in as they flew. It was a brilliant idea, one they had both worked on.

Kellan laid his hands on each of Neil's shoulders and waited for him to corral Dylan into the bag. With a little coaxing and a couple doggie treats, Dylan got in and let Neil zip it up.

While they prepared for takeoff, that busy hummingbird hovered due south, watching them the entire time.

"This might be tricky at first, but once we're airborne, it should be smooth flying." Unable to run into the wind and fly the way he would have normally done, Kellan stood in place and beat his wings several times to gather the wind he needed for liftoff. They climbed straight up, and as soon as they were high enough to plane out, Kellan rolled his wings front to back, flapping them faster until they moved forward like a typical angel should.

By the time Kellan reached a decent soaring speed, the light pollution in the air and the big city lights reflecting off the cloud deck made him think they might be flying over Minneapolis. If that was the city he'd thought, and he held his one hundred forty knot speed, they'd probably make it to AZ in about thirteen hours.

"I can't believe I'd forgotten how great this feels," Neil said, the headwinds meeting his face and pushing through his hair. He looked down below and saw a lot of blackness. In the distance, he could see tiny street lights flickering, headlights of cars maybe, like the stars were beneath them instead of overhead.

Hawk-like with outstretched wings, Kellan soared most of the way, dipping and swooping a few times to make the flight less boring. Every once in a while they spotted the hummingbird.

They were about two hours into the flight when Kellan noticed several dark areas down below, and he figured they were somewhere over Iowa. Black patches on the ground were a good sign for them. No lights meant no people, possibly no trouble, and made it a secluded place to take a break. As they got closer to it, Kellan could see the major part of the dark spot was a small lake, and surrounding it were heavily wooded parcels. That would be perfect for keeping them out of sight and to themselves.

At the very moment Kellan started back flapping so he could touch down, the phone in Neil's rear pants pocket buzzed. Unable to easily reach it, he insisted Kellan get it.

Kellan pulled the phone out, tilted it so Neil could glance at the screen, then pulled it back and answered without breaking his winged rhythm. "Hang on, Seth, we're landing."

Chapter 21

Kellan was strong enough to hold the phone to his ear in one hand while he removed the sheet from over his shoulder with Neil still in it. Neil hit the ground with a thud, and without meaning to, Kellan laughed when he heard Neil grunt.

Within a few moments, Neil was out of the tangled hammock and on his feet. He reached for the phone and turned the speaker on so they both could hear.

As soon as Neil said hello, Seth didn't hold back. He told them he didn't have much on Kaleb, but mentioned he'd come inches from bumping into a man name Trotsky.

"Who's Trotsky?" Kellan asked. "Should we know him?"

"Oh, sorry. He was Kaleb's instructor, and still might be. He's taken care of him since he was born, like I had taken care of you—same role."

"Are you saying that Kaleb could be there at AZ?" Neil asked.

"From what I'd found in the files so far, they disclose a

young male angel was at AZ, and had been taken to another part of the country to live. The documents also indicate that they bring him back to AZ from time to time for extensive examinations they wouldn't do anyplace else, equipment reasons, I presume. Because I saw Trotsky in the hall makes me believe Kaleb might be here now for that scheduled exam."

"But if he's not there, do you know where they took him?" Kellan leaned into the phone and asked.

"By the records I've dug up, there's a house in the secluded hills of southern Colorado, just outside of San Juan National forest," Seth answered. "I don't have the exact location, but I'm sure I'll come across it somewhere soon."

"Why would they put him there instead of keeping him near Trotsky and those who are able to protect him?" Kellan raised his voice, and when he did, he took in a deep breath that puffed his chest up like he was about to fight.

"I'm not sure about that either, but I figure, the possibility of somebody discovering a kid with wings out there is less likely than seeing one flying around a big city such as Phoenix. But what I am pretty certain of, he's not unprotected out there. The government wouldn't let a valuable asset like that be left alone," Seth said.

Thinking sensibly, Seth brought up Kellan's past. "Remember what it was like for you, Kellan—stuck in a facility that seemed like an institute. I mean, you turned out well, but perhaps they're trying something different with Kaleb. Maybe they put him there to live a more normal life between his occasional visits to AZ."

"Colorado and AZ are quite a distance apart to be moving an angel from one place to the other all the time." Kellan said, shifting his weight from one foot to the other as if he was agitated, then mentioned. "Plus, wouldn't the climate differences put a toll on his little body?"

"It is cooler than Arizona a few months out of the year, but not drastic," Seth answered.

Kellan opened up. "I know I've had a decent life at TC, with you by my side, Seth, but something tells me Kaleb's is different. He's my kid, and I have an idea he might be unfortunate in some way. Don't I have parental rights or some shit like that?"

Kellan knew his life was different from a naturally born human being, and potentially having the rights of a parent seemed a stretch, but he said it anyway. He was fairly clear on how he fit into the scheme of things when it came to the military. He was their creation, brought up by them to spend his life doing what he was told, because he had no other choice, and to expect and submit to that reality. It was like they owned him, and he hadn't cared for that feeling for quite some time, which was the main reason he escaped the military's control. Now that he'd met Neil and, knew how it felt to be close to somebody he considered family, it was only natural to expect the same treatment and consideration as any other person, especially now that Kaleb was involved. He wasn't asking for anything more than an ordinary human would want and deserve.

Not getting a response from Seth, Kellan asked, "Doesn't Kaleb truly belong to me?"

Seth explained, "It doesn't work like that with the government. They have their own rules, and those rules don't allow you to step in and be granted custody because a judge said so. First of all, it would never come to that. They are the judge and jury. Give me time. I've got some things to work out."

For several moments there was complete silence.

Seth realized it was going to be way more complicated than he originally thought. He needed to establish a foolproof plan that laid out how he was going to proceed at the facility, work out a timeline, and then figure out when might be a good time to set the plan in motion.

He was determined to make it all happen, he needed to. Kellan was his friend, probably his only one, and he understood completely that Kellan wanted nothing more than to live as a family with the boy and Neil. Kellan's upbringing, isolated and controlled as he'd been, was surely eating away at him. That kind of life wasn't going to be good enough for his son.

Seth had a soft spot for many of the creations that had come out of TC, almost as if the ones he cared for were his pets. His heart seemed much bigger than the rest of the clinicians at that facility. He'd proven that to himself time and again by how he'd gone the extra mile to help those creatures when no one else wanted to. He never understood how somebody could just walk away from crying eyes. He itched to comfort a suffering soul, ached to make a sad face smile. His heart warmed every time he gave them a helping hand.

What had frozen his heart at times were the things he'd seen over the years while at TC. Even as he tried to block those dreadful images from his mind, bitterness toward the military had been instilled in him. He knew that some of the creatures were the way they were because of how the military made them, and many of the doctors seemed not to care if the things suffered or not.

In the beginning, he hadn't witnessed much of the ugly stuff that went on inside, only the fascinating, like watching a baby angel grow. Over time he was privy to the uglier side of their research—failed experiments, deliberate attempts to subvert nature into something hideous and evil. Weaponized biologics. The more he saw, the more he feared for his own soul, up until he was paired with Kellan.

Because of his angel, Seth's heart wouldn't allow him to cross over to the darker side. It wasn't in his nature, and he preferred to stay neutral as much as possible. The entire time he was part of the TC team, he always balanced both sides, and tried to keep the playing fields equal between the military's directives and Kellan's needs. After Kellan escaped, the military revealed how far they were willing to go by sending the vicious Seekers after Kellan. When Seth had protested, fearing for Kellan's life, it had created a schism between himself and those with less investment in Kellan's welfare. When push came to shove, Seth's loyalties were tipping toward Kellan's camp.

In order for it to appear he hadn't closed the door entirely on the military, Seth made sure he was passing small details over to them, like where Kellan and Neil were, and not bothering to hide the fact he was browsing the database. He was pretty certain the government was keeping tabs on him, so by feeding them bits of material, he hoped it would keep them from hovering so closely over him. Because of what he knew, Seth felt trapped in his position. He was aware he could do more from the inside than out, and that the military offered the best chance for Kellan to get what he most wanted.

After a long pause, Kellan looked concerned. His brow lifted and so did his wings. "What's to work out, Seth?"

"It's office stuff. I'll fill you in on that when I have more time. Just get to AZ as soon as you can," Seth said. "Where are you?"

Kellan answered, "Considering the time we left and how fast I flew, I believe we're in central Iowa someplace."

"Great! Then you should be here sometime tomorrow if you fly most of the night," Seth predicted.

"I was planning to fly through the night so we were in Arizona by morning, but now that you've mentioned the San Juan National Forest, maybe we'll circle the place and see what it's like." Kellan really wanted to get a bird's eye view of what his future might hold sooner than later. "What do you think, Seth? Can you hold down the dogs for a bit until we get there? It'll be quick."

Seth huffed, "Kellan, skip that. No detours right now."

At first, Kellan hesitated with sticking to the original course because he knew how much Neil was bothered by the way he always gave in to Seth. But because Kellan trusted Seth, he agreed with sticking to the original route, figuring Seth truly knew what he was doing. "If you think so, Seth. We'll be there first thing."

"Good. Glad you wised up. Now fly safely, Kellan. See you tomorrow," Seth said.

"See you soon, Seth." Neil pressed *end call* and dropped the phone into his pants pocket.

Kellan was facing Neil at that moment, looking into his eyes, seeing the stars in the sky twinkle in them. If he didn't know any better, he'd have mistaken them for the real thing.

Neil inhaled through his nose and exhaled through his mouth, almost as if he were trying to ease a heightened stress level.

Kellan removed Neil's shirt, placed a hand on each of his shoulders and pulled him close. "We have a few spare minutes before we need to take off again. You want to-o-o-o..." His voice trailed off. He rocked his head, shifting his gaze to the ground then back at Neil.

"To-o-o-o what?" Neil grinned, knowing what Kellan was thinking, but wasn't sure who would take the top now that they had traded places. Neil preferred to be under Kellan, but was okay either way.

"Well…" Kellan glanced around, "it's dark out. Nobody seems to be nearby, we're alone. Soo, we have time to bond." He wrapped his wings around Neil, holding him in place, hiding him, hoping he'd forget about everything around him.

They'd even overlooked Dylan who was lying next to them chewing a stick he'd found, and looking up at them between bites, obviously content with whatever they were about to do.

Neil's hands sought Kellan's chest, pricking his fingers on the short hair growing back. He liked how the chest hair made Kellan look more masculine, turning his angelic appearance to one that was tough and reckless. "Trying to be discreet isn't getting you anywhere, Kellan, and your erection seems like it wants to find a cozy spot inside of me."

Kellan smirked, no longer holding back. He went for a killer kiss, forcing his tongue into Neil's mouth and then sucking Neil's into his. Instantly, their erections came to life, fiercely pushing against the inside of their jeans, trying to get out.

Neil lowered himself to the ground, bringing Kellan down on top of him. He took pleasure in Kellan's weight crushing him into the soft earth. He relished how his wings fluttered above, reflecting the dim light that lit Kellan's face, making him seem even more angelic. It was moments like these where he realized how much he was in love.

Kellan shifted his body at Neil's side. He slowly slid a hand down the gutter of Neil's abdomen where he briefly stopped above his waistband. "I love the feel of your skin, Neil," he crooned. His hand moved further, palming Neil's erection that was growing thicker within his jeans.

All around them under the milky moonlight glinting off the lake, curious sounds filled the air. Crickets chirruped, frogs croaked, and a warbling loon yodeled to another. The canopy of leaves on the few trees scattered around the perimeter of the lake rustled together in the light breeze as if trying to outperform the gentle lap of waves coming onshore.

After several exhilarating moments of Kellan exploring, Neil huffed and kissed his plump lips lightly. "Let's be daring. Make love to me right here, Kellan." Neil's hand reached for Kellan's chest, palming one muscular pec. Little by little he moved his hand to the back of Kellan's shoulder. The muscles supporting his wings were thick and hard, so different from his own. He relocated his hand to the underside of the wing, gently running his fingers over feathers. When he stroked the quills from tip to base, his touch sent exquisite sensations through Kellan's entire body, making him growl and flutter his feathers uncontrollably.

The placement of Neil's hand drove Kellan into a frenzy. His nerves fired with anticipation, and he dove into Neil for an intense kiss, the sound noisy and all so wet. Thoughts of penetrating Neil quickly ravaged him, making him feel exhilarated and alive. Unable to contain himself any longer, he got to his feet and flapped his wings that lifted him higher. Hovering, he removed his jeans and let them go. His rock hard dick sprung free, ready to burrow inside Neil.

Before Kellan descended, Neil shed his clothes and lay waiting, spread eagle and exposed.

Catching a glimpse of Neil down below, Kellan vigorously changed the angle of his wings, flapping them higher above his head to increase drag. Once his feet touched the ground, he brought his wings in at a slower beat, and he landed smoothly on top of Neil. Rolling his hips, Kellan slid his erection back and forth against Neil's. The friction, mixed with the anticipation of penetrating the man under him, drew more semen from Kellan. Leaning into Neil, Kellan kissed his lips, his neck, and the lobe of his ear. When he ran his wet tongue along Neil's jawline to his mouth, his lover's body quaked in anticipation, so much so Kellan sensed Neil was close to cumming, even after so little stimulation.

Unexpectedly, Kellan broke their kiss and sat back on the heels of his feet. He gripped his dripping erection, keeping it hard for Neil. Gut clenched, thigh muscles quivering, Kellan groaned, "Oh Gawd, I need to fuck you, Neil," his voice betraying the unbridled passion he felt for his lover. Soft moans of lust gave way to wordless whimpers of desire.

Watching Kellan, Neil's own hunger for him increased, the anticipation so strong it was close to taking over his entire soul, especially with Kellan propped on his knees and a hand moving back and forth over his glorious wet cock. Neil's excitement was pushed to the limit when Kellan's other hand circled and finger-poked his twitching entrance. Neil wanted it, he needed it. He could hardly breathe, and if the world ended, he wouldn't care, because all he wanted was Kellan to take him to a place he'd never been before. An overpowering scent of sex and musk wafted toward Neil as Kellan's wings fluttered in the fresh air. It smelled woodsy, bringing a hint of rainfall with it. His nerve endings sparked. Blood pounded harshly in his ears.

Craving every bit of Kellan, Neil aggressively gripped his wingtips, tugging him closer. He needed to feel the angel's cock forcibly moving in and out of his hot channel, so badly he ached for it. The punishing pleasure of Kellan's cock bearing down against his caused Neil's hips to uncontrollably thrust upward, and the sudden jolt ruined the grip he had on Kellan's wings. He was gentle when he needed to be, but right then didn't seem to be the time to be tender. Completely worked into a frenzy, Neil begged, "Fuck me, Kellan. Right now. Don't wait another second."

Neil growled at the initial sting of Kellan's angelic cock being pushed to the hilt.

Kellan cried out, "Sweet surrender, you feel good."

Even though Kellan's dick was a sudden shock to his system, Neil arched into the intrusion, his body vibrating with need. He grabbed hold of his legs behind each knee and pulled them to his chest, opening himself up further to Kellan. "Do it, Kellan. Split me in two."

Kellan pulled his dick out and quickly jammed it back in, power punching his up curved cock into Neil's G-spot. "Like that? Is that how you want it?" He could feel Neil's channel squeezing tighter, as though the more dick he gave him, the more he wanted.

Prompted by Kellan's bulbous crown banging against his prostate, Neil suddenly felt like he was out of body, his head spinning in fucked up circles. Kellan's erection was able to do incredible things to Neil that no one had ever been able to do, making him cum by penetrating his asshole alone. The internal massage by Kellan's dick against Neil's prostate could push semen out of him without a single stroke to his cock. Neil's dick, crazily bouncing against his tightened abdomen, leaked pre-cum that Kellan's nine-plus inches of cock had effortlessly worked out of him. Neil could feel his fiery cream brewing, moving from his balls to the seminal chamber that would soon find release through his dick. He lost control and the grip on his knees. His arms dropped to the dirt above his head, exposing the sensual pockets of his pits. He wildly shouted, "Fuck... fuck... fuckin' fuck me, Kellan. Don't fucking stop."

All of a sudden, Neil's ankles were locked in Kellan's grasp, and his legs were being opened like a wishbone. As Kellan vigorously fucked him, Neil could feel the tingling in his nuts that a full release was about to erupt. Driven to frenzy beyond returning, Neil's slick channel worked Kellan's cock, the flexing muscles relentlessly sucking on his angel's dick ever further, stroking up and down his length, pulling on it, as if his sphincter was hungry for the man's complete release.

Kellan possessed Neil like he owned him, and growled broken words, "You're amazing, Neil..." — he gasped — "are you ready..." — he groaned — "...for me?" Kellan forced his hips into Neil again and again, eager to cum inside the man he loved.

Reveling in the sensation of his own rising orgasm, Neil struggled to answer. "Yes... Kell."

Then it happened. A fiery rush in his pelvis made Kellan light-headed, and searing pleasure raced through him as if his insides were being torn apart. He shot the frothy semen Neil had been waiting for, pumping so much into him that it overflowed Neil's channel and soaked the ground, his butt cheeks bathing in Kellan's juices. Kellan continued shooting one massive load after another that didn't seem to want to stop, cramming it all up in Neil's channel.

Neil heaved forward, shoulder blades leaving the ground. The sensation of his insides expanded from Kellan's hefty release, pushing him to the orgasmic edge and then over. His head snapped back as the moment came. Like fireworks shooting to the sky, he sprayed his spunk, squirting everywhere, flooding his chest.

"Fuck yeah, that's my man. Give me all of it," Kellan cried out as he continued reaming Neil's crater of a hole his stovepipe wide cock had shaped.

It took a while for Neil to settle down — his heart raced,

beating in time with every pulsing clench his asshole imposed on Kellan's cock, taking what he had and milking it clean. There was no way he was getting off Kellan's dick just yet. He was locked on it, determined to hang on, and it felt too good jammed up inside of him to let it slip away. When the inevitable moment arrived, sensing Kellan's cock soften, he had no choice but to allow it to slide free.

Kellan was still breathing heavily, but was able to say, "I wish you could see this."

"See what?"

"My thick veiny dick looks just as spectacular slowly snaking out of you soft as when I stuffed it into you rock hard." Kellan lowered himself down on top of Neil and waited for the vibrations racing through his body to subside. His fingers tangled in Neil's hair, holding his head back at a sharp angle. Their cheeks pressed together, wet with Neil's creamy release.

Syncing breaths, they waited for their heart rates to settle back to normal as lust slowly drained once more into affection. As they lay there, a cool breeze stroked their overheated flesh.

Kellan let go of Neil's hair, lifted his weight off him and looked directly into his eyes. "What?" He shifted, balancing on his balled fist on either side of Neil's shoulders.

Neil couldn't believe how much they'd had to go through to get to that moment in time, and the idea of having Kellan to himself made him chuckle. "I just love you, Kellan. A lot. Being here with you makes me so fucking happy." Neil had developed so much love for Kellan that it overwhelmed him with new emotions. Every time he was with Kellan, it was amazing. Every time Kellan held him, Neil felt protected. Every time Kellan moved inside him, it was the most incredible connection he'd ever experienced.

At the moment Kellan wanted nothing more than to show Neil he was also capable of gentleness, of quiet, sensual love, of tenderness. Slowly he brushed Neil's kiss-swollen lips, putting all his love, all his wants and desires into a simple act of affection.

Neil's head rotated with Kellan's as he relished in his angel's softer side, accepting his kiss, surrendering to the lighter side of passion.

Between kisses, Kellan told Neil he loved him, too. He turned his voice deep and sexy, and said, "How about we trade places, hot stuff?" He really wanted to feel Neil's dick inside him again. But unlike the last time, he wanted the sex with Neil to be slow and sensual, as in making love. Without waiting another second, Kellan gripped Neil's shoulders and rolled him over. The shift in weight made Kellan grunt, and his wings thwacked against each other when they laid out flat across the cool ground underneath him.

Neil's hands landed on Kellan's chest, his fingers interlacing with hair that seemed to have grown longer within a few short hours. While sitting on top of Kellan, Neil looked down into his cerulean eyes and the lustful thoughts about being back inside him returned with a vengeance. Like Kellan, Neil was determined to give as much pleasure to Kellan as he'd just experienced. Neil didn't want it to be the way it happened before, the ram-bam-thank-you-man kind of fuck that made them both cum in less than five minutes. Even though it was hot and thrilling, a long, slow fuck would be so much better.

Kellan lifted his hips, bumping Neil forward into a kiss.

Neil whispered into Kellan's mouth while their lips brushed against each other's, "Name the place and time, and I'll have my hard-on ready to make contact with that sweet, sweet dildo sleeve of yours." He secured their lips in another killer kiss, not letting Kellan answer.

Never hearing his asshole described in such a way made Kellan laugh. He admitted that was funny. "Okay, stud. You can stick that dick of yours inside me later. Right now, let's fly."

Chapter 22

Before the morning light crept in and revealed their hiding place, Neil pulled himself away and got dressed. It was better to be prepared rather than sorry.

Standing up, Kellan shook his wings. Loose blades of grass clinging to them flittered back to the ground.

They put themselves back together the same way they had done during the first part of their flight, the sheet holding Neil against Kellan, and Dylan inside the bag strapped to Neil's waist. They took to the air, leaving the secluded place in the middle of Iowa behind.

The weather couldn't have been more perfect for flying. No clouds, no threats of rain or heavy winds, just a mass of twinkling stars that helped light the way.

It took them the rest of the dawning hours to reach the dry state of Arizona where they located a place in the mountainous zone that was not too far east of Phoenix. It was a hot place, clearly one that would roast their flesh if they hung out in the sun for too long. There were several rocky hills and valleys with little to no vegetation. In the deepest parts of the gorges were a few lakes that had narrow streams connecting one to the other, all part of the Salt River Watershed. It was home for trout, maybe a frog or two, but not people.

On their way in, Kellan remembered seeing a sign that mentioned Tonto National Forest, and because the reservation seemed to have only one road running through it, he figured it would be a good place to stay until they got word from Seth to make a move.

Surprisingly, for such a dry place small bristly trees lined the narrow streams there. From those few sporadic bushes, small amounts of shade were cast along the ground, bringing the temperature in those areas down a few degrees.

Even with a bit of shade where they were, it was so hot and stagnant that it felt like there was no oxygen in the air when they breathed. When the midday sun found its spot in the sky straight above them, it got worse. The heat index went up so quickly it gave them the feeling they were sitting on the edge of hell.

Because of the fast weather change, Neil wasted no time sending a text to Seth that told him they had arrived, and asked to let them know where they were to go next. Any place would be better than the scraggly bush they were under at the moment.

Kellan sat next to Dylan, fanning everybody with his wings to cool them down. It generated a little breeze, but it mostly just moved the desert heat around and lifted gritty dust. The gusts stirred other creatures on the ground. A few bugs skittered from one dry leaf to the next.

"Shit! A big ass spider," Neil shrieked. He pointed as he leaped to his feet.

Dylan barked when Neil hollered, looking at him and then at Kellan. His little mind probably thought, *"What the heck are you screaming at?"*

Neil screeched again, turning to Kellan and then tried to locate the furry tarantula that scampered across the ground from beneath a stone. "Did you see that freaking arachnid? The bitch was the size of my hand — I swear."

Kellan stood up and snapped a branch from the bush they were all trying to fit under, planning to use the crusty twig as a weapon if the eight-legged fur ball came at them with its fangs exposed. He laughed when he saw Neil skip across the ground, raising dust and bringing more bugs out of hiding.

Neil knew little about tarantulas, but what he did know, as long as they were left alone, there was no need to worry about being attacked by one. Not taking chances, Neil kept an eye out for that monster-sized spider's return, as well as anything else that scurried. He was already on edge, and for a legitimate reason, so the vibration in his back pocket made him think the tarantula had bitten him on the ass cheek, possibly infecting him with venom he understood to be deadly. The buzz and the spider ramped up his anxiety level, and he knew he wouldn't calm down until they'd left the creature ridden desert. "Fuck me in the asshole. We need to get out of this place."

Kellan took a couple steps forward until he was standing at Neil's side. Together they viewed the screen on the cell phone and saw that there was a message from Seth. The text mentioned that it wasn't safe to stay wherever they were, and it was best if they found their way to AZ as soon as possible.

Wondering why Seth had a different view on their current situation from what he had mentioned earlier, they speculated Seth wasn't the one on the other end of the phone. The last time they spoke with him, he told them to hang loose until he could figure out a safe place for them to go. What had changed?

The only way for them to know for certain it was Seth who had sent the message was to speak with him directly, to hear his voice. Neil sent a text back that asked Seth to call them.

Within a few minutes, the phone rang and the screen showed it was Seth.

Neil and Kellan exchanged glances at the same time, suspicious of who might be on the other end making the call.

Kellan swallowed, tapped connect and said, "Hello?"

Thankful to hear Seth's voice, Kellan activated the speaker so Neil could hear the conversation too.

Neil asked Seth if everything was okay, listening for tone changes in his voice that would indicate he was being coached. From what Neil could tell, nothing sounded out of the ordinary. Other than being loud, as if he was trying to talk over background noise, Seth's voice sounded cheerful enough, perhaps unreasonably so.

Seth's attempt at a cover-up was blown almost immediately when he told them why they needed to put on their hiking boots and get the heck out of Dodge. Keeping his explanation to a bare minimum, Seth mentioned the government had suspected the "Seeker-on-the-run" might be trailing them, that it could even be closer than they thought, and the only safe place for them was at AZ.

First monster sized spiders and now this?

Neil cocked his head to one side as if trying to hear sounds in the phone that shouldn't be there. "How would they know the Seeker might be right around the corner?"

Seth answered, "They don't. Nobody knows exactly where that thing is. But... because it was originally programmed to seek Kellan, they are counting on it to do just that. That's one of the reasons they left you guys alone for the past few days. They were expecting it to find you, there'd be a scuffle, and somehow you'd lead it to AZ or they could net it themselves when it showed up again."

That made some sense because the Seeker had found them and caused a ruckus, but Kellan had messed that plan up by beating the shit out of it at Lake Michigan, causing it to scurry away.

Seth continued. "The military always had me in place as part of the plan to get you back, and I was okay with that because I had a plan of my own. They placed me on their imaginary chess board, used me as a pawn to get you to move where they wanted you. They knew I'd reach out to you, which I did. And guess what? You are here, out west."

"Unbelievable," Kellan griped.

"It's all right though, Kellan. You'll always be of great value to them, so they're going to set you and Neil up in a secure place to live off the premises of AZ. You guys will be able to live safely together and they can keep watch over you. Sorry for making you out to be an alien with what I'm about to say, but the military can't afford to have the human race see you. Not yet anyway."

"How can we trust them to do what they say?"

"We have to, Kellan. I believe them because they need that Seeker back just as much as you, if not more."

"Why's that?"

"You're tamed. That thing isn't. It doesn't know enough to keep itself hidden as you do. On the other hand, it's a trained killer and if anybody outside AZ gets hold of it or it of them, some crazy shit could happen. You know that as well as I do."

"This is so fucked up," Kellan yelled.

"It seems so, but you have to trust me on all this, Kellan. It's going to be fine."

"You better be right about that." Kellan glanced at Neil, unsure of anything that was being said.

"Can you ping your location on the phone?" Seth asked for a screenshot and mentioned it might be best for a chopper to pick them up and bring them to AZ.

Everything truly seemed almost beyond fixing, and all they could do was listen to what Seth was saying and hope for the best.

Neil wasn't comfortable with any of what he had heard, but he went with it because there didn't seem to be any other choice. All the hiding and running was beginning to take its toll on him. Why the government didn't just send out a missile loaded chopper to pick them off already like they tried to do the last time never made any sense to him. Logically, if they had, it would have made everything a lot easier. But the idea of being near a military chopper again had Neil shaken. It brought back some bad-ass memories that he wanted to leave in his past.

In less than thirty minutes from when Neil sent Seth a snapshot of where they were, a chopper flew in and circled them. The thump of the blades against the wind immediately brought back all the unwanted memories Neil had been trying so hard to put out of his mind. The repetitive thwack gave him that uneasy feeling, and it seemed to do the same to Kellan and Dylan by what he saw in the way they reacted.

The chopper ultimately landed in an open, fairly flat area that was about fifty yards away from them. As soon as it touched down, Seth quickly became visible to Kellan and Neil when the door of the aircraft opened. Without getting out, he rolled one hand into his chest as if coaxing them toward the chopper, while holding the other arm above his brow as though he was trying to block out the sun.

Having doubts about getting into a helicopter like the one

that tried to take them out without warning not so long ago, Kellan grabbed hold of Neil's arm, not letting him move. He rolled his eyes until he was looking at the spinning blades while dragging a finger across his throat that signaled he wanted the engine cut before any of them took another step forward. He'd seen what those blades could do when a Seeker got tangled up in them, so stepping under a spinning blade wasn't going to happen until the chopper was shut down. He thought life was better with wings and a head.

After his signal was acknowledged and the blades stalled out, they made their move toward the open door of the helicopter.

Taking no chances, Kellan still pulled his wings in tightly against his back and lowered his head before making any attempt at walking under the helicopter blades, spinning or not. Keeping pace beside Kellan, Neil hung onto the carrier Dylan was tucked safely inside.

They crawled into the chopper, greeted Seth before sitting opposite him inside the fuselage. The two MP Officers next to Seth stared at the three of them like they were ghosts from Casper's castle. Since the MPs were from the Lab, Kellan was sure they'd seen angels before, but couldn't figure out why they were looking at him the way they were. Perhaps it was the way Neil was sitting so close to him, their shoulders pressed tightly together, holding his hand at his thigh and his other crossing his chest with a secure grasp around Kellan's bicep. There was no separating them now. No point blank pistol, spear or machete could keep them apart.

Seth knee-walked across the floor until he was centered in front of Kellan and Neil. He smiled softly at Kellan, and then asked if everything was all right, how he'd been and if he was okay with the events that were about to take place that day.

Kellan responded positively even though his face betrayed his reluctance to buy into the story.

By the way Seth spoke, Neil guessed he was keeping his conversation short to prevent nearby listeners from suspecting they'd had previous contact with each other, or had been making plans to find Kellan's son, Kaleb.

After the brief conversation and a side-winder smile to Neil, Seth unlatched the aviation headsets from the wall above their heads and motioned that they needed to put them on. Using ear protection would knock out the deafening whistle the spinning engine emitted, as well as ease communication between them inside the noisy craft.

The high pitched whistle of the engine was more ear-piercing to a dog than to a human or an angel. To relieve Dylan from the noise of that, cotton balls were stuffed in his ears and held in place by wrapping his head with a ribbon of gauze. He looked mummified-silly, but if he didn't have the security wrap, one shake of the head and the puffballs would be ejected without a doubt.

Within seconds from when the blades started spinning again, there was lift off.

In the air the flight was rough, not as smooth the way Neil thought it would be, nor as graceful as flying in Kellan's arms. The banging of the blades against the wind was just as unsettling as if standing next to them outside the craft. They thumped so hard that they seemed to take the place of his heartbeat, making him feel like his heart was on the outside of his chest. After the initial shock, the heavy thumping faded into the background, the way so many annoying things eventually did.

It only took about fifteen minutes to fly from Tonto National Forest to AZ Genetic Manipulation Laboratory, and when they landed, a sense of relief returned to all of them. For Kellan, used to flying under his own power, it was a relief to once more be in control of when and where he could use his abilities. For Neil, flying with someone else in control—someone not Kellan—wasn't going to be comfortable ever again.

Once inside AZ, Kellan and Neil were told to go with Seth and the two lurking MPs. Knowing how the MPs reacted to any sudden movement found to be threatening, Kellan kept his cool, acting as normal as an angel in captivity could. Together, Kellan and Neil walked behind Seth in a tight clump, holding hands, taking precautions not to cause any reason to be treated as prisoners. Even with Seth's assurances that AZ was a safe haven, the feeling of dread and fear still hung with them. For all they knew, no more than sneezing the wrong way might set off alarms that would put them in detention. Could they really trust Seth in the face of mounting evidence against the assurances he'd given them?

Even though AZ wasn't TC, everything inside looked as if it was the same to Kellan, bringing his thoughts back to where he'd grown up and lived for the past twenty-eight years. The medical labs and rooms were very similar to TC, institutional-like, with a comparable set up and only a few minor differences in room shapes, sizes and placement.

An eerie feeling came over Kellan as he walked the halls of AZ. Everything he looked at brought back unwanted memories. Some good. A few bad. Other than the wall color and the smell of formaldehyde, the similarities of the two places were even more apparent in the way the clinicians traveled from room to room, their actions dredging up old memories.

Feeling moderate heat coming off Kellan's skin, sensing tension in his grasp, anxiety threatened to bury Neil, the memories tainted by what had occurred the last time he was at TC, which made him want to get out of AZ straightaway. If it weren't for the need to unite Kellan with his son Kaleb, he'd have been long gone, dragging Kellan with him so they could take to the sky and fly far, far away.

They continued down the corridor, and when they made one final turn, they saw that the flooring and wall color had changed. The difference seemed to make the place feel more like a home for the elderly than an institution for the mentally insane. It wasn't the best looking place to call home, but it was better than living on the street or in one of the rooms that looked like a hospital examination chamber.

Seth and the MPs stopped in front of a six panel door that resembled a mid-class apartment entry or a classy hotel suite. The only thing that seemed bothersome was the mail basket on the wall next to the door, one that appeared to hold hospital records for whoever was in that room.

Seth turned toward Kellan, but held his gaze on Neil and said, "Okay guys, this is your home for now. It's all set up for living comfortably and the good news is that it's a dog friendly hotel."

Surprised at the thoughtfulness, Kellan and Neil smiled.

Seth reached for the mail basket next to the door, pulled out a folder and opened it. Inside the folder, instead of the expected medical records, were slot key cards for their new accommodations. Seth handed one of the cards to Neil and the other to Kellan. "These are the keys to this door, your temporary home. Don't get too attached to the place because I'm not sure how long you're staying here. These keys also give you access around the property where you and Dylan are allowed to go. That's their idea of giving you free rein without letting you get too far."

That didn't sound like freedom to either Kellan or Neil, but more like prison as they'd expected, only this cell was supposedly designed for the rich and famous.

Taking the key, Neil asked, "May we?" He pointed at the door and took a step forward.

Still holding Neil's hand, Kellan moved with him. His wings extended as if shielding them from possible danger.

The whole idea of being in the government's custody was unpleasant, and it felt like they were being put in jail. But, if they were going to put a rational spin on it, their situation was better than being on the run, hiding in trees or putting up a tent on uninhabited islands.

Chapter 23

Seth moved aside to let Neil swipe the card over the magnetic reader that would unlock the door and allow passage. The latch clicked and the door smoothly opened when he pushed a hand against it.

Everybody entered except the MPs. Inside was more than just a hotel room. It was an actual apartment with everything they needed, consisting of a large open floor plan that was fresh and airy. Lining the back wall of the ranch-style apartment was floor to ceiling glass sliders that opened up to a patio and a backyard enclosed by a twenty-foot-high brick wall.

When Seth noticed a look of dismay on Neil's face, he quickly explained the barrier wasn't there to keep them in, but to keep people and wild animals out.

His explanation helped a little, but Neil was still a little suspicious of Seth and mixed messages he was getting from AZ.

The apartment was actually nice in Neil's opinion. A far cry better than the dilapidated lighthouse they'd come from. The only thing missing was the lake view Neil was used to.

Seth took them on a quick tour, showing them all the rooms, with the last stop being the master bedroom suite. Before ending the tour, he opened the dresser drawers and closets so they could see they were totally stocked. "This should make your stay pleasant. You two shouldn't have to worry about a thing. It's all taken care of."

After shaking hands, Neil grabbed Dylan and left Seth and Kellan together. The vibe he'd gotten was that both men required some one-on-one time to re-establish their old connection. Given their history, Neil got that, but it still didn't sit well with him.

Kellan took advantage of the time Neil was away and pulled Seth alone into the living room. Keeping his voice low, he said, "Be up front with me, Seth. Please tell me we're going to be okay here. I don't give a shit about me, but I don't want anything to happen to Neil. I love that man so much, that if anything did happen, I couldn't live with myself. Can you promise me that he will be all right?"

Seth stepped closer to Kellan, tucking himself under his wing to buffer what he was going to say. "There's nothing to worry about, Kellan. They promised me that all three of you will be one hundred percent protected. They know you're extremely valuable, and they don't want anything to happen to you. They've told me that and I believe them."

"Okay. If you trust them, then I do too. That's all I needed to hear." Kellan inhaled, taking in air that puffed up his chest. He slowly let it back out before saying, "One more thing before you leave. Why are we really here?"

"We have an appointment with the Chiefs of Staff tomorrow. They'll tell you about it then."

In the meantime, Neil had been placing the few items they brought along into the bathroom closet. In case the tranquilizer pistols and darts were needed again, he stuffed those under the sink where he'd easily remember their location. Then he stashed the toys in the bedside nightstand, feeling the entire time that he was being watched. Trying to locate the spy cameras that made him feel that way, he coolly glanced around the room.

Kellan lowered a wing and looked over his shoulder, making sure Neil was still in the back bedroom. Turning back to face Seth, he said, "Those are some pretty high ranking people who will be at the round table. Seems major, and it would make more sense to me if you'd give me a little bit of information on what's in store. I can see by the look on your face you know something. Why can't you tell me now?"

Kellan could tell by Seth's shifty eyes, pinched face and jerky movements that he wasn't comfortable revealing what he knew. To persuade Seth to give him something, Kellan made sure Seth understood he was fully prepared to fly out of there. Giving in to Kellan, Seth told him, "It's about the Seeker that's on the loose. They can't find it and they want you to help get it back."

"That's it?" Kellan squawked. "No big deal, I can handle that. The only thing that worries me is after all that is done, and the Seeker is back behind bars, what happens to us?"

"They assured me that there were plans for you, safe ones. But, I've been working on a way to guarantee that, and you'll find out what I've come up with tomorrow," Seth confidently said.

Kellan anxiously whispered, "What? Tell me now, Seth. Don't you think it's a good idea that I'm prepared?"

"My ace-in-the-hole means I need everybody to be blindsided, even you. We can't afford to have a leak. That's how it's gotta be. I'm stuck with sealed lips whether you like it or not. Now don't ask me again." Seth's tone went even lower. "Shush, here comes Neil."

When everything was in place where Neil wanted it, he romped with Dylan at his side into the living room where Seth and Kellan were. "Hi guys. Everything okay?"

Just as Neil entered, Kellan retracted his wings and spun to face him. "Hi, Hun. All is good. Did you get everything put away where you wanted it?"

"I did," Neil said. "Everything." He grinned and waggled his brow.

Kellan knew what Neil was talking about when he said "everything," and Seth probably did too.

Seth stepped around Kellan with a grin of his own. "I've got office crap to do before the clock strikes twelve, so I need to get going. I'll see the two of you tomorrow morning. Now relax, make yourselves at home, and be sure to get some rest. Your heads need to be clear tomorrow."

Chapter 24

Standing together at the door after Seth left, Neil asked Kellan, "Now what do we do?"

Kellan reached out and took Neil's hand in his, swinging them like a jumping rope. "I could certainly eat something. That flight over sapped all my energy."

"There's a good sized kitchen here and I'm sure it's fully stocked." Neil was feeling weak from lack of nutrition too, a little dizzy and borderline nauseous. Looking forward to finding something to eat that would give them strength, he towed Kellan into the kitchen by the hand and opened up the refrigerator. As suspected, food galore.

Kellan conveyed his appreciation by saying, "So far the government seems to be fulfilling their side of the bargain. How well can you work a kitchen?"

Catching a glimpse of Kellan's smirk, Neil answered, "I'm not much of a chef since I don't do much cooking, so for now how about we just select something from the freezer and nuke the bastard?"

Kellan moved his wings out of the way and stepped closer to Neil's side, hugging him with an arm draped lightly over the back of his shoulders. They stood there looking in the refrigerator as if food was going to jump out of it already prepared on a plate.

Neil then said, "Did you happen to notice if there was a grill on the patio out back?"

"No, but I can check." Kellan removed his arm from Neil's shoulders.

"No! Wait! I'll go look. It's still light outside." Neil pressed a hand to Kellan's chest, holding him in place.

Kellan inhaled, expanding his chest, pushing forward into Neil's hand. "It's fine, Neil. Remember where we are? We're in the middle of the desert and there are twenty foot walls all around this compound. Nobody's going to see me."

"You're right. I forgot. I'm not used to you being in the sunlight. It's okay, go check, and if there is one, how about getting it started." Neil kissed Kellan and stepped out of his way, opened the refrigerator again and took out a breast of chicken.

"Yes, love. I'll do it for you." Kellan scowled at the chicken breast in Neil's hand as he walked out the door, clumsily bumping the tips of his wings against the door frame.

Right then Neil realized why Kellan looked at him the way he did before leaving the kitchen. Neil mumbled, "Oh shit. I'm such a schmuck. Chicken? I might as well feed him eggs. Oh Gawd." Understanding birds probably don't eat other birds, at least normal ones don't, Neil laughed at himself while he put the chicken back in the refrigerator, wondering why it was even there in the first place.

Outside, Dylan raced at lightning speed to Kellan's side and stared at him. It was as if the dog was trying to mentally tell Kellan to press the igniter button and turn the burners' knobs to the ON position, like he knew Kellan had no idea what he was doing. Or he was just as hungry as they were and wanted to take part in the feeding ritual.

"What are you looking at? I've got this. Aw crap, you haven't eaten since yesterday. Do you like chicken, Dylan?" Kellan brushed Dylan's back with his wingtip while he took a few minutes to figure out how to get the fire going on the grill. He'd never used a contraption like that before, so it took some tinkering to make a flame appear.

At the moment Kellan got the grill started, Neil stepped through the doorway and said, "Change of plans. No chicken" — he laughed — "I couldn't bear to see you having at another winged creature or watching me go to town on one. From now on, we're vegetarians."

"Don't be silly, you can have whatever you want. I'm able to survive on bird seed," Kellan joked while closing the lid on the grill, enclosing the fire inside.

"Huh? I thought..." Neil started to say.

Kellan placed a cupped hand over Neil's mouth to stop him from chattering. He laughed at Neil before changing his grin into a smile. "You're so fucking cute when I'm having you on. It's grass I like, not bird seed."

"What?" Neil squawked again, skipping around Kellan to douse the flame inside the grill before his wings went up in flames.

"You are so easy to fool, my gullible lover. Now shut up and kiss your angel." When they kissed, Kellan felt his feathers twitter. The orgasmic buzz raced through the plumes to his crotch, giving him that instant erection he always got whenever Neil touched him.

Neil went straight for Kellan's tongue and sucked it into his mouth, the slippery sensation aroused him and made him want more. Grabbing hold of Kellan's jaw in both hands, Neil held their kiss in place, taking his time to enjoy what Kellan offered. There was hardly any space between them and their body heat seemed to have reached the same temperature as the grill did when it was fired up. If there was anything hotter than them at the moment, it would have gone up in flames. Neil gulped when he felt Kellan's thickening cock press against his thigh and the thrill of feeling him made Neil stiffen too.

Remembering it was daylight and there might be an audience, Neil kept their connection restrained to just a kiss. He backed away first, looking at the corners of the apartment for possible cameras.

Kellan leaned back a little and looked at Neil the same way he did the chicken breast earlier and asked, "What's wrong?"

"Cameras," was all Neil said.

"Who cares? They already know we've been fucking." Kellan laughed at his raunchy statement regarding sticking his dick into Neil.

"But they haven't seen us in action. I hope." Neil pecked Kellan quickly on the mouth with dry lips and then took a few steps back to give their auras space to expand. "I'm fine with them seeing us kiss, I don't care if anybody does for that matter, but I'm not too sure I want them zooming in on my hard-on trying to sword fight with yours, which by the way is leaking like a muthuh."

Kellan looked down, knowing the front of his jeans were getting wet. He smiled at the effect Neil had on him. "But when the lights go down, can we try this again? I'm dying for a long lasting sword fight with you that will end up with one of us getting stabbed."

There was something funny about what Kellan just said that made Neil laugh. "Why don't we think about eating first, and then we fence."

"I so agree with that." Kellan pecked Neil back, on the lips once and then again to his cheek.

Before they discussed sex any further, Neil dragged Kellan into the apartment by a wing, like he was holding a hand.

Once inside, they worked around each other like a couple who have been together for several years. Kellan darted for the shelves and started flinging appetizing items onto the counter while Neil grouped together the things that would make a decent meal.

While whirling from cabinet to counter, Kellan had come across a science diet kibble for Dylan, gave him plenty to satisfy his empty stomach while Neil filled a water bowl to wash it all down.

Within minutes after emptying his dinner bowl, Dylan looked bored stiff. He yawned and took a place on the floor near the door where the warmth in the room and the sound of the two voices lulled him to sleep.

From time to time, Kellan's wings got in the way, but no more than they usually did. Aside from that, they had a relatively stress-free afternoon for the first time in a while. They quietly ate at a table like a normal family instead of standing at a dusty counter top or propped on a sofa with a bag of chips and a couple of candy bars. After they finished their meal, the time seemed to fly by.

"Are you nervous about tomorrow?" Neil asked Kellan. "I am, and it's not me who's on trial."

"A little, because I don't know what to expect. But I'm sure things will be fine and hopefully we can get the help we need to find Kaleb."

"That I hope," Neil agreed, but soon became fidgety, unable to contain his anxiety.

Kellan watched him, and said, "Hey. It'll be all good. Why don't we crack open some wine and relax a little. Take our mind off everything except the two of us."

Neil pursed his lips and smiled at Kellan, giving him the sign that he agreed.

With the sun on slow descent, the heat strangely dissipated in a way they weren't used to, making the air feel as though the temperature had dropped twenty degrees. Because of the lower heat index, they were able to comfortably sit outside on the patio with Dylan. Neil sat in a chair looking at Kellan who was perched shirtless on a stool, looking heavenly gorgeous.

The bottle of wine Kellan mentioned earlier had been opened, and he made it a point to get Neil a bit tipsy and keep him that way, for good reason in his opinion. He wanted to make sure Neil was relaxed and to help him forget about any cameras that might be hidden around the house, which was pretty much a guarantee. Getting into Neil's pants was Kellan's ultimate goal that night, and in order to pull it off sooner than later, he made sure he kept the wine glasses filled.

Kellan watched as Neil slowly undid his shirt one button at a time until it was completely off. With the air feeling chilly that evening, Kellan figured the wine made Neil's body hot and instigated the need to put himself on display the way he did.

Kellan went on admiring the view — Neil's smooth muscular chest and the hairy trail running down the center of his rippled stomach. As would always happen, Kellan's body responded instantly. His hard-on sprung to life, making his jeans feel as if they had shrunk two sizes.

While chatting about what might happen the next day, Kellan noticed Neil's speech beginning to slow, some of his words slurring. His body language was also becoming woozy, slipping into what looked to be a peaceful state. Smiling at his accomplishment at getting Neil to relax, Kellan asked, "How's my man doing?"

Neil dropped the back of his hand into the cushion next to him, as if his limb was either super loose, or way too heavy to hold up, and said, "I'm good. Real good. How 'bout you?"

"I'm good too. Relaxed and enjoying the view?" Kellan replied.

"What view? All we got is that beautiful brick wall," Neil sarcastically said, rolling his head against the back of the settee, trailing his gaze from Kellan to the twenty foot structure at the back of the property.

Kellan held the wine glass in both hands, brought his wings above his head and beat them downward, taking him on a quick flight. When he returned, he landed between Neil's knees. "Not that, silly. The view I'm talking about is you, my stunning boyfriend with no shirt on." He swallowed the rest of the wine in his glass and set the empty crystal down on the ground next to where Neil was sitting.

Neil smiled at Kellan, one side of his mouth higher than the other.

Kellan inched closer to Neil, lowering himself to his knees until their eyes met. He ran a finger up the hairy trail on Neil's abdomen and then down again, gripping his waistband by tucking his fingers inside. Leaning forward, Kellan kissed Neil gently. His lover's eyes fluttered at half mast, and the slow rise and fall of his chest stuttered to a stop, almost as if Kellan had stolen his breath. "Let's go inside. I need to feel you close to me. I'd like you to make love to me, join my soul."

With an increasing desire to feel Neil's bare chest against his, Kellan stood and held a hand out for Neil to take it. Affection gripped Kellan when he took Neil's hand in his and laced their fingers together, noticing his touch was gentle and warm. Their lips met in a passionate kiss that within an instant, turned aggressive, tongues eagerly skewering each other's mouth.

Kissing and holding onto one another, they stumbled

through the apartment while making a beeline to the bedroom.

On the way, Kellan pulled Neil's hair from behind, exposing the thick vein in his neck. Like a vampire, he dragged his tongue up the jugular, and then bit down where jaw met ear.

As if his lifeline had just been severed, Neil howled, releasing a low roll of satisfaction from his throat. But the intense attack didn't stop his need to mate with his angel. Overpowered by lust, Neil gripped Kellan's wing where it joined his spine, unconsciously thrusting the newly discovered erogenous zone into overdrive.

Kellan roared, and his wings snapped erect, knocking wall paintings off kilter as they made their way down the hallway to bedroom.

With both hands firmly pressed to Neil's shoulders, Kellan pushed him backward onto the bed. He aggressively climbed over top of Neil, straddling his thighs that pinned him in place. Deviously, Kellan covered Neil's eyes with his wingtips while dragging a finger from one of Neil's pectorals to the other, flicking at a nipple each time he circled it. His other hand artfully gripped Neil's dick, and each time he stroked its full length, he felt Neil thrashing under him.

Kellan stood to remove his jeans, and the way Neil looked at him, had Kellan believing his lover was keen on the hairy trail traveling up his abdomen, and the way the feathery wisps branched out like tiny leaves on a tree across his chest. After several moments of ogling, Neil's gaze traveled down Kellan's torso, becoming transfixed by the thick cock within his white undies.

Intruding on what might have been a fantasy going on in Neil's head, Kellan pulled Neil's pants off, leaving him lying only in black briefs. He leaned into Neil, and delicately kissed his six pack. With each kiss, Kellan burned to make a physical connection with the striking man under him. His heart banged behind his ribcage as his eagerness to make love intensified.

Neil's legs moved further apart, and Kellan accepted the invitation by settling between them. To increase the pleasure he'd already started, Kellan stretched the elastic waistband under Neil's sagging scrotum, lifting his warm balls into view. He effortlessly tucked a hand into the leg opening of Neil's briefs, thumb stroking his taint while finger punching his puckering knot.

Working slowly, Kellan leaned forward and traced his tongue along the underside of Neil's dick, following the pronounced veining from tip to base. He stopped for a moment and inhaled, savoring the scent of Neil's musky nuts before taking them into his mouth. He sucked them in one at a time, tugging and releasing, first gently, then drawing them both in with greater assertion.

Neil's head fell back as he cried out, "That's it, eat my big nuts."

Slowly, Kellan let Neil's balls slip free, and as soon as released, he eased his soft lips around the wedge shaped head of Neil's cock. He circled the plumpness with his tongue, exploring the sensitive slit, darting the tip as far inside it as he could manage. Kellan enjoyed the smoky taste of Neil's dick, the warm muskiness of the hair surrounding it, and the sweetness of the silky juices seeping from the velvety crown. As Kellan took Neil's cock further into his warm, wet mouth, swallowing to the base, his hand explored the hot spot between Neil's legs, fondling his sagging balls and finding his asshole with roving fingers.

Kellan sucked Neil's hard cock, drawing it deep down his throat as his semen slicked fingers pressed up into Neil's tight channel, pushing on his prostate and forcing him to give up still more of that precious, hot juice. A warm wave of carnal energy pulsated through Kellan as he finger fucked Neil and swallowed his entire dick at the same time. The dual action clearly stimulated Neil, so much so that it caused his butt to respond as if a secret button had been punched, flexing and sucking Kellan's fingers deeper until all but his thumb was reaming his hole. Neil's hips wildly lifted and fell in a face fucking rhythm, the head of his dick colliding with the back of Kellan's throat. His throaty cries got louder the deeper Kellan's fingers sank into his soft pliant asshole and his angel's slippery mouth worked up and down his stiff shaft in a vigorous manner.

Neil urgently pleaded between gasps, "Shit, Kell... you need to stop. I don't want to cum yet. Fuck... you need to stop." He inhaled and held his breath, as if luring himself away from a cum-filled rush that his boyfriend was trying so desperately to suck out of him.

As much as Kellan wanted to get a mouth full of cum, he slid Neil's cock from his mouth and let it fall into the gutter of his abdomen. While slowly slipping his fingers from Neil's asshole, Kellan licked his lips, savoring the peach-flavored tang of his lover's pre-cum.

Kellan removed his and Neil's briefs, tossing them to the floor.

Neil admired the way Kellan's muscles flexed as he moved. He expelled a smooth sigh and crooned, "I want so badly to make love to you right now, Kellan."

Kellan smiled down at Neil.

"I'd like you lying back, with me looking into your eyes while I move inside you." Neil hesitated a few seconds, thinking about what he had asked Kellan to do, and then added with concern, "Can we do that without hurting your wings, you know... bending or breaking them?"

"Don't worry about that. They aren't as fragile as they might look. You've seen those recordings of me. I was on my back in most of them, cuz that's the way I like it." Kellan took hold of Neil's hands, lifted him off his back and spun him out of the way. Taking Neil's place, Kellan used his wings skillfully to lay himself back and rest his head against the pillow.

While watching Kellan spread his legs, Neil caught a seductive look in his eyes that appeared he was giving approval to stick his cock inside him.

Like a panther, Neil crawled on top of Kellan, positioning himself between his open legs. With care, he kissed Kellan's cheeks, his nose, and his lips, loving him with each gentle kiss.

Neil's tender touch seemed to strengthen Kellan's urge to be penetrated. The signs were all there. There was aggressive whimpering. His submissive body was trembling, and his abdomen flexed from the frequent gasps. The pungent scent of semen that had collected in the gutters of Kellan's six-pack whirled between them, omitting pheromones from every pore of their flesh, pushing each other's libido into overdrive.

Drawn to the glistening semen on Kellan's abs like it was unlocked treasure that spilled across a ship's deck, Neil greedily swiped a hand through it and coated his own erection. He worked his fist back and forth over the entire shaft before going for more and transferring the slippery juice to Kellan's asshole. One finger at a time slipped inside Kellan until three were buried passed the knuckle.

Kellan released grizzly groans as Neil's semen slippery fingers sunk inside him. Even though the three fingered prostate massage was insanely ball busting, Neil's long, delicate fingers weren't nearly enough. Kellan craved more than that, and Neil's eight-inch cock that bent slightly upward would surely satisfy his scorching hole instead. Kellan pulled his knees to his chest, submitting to Neil completely. He rode every digit stuffed inside him with oscillating hips, lifting up and down, rotating, and shifting left to right, using his ass muscles to help pull Neil's fingers in to where he wanted them. Kellan emitted guttural noises each time pressure met his prostate. On contact, his head snapped forward, driving his chin into his chest that forced air from his lungs through jaw-locked teeth. At that moment, Neil's eyes locked on his. The glistening slits made Neil appear as though he was under a spell, as if he was concentrating deeply, perhaps starving to please the greedy hole his fingers were penetrating.

At no point while being reamed with bony fingers had Kellan shown an ounce of resistance, and by the way he gyrated and pushed his ass end into Neil's hand, clamping down around his knuckles, it was clear he needed to get speared by something bigger. Neil was immersed in the cozy grip Kellan's channel had on him, riveted by the pulse he felt stemming from inside Kellan, but was just as eager to feel that hot channel wrapped around his cock as Kellan was to feel his corded cock inside him. Neil splayed his fingers one last time before slipping them out of Kellan's warm sphincter, and without giving it a chance to snap shut, pressed his erection against the softened entrance.

Kellan could feel the mushroomed head of Neil's cock easing in. He took a deep breath to loosen up, preparing for penetration. His puckering hole started flexing as though it couldn't wait any more.

Feeling that, Neil pushed harder, and the crown of his dick eased in further. The embrace of Kellan's snug channel and intensity of the heat radiating from it felt like fire. It raced up

Neil's dick, making him feel hot all over. He paused a moment, allowing Kellan to adjust to the thickness of an invasion larger than three fingers.

Kellan couldn't hide how good Neil felt sliding in. Evidence of that appeared in an unmanageable whimper. The pleasurable intrusion forced his mouth to spring open and his head to fall back. His neck stretched, revealing his Adams's apple and almost every cord from shoulder to skull became prominent. His wings fluttered and went rigid under him. His hips lifted and he pushed his legs in tighter against his chest, opening himself for Neil. After a few moments passed, he was able to make eye contact with Neil's brown eyes that had gone smoky with lust. Kellan breathlessly spoke, "Damn, Neil, I so love you."

Neil gazed down at Kellan, raising himself up a few inches to watch his angel's reaction while pulling his dick out.

Stirring, Kellan whined, "No. Don't pull out." His wingtips moved to Neil's hips, holding him in place. The feathered tickling made Neil smile.

Knowing how much Kellan wanted him, Neil lowered himself, letting the head of his dick tap a few times at Kellan's wet pucker before slowly sinking back inside.

Neil edged Kellan, penetrating just a few inches, and then denying him the entire length he wanted. Neil teased him, rewarding Kellan with more, and then punishing him by taking it back. He repeated the bantering motion, making sure Kellan could only think about having that cock and the promise of it being all his.

Kellan could feel his body being played like an instrument, Neil controlling the notes in the rhythm he orchestrated. Long slow strokes followed by rapid withdrawal, the dramatic pause and build-up of tension. Kellan's body vibrated to angelic strings, his feathers in a timpani, like leaves rustling in a soft breeze. The sting of Neil's intrusion lifted Kellan's torso, driving him backwards, the feathers creating a frictionless surface. Within that motion, pain morphed to pleasure as Neil stroked his prostate, again and again and again. Exhilarated beyond passion, all Kellan wanted then was to have Neil hammer him, bludgeon his ass, shove his dick so far inside him that his tonsils would feel the impact. Wanting nothing more than to trap the demon controlling him, he wrapped his legs around his lover.

Neil pushed himself upward and met eyes with the man he was connected to. Gazing back at him, Neil noticed Kellan's eyes had changed, his pupils were as black as coal, and a smoky haze resembling desire almost hid all traces of each iris. Motivated by the warmth emanating from Kellan's eyes, Neil arched his back to push his erection deeper. When he heard Kellan moan, he picked up his pace, cock-probing the heated depths of his slippery hole, violently drilling into him faster and faster. Each ass gripping stroke sent tingling sensations from the head of his cock to his groin, intensifying when the tremors reached the pivotal point of his prostate. The harder he rammed his pelvis into Kellan, the stronger the electrical sparks crackled across his crotch in waves, spreading to his spine and racing throughout his entire body. His breathing was in rhythm with each reaming plunge. His orgasm grew, overwhelming him with an urge to explode.

Before there was a chance of cumming too soon, Neil held still and tenderly kissed Kellan, taking pleasure in their bodies being so intimately linked. Slowly sliding out and then back into Kellan, Neil gave him another inch every time he moved his hips forward. When Neil's hairy pelvis ground into the flesh between Kellan's balls and asshole, he stopped fucking and held still. His breathing jammed in his throat when he felt Kellan's tunnel naturally massage his entire cock as if begging for him to keep his rhythm going.

Neil gladly started up again, smoothly rolling his hips back and forth, giving Kellan what he wanted. Bringing himself down against Kellan's chest, Neil murmured into his ear, "You feel amazing, Kellan. I'm going to have a hard time pulling out of you now that I'm in you."

Rolling his head over the pillow, Kellan kissed Neil's cheek and whispered, "You can stay inside me as long as you want."

Neil rocked against Kellan, keeping his rhythm slow and sensual so his angel could feel all of him. "Omigawd, Kellan" — his eyes closed — "I love you."

Reaching around Neil's shoulders, Kellan lured his lover tighter to his chest and locked him into a passionate kiss. Sucking Neil's tongue, he mimicked each slow thrust of Neil's hips with deep swallows, like a double-ended plug linking mouth to ass.

Kellan's breathing became labored as Neil rubbed his whiskered chin along the length of Kellan's jaw, leaving his flesh stinging and raw. The burning sensation was replaced by quick nips to his ear lobe and kiss-swollen lips, every surface tender and ripe for Neil's special attention.

Neil had set up a conduit like an electrical current that raced from mouth to nipples to groin to that place deep inside where they were linked so intimately sensation ruled all, where insanity and love ruled as one.

The war between allowing his orgasm to consume him and not wanting it ever to end drove Kellan nearly to the breaking point. If he burst, it would be over, and the last thing he ever wanted was for their precious link to be severed.

Neil felt Kellan's body begging him to keep going, sucking him in. Neil lay still while Kellan's insides stroked him, clutching his cock and demanding its due.

Neil pressed his lips into Kellan's neck and vocalized his extreme pleasure while rhythmically rolling his hips, fucking Kellan deeply. With Kellan squirming underneath him, the contact ramped Neil's excitement to stratospheric levels. Mind nearly blown, his hips, groin, and cock took over, driving with fierce thrusts until Kellan wailed to the high heavens.

Kellan cried out each time Neil's pelvis thumped against his ass. Neil recognized how close Kellan was to cumming, the sensation probably too intense to contain himself any longer. Kellan roared to the high heavens.

Staying connected to Kellan's increasing demands, Neil lifted his upper body, propping himself on fisted hands. Neil increased the pace even more, hips relentlessly banging into Kellan, giving him what he craved.

Kellan's body convulsed as the sensation of his internal climax climbed to a level he wasn't sure he could return from. His rectum flexed madly, stroking Neil like a fisted hand. Squeezing and tugging, pulling him in, working hard at taking what he needed.

With Kellan so close to losing control, Neil knew it was time to let go.

Neil groaned, "Oh Gawd, here it comes." He winced. "Are you ready for me?" He pushed forward. His pelvis ground against Kellan's taint.

"Yes. Give it to me. Everything you've got. Cum inside me, Neil." Kellan fanned his hands across Neil's chest, feeling his heart bang behind his ribs. While getting fucked, his eyes squeezed shut and his mouth sprung open. He yelled, "Fuck, Neil. I'm so close. Keep fucking my hole." Kellan pulled Neil against him, diving for his mouth with intense obsession, kissing hard, sucking in air with flaring nostrils, feeding off Neil's essence.

Kellan took hold of his own erect dick, stroking it, meeting every one of Neil's forward thrusts. He felt Neil's body go rigid and saw his eyes clamp shut.

Moans of pleasure escaped Neil's vocal cords as he hammered Kellan, practically splitting his angel in two. Every part of Kellan was lurching as Neil thumped against him. His legs, his arms, and his wings jerked under the relentless assault. He growled while powerfully fucking Kellan, ramming his dick in and out of him fast and forceful. He was on the verge of cumming, he felt it boiling inside him, sparking and quickly spreading out across his pelvis. Suddenly, he lost all his sanity. Along with a gut expelled rumble, his abdomen tightened, and semen shot through his stone-hard cock straight into Kellan's sucking channel. He collapsed on top of Kellan, his entire body stiffening as his dick surged.

Neil's body jerked as he pumped every ounce of sperm from within him, heaving until the last of his convulsions subsided and everything he had was inside his man. Neil's heart nearly burst knowing his cock had taken them both to a place that was theirs alone—bound together with passion and a connection that defied explanation. With one last huff, he propped himself up, looking at his dick still inserted in Kellan.

"Fuck, I'm almost there." Kellan gripped his dick and savagely stroked it.

With a dick no longer able to stand stiff, Neil slipped out and hooked three fingers inside Kellan's asshole, massaging his prostate to strengthen his orgasm.

Breathing heavily, Kellan's upper body convulsed forward off the bed and his mouth uncontrollably gaped in an aggressive wail. Yelling Neil's name, he shot ribbons of semen from his dick, splashing his chest and face. His abdomen crunched in time with every stream of cum his spasmodic prostate squeezed from inside him. Kellan's groans turned gritty, "Right there, Neil. Fuck! Don't stop."

As ordered, Neil kept thrusting his digits into Kellan, stroking his G-spot for all he was worth. He watched Kellan jerk as he unloaded his sperm.

Waves rolled over Kellan's abdomen as he breathed, and didn't stop until he finally settled down and opened his eyes. He felt closer to Neil than he ever had been, felt like Neil had taken the core of his soul, like they had shared each other's energy.

Neil pressed his chest tightly against Kellan's. "Damn, I love you." Neil tasted Kellan's semen when he kissed him. "Seeing you cum like that was really hot. I could have watched you shoot your spunk all night long."

Somewhat embarrassed, Kellan laughed. He wrapped his arms around Neil's neck, pulling him closer. "Now that I have your cum inside me, I feel even closer to you, like you've marked me as yours." He hugged Neil.

Neil ran two fingers across Kellan's brow as if he was pushing away loose strands of hair that were covering his eyes. Nothing was there, but he still did it. "I love you very much. You do know that, right?" He gave Kellan a loving kiss on the lips and held it.

Kellan squirmed under Neil, curling his wings around them like a cocoon. "I do," he said.

They lay motionless for quite a while, Neil deeply connecting with Kellan, not wanting to ever leave him, or have him taken away.

Neil slid off of Kellan, slipped the casing off one of the pillows and used it to clean up the juicy mess they made across their chests. After tossing the cum soaked casing aside, he settled in next to the man he was in love with and covered up with the blanket that had found its way to the foot of the bed during their sexual escapade.

After kissing Kellan, Neil rolled over and backed into Kellan's arms. They lay comfortably in a molded position—spooning.

Neil moaned as he backed his ass tightly against Kellan, feeling satisfied and full as his angel entered him from behind.

The warm hair on Kellan's pelvis tickled Neil's smooth muscled butt once full connection was made.

Kellan kissed Neil below the ear. "I love you, Hun," he whispered.

Neil rotated his head over his shoulder and snatched a kiss from Kellan's lips. "I love you too, Kell." He squirmed, his asshole sucking Kellan in.

No one had ever called him Kell before, but he smiled at the nickname. He didn't mind the short play on his name. He actually liked it, especially coming from Neil.

In less than five minutes, Kellan whispered into Neil's ear, "Damn, Neil. I can't sleep with my dick inside you like this. I either need to pull out and jack off or I need to fuck you until I cum." Kellan moved his cock in and out of Neil, slowly fucking him, leaking semen inside of him as he did.

Neil's cock jumped each time Kellan's cock rubbed against his prostate. The pressure from inside milked pre-cum out of him that spilled to the sheets on the bed.

Kellan slowed his pace, almost stopping.

The hesitant rhythm gave Neil a moment to breathe. "Damn, you feel so fucking great inside me. But..."

Kellan stopped fucking. "But what?"

"But this." Neil pulled his ass off of Kellan's cock, dragging semen with him. "Get on your back again. I want to look into your eyes while you plant your seed."

"What?" Kellan laughed, sitting up. His wings wavered behind him, stretching toward the ceiling.

"Yeah. Plant your seed"—Neil laughed too—"It wouldn't surprise me if something actually came of it. We've seen crazier shit recently."

"I suppose this is as good a time as any. After all, it seems we might actually have a kid on the way. We may as well go through the motions." Kellan rolled onto his back, his dick already hard as stone, anticipating having Neil hop on and ride it. The thought of him and Neil being parents of a small angel made him smile, or actually beam. It hit him for the first time. It was a happy thought, a feeling that it was going to happen soon and work out in a good way. He gripped his erection, standing it up straight and told Neil to take his place.

Due to exhaustion from having at each other's bodies only a short time ago, the moment of passion this time went quickly. In a matter of minutes, they made their connection and were drained again.

Several moments had passed and they were still lying naked and attached, Neil on top of Kellan, and neither had any desire to let go. But, being alert the next morning was crucial, and because duty called, they needed to separate and get a good night's rest.

Kellan hugged Neil hard before letting him go, and then said with a grin, "After a fuck like that, there has to be a kid on the way."

Neil chuckled as he pulled himself away, letting Kellan's dick slide free.

"Wait a minute. Where are you going?" Kellan reached out and placed a hand on Neil's thigh, stopping him from leaving the bed.

"To get the pillow casing so we can clean up."

"No, sweetie. Leave it. I like it where it is."

Neil contemplated, but instead said, "Stay there, I'll get the wipes." While cleaning up, he examined Kellan's frame, from his beautiful white wings to his sexy toes, becoming more obsessed with every part of him. To Neil, the entire package was magnificent. Inside and out.

The time came for Neil and his angelic boyfriend to get some sleep. The next morning was probably going to be a stressful one, so it made perfect sense to get a decent nights rest.

Kellan flipped his wings behind his back, slid beneath the covering and met Neil in the middle face to face. Pulling Neil close, Kellan held him firmly against his chest, interlocking mouth-to-mouth in a sensual kiss.

"Okay, Hun, time for sleep." Kellan lifted the sheet above Neil, exposing his naked body. He motioned for Neil to turn over while pushing his shoulder in the direction he wanted him to roll.

Neil flipped onto his side with his back toward Kellan the way he was asked to do. He settled in, pushing his rear into Kellan's hairy pelvis, liking how comfortably his angel's dick rested between his ass cheeks.

Kellan threw the sheet into the air and waited for it to slowly float down over top of them. He inched his naked body against Neil from behind, tightly spooning him with an arm wrapped securely across his chest. Kellan held him close, nuzzling his cheek alongside Neil's ear, and once again whispered that he loved him.

Neil rotated his chin over his shoulder, and kissed Kellan. "I love you, too, Kell."

There was that smile again. He would never tire of Neil calling him Kell.

Kellan brought a wing around and laid it over top of them like a blanket. "See you in the morning, my love."

Chapter 25

The next morning seemed to come fast, as though the minute Kellan and Neil closed their eyes, the sun came up.

"Up and at it, stud. We need to get ready." Kellan stood fanning his wings over Neil who was still in bed.

Without questioning the time, Neil groaned and sat up.

ଔ ଞ

That same morning, Seth was at his work station in the genetic manipulation wing. He'd been placed there to perform similar roles he had while at TC, as lead lab technician and personal nurse to those like Kellan and some newly developed creations. This particular morning's agenda, however, had a twist to it. He was preparing for the scheduled conference with the Chiefs of Staff about Kellan: possibly encourage them to extend his boundaries beyond their already decided limits, let him be his own person, and allow him to extend his wings outside of a ten by ten foot room. His main plan was to set him and Neil up in a house of their own that was other than a medical facility. One secluded, yet still monitored by the military. He was a bit on edge about the whole thing, yet anxious to get the meeting going and his idea implemented.

The promptness of the military was always spot on, never a minute too early or a second too late. The time was straight up seven A.M. when the MP stepped into Seth's office to escort him to the conference room where the morning's meeting was scheduled. Seth knew who the man was, which made the four-minute walk to level O-four negative less daunting. The floors were numbered that way because the levels went down instead of up.

On the way to "the situation room," Seth fidgeted with the badge hanging around his neck. There was good reason to be nervous, since the men were military brass who rarely met with civilians, and certainly no one at his pay grade. These men picked and chose when they wanted and needed to be seen, and normally had admins who communicated between the two parties so they didn't have to. Aside from that, they were at the top of the command chain and for Seth to be in the same room with them was next to being in the presence of a King or a Queen.

When Seth and his escort reached the situation room, a burly MP corralled only him into a tunnel-like alcove with full body scanners, conditioned air, and carefully controlled temperature and humidity levels. To Seth, the sensation within the small area seemed sterile, and the air circulating inside smelled of ozone.

After being scanned and sanitized, Seth was given the okay to move ahead. The room was private, soundproof, secure, and had state-of-the-art communication devices and monitors that maintained control of sensitive information flowing in and out of government facilities, whether located domestically or abroad. The same carefully controlled atmosphere that was in the alcove was also in that room. The only difference, the room temperature was slightly cooler.

As Seth had expected, the situation room was similar to the rest of the place, institution-like, with gray-green walls and gray-white trim. The large table in the middle, surrounded by black leather chairs and flat screen communication monitors lining every wall, gave it the appearance of a typical conference room. The space was intimidating to Seth, even more so after sitting directly across from the three military men on the far side of the table. They sat with threatening glares, looking at him in a way that immediately put Seth on the defensive.

Seth sat down, eyes scanned the room taking in all the details, until his gaze rested on the figure in the corner, and that figure amounted to a bombshell he hadn't expected—someone from the head of NSA branch operations whose clearance probably trumped everyone else's in the room. With a board-like posture, the officer stood quietly with a blank face. Hardly a movement out of him, just an occasional cop-eyed stare, curiously observing every move Seth made.

Although the NSA's presence, especially the Director, was unexpected, it made sense in a way since they'd have reason to oversee the TC and AZ programs. The D.O. was at the top of the command chain and was normally only called when an attack on the nation was reaching a catastrophic level, which could mean something more serious was lurking that Seth might not be prepared for. After briefly observing the D.O., Seth quickly glanced away before anybody in the room noticed.

At the moment, Seth knew he was being watched by more than just the NSA D.O., possibly the watch team who ran all the complicated equipment fastened to the walls. It probably wasn't important, but he wondered where they had been tucked away as he glanced around the room and back to the men facing him.

The tense silence lasted a few short minutes, just enough time for everybody to get a good look at one another. The wary glances and the silent treatment got Seth's heart pumping, and he wondered what all the staring was about. His first thoughts were that something bad might have happened to Kellan or Kaleb. Or they knew what he'd been up to and the meeting was for no other reason than to give him his walking papers. The whole situation at the moment made him uneasy, and all he wanted to do was settle the issues of Kellan's freedom. In his own head, he resolved, *"Let's get the fucking ball rolling."*

As a privy to Seth's thoughts, the chief of staff, Colonel Riley, spoke. The Colonel first extended his gratitude to Seth for getting Kellan to AZ without any problems, and he reiterated how the government wanted him to continue being Kellan's guardian, as he had when they were at TC in Michigan.

Seth's eyes narrowed after hearing what the Colonel just said. While Seth was relieved to hear he was going to be with Kellan again, he wasn't thrilled about falling back into the same old pattern from when they'd been at TC, on lock down twenty-four seven, flying only at night. Kellan left because he could no longer tolerate that kind of life, and Seth vowed he'd fight tooth and nail to prevent that from happening again.

Colonel Riley spoke again, reviewing for the assembled group that after losing complete contact with the Seeker for the past few days, its last known position was when Kellan supposedly killed it in Michigan under the Mackinac Bridge. When that couldn't be confirmed, they were forced to consider other possibilities, such as the tracking device might have been destroyed or extracted. The other possibility was that the device was experiencing intermittent faults.

The original placement of the tracking chip was between the Seekers wings, which would have been a challenge to remove or destroy on its own without causing major injury, maybe even spinal damage. If the Seeker hadn't been the one who deactivated the chip, who would have? The possibility that somebody managed to disengage the tracker raised the military's concerns and bumped the severity level of the situation to critical.

The entire time the tracking chip was being discussed, they determined the only logical reason was that Kellan destroyed the device if the Seeker hadn't, and probably had happened during the first fight under the bridge because that's the last time it was able to be traced. The military hadn't been able to pinpoint the Seeker's location since then, and without the ability to keep track of the Seeker, finding and containing it immediately was crucial.

When Kellan escaped it had been bad enough to lose a valuable asset, one that was spectacular to look at but not prone to being lethal or vindictive. The Seeker going rogue and following Kellan had been unexpected and opened up questions about controlling the creatures. The government, and the military in particular, were masters at keeping secrets, but to have two of their genetically altered specimens loose on an unsuspecting population had taken the risks to stratospheric levels.

Until the Seeker was on lockdown at AZ, the military was intent on recapturing the creature in order to safeguard the public and keep their research secret, and from what had already been confirmed, the Seeker was still following its original program and looking for Kellan.

The military's purpose for building Kellan was to take on secret missions, fly under the radar and carry out their stringent commands. It was the plan from the very start, Kellan's reason for existing, and now was a time to use what they've created. He was better than a chopper could ever be at corralling and detaining the winged monster. He could maneuver in ways a chopper couldn't and was able to go after it like a falcon hunts a sparrow, plucking it from the sky in mid-flight and debilitating it before they hit the ground.

For the next half hour, the Colonel established operation parameters for recovering the Seeker, explaining the order of procedures, who would do what, where and when. From the start, they decided to use Kellan as bait—the primary reason for making sure he got back to AZ uninjured and in one piece. He, after all, was what those particular Seekers were programed to go after, making him the logical choice to lure the Seeker out of hiding.

Even though Kellan was in the government's custody, with only vague assurances about seeing to his welfare, he could still tell them to go find their own damned Seeker. There was no obligation on his part to follow through with the Seeker problem, unless they tortured him somehow. Maybe being shot down with a bullet in the head would be better than spending the remainder of his life behind bars. His only incentive, and he wasn't sure if they knew he knew, was his kid. If it wasn't for the little angel, Kellan might be long gone, flying away while holding up a fuck you finger.

Seth was brought in to be part of the team because of how close he was with Kellan, and out of anybody, he might be the one person who could influence the angel to do what was needed without using military force. But if Kellan failed, a second unit would be on deployment standby to finish the job.

During the short time they let Seth speak, the Directing Officer listened from where he stood in the corner, his gaze sweeping around the room, resting briefly on one after the other, shaking his head and nodding every now and then, signaling what would be allowed and what wouldn't. The entire time it seemed to Seth they were only hearing what would benefit the military, not taking into consideration that Kellan was a living, breathing life form, very similar to them, and deserved more than a life of incarceration.

Before the conference ended, the one thing Seth wanted to hear was that they were still going to honor the decision made about giving Kellan and Neil a secure place to live. He believed he had convinced them earlier and reminded them it was the only leverage they had to push Kellan to do what was being asked of him. All Seth needed was the surety they were going to fulfill their promise. There was a partial nod from the Director when Seth brought it up, but not an unequivocal yes, leaving Seth unsatisfied. Not for the first time, Seth knew so-called conditions that were set in stone could be easily overturned. His short pitch to arrange for suitable living quarters for Kellan had received only a half-assed nod, not exactly a confidence builder. He was left frustrated, wondering if this was one of those times they were going to change their mind. He wasn't really sure any of them were on his side, or if Kellan was getting out of there alive after he completed the task. The idea of it all being bullshit was eating him alive, but he'd done all he could not to let it show.

When the conference adjourned, Colonel Riley pulled Seth aside for a one-on-one talk out in the hallway. He filled Seth in on a few details planned for Kellan and Neil that weren't mentioned in the meeting, making sure to heighten Seth's assurances pertaining to the outcome of the upcoming mission as long as Kellan cooperated.

Seth agreed to listen, but remained a little apprehensive about holding on too tightly to what he was being fed.

Chapter 26

After the conference was over, Seth went straight to see Kellan and Neil. The four minutes it took Seth to reach their apartment seemed like an hour. The creaky elevator ride added to the urgency, and he was relieved to be out of it. In the meeting it was brought up that there was only an hour until Kellan was needed back at the situation room, which could be the reason Seth felt that time wasn't on his side.

When he got to the door of the apartment, he thought he heard muffled noises on the other side that would suggest mischief between two men. He became irritated they were letting lust run their lives when they have more important things to consider.

Instead of standing outside picturing two men screwing around, Seth pounded on the door. When Neil opened the door, Seth was about to make a comment but saw Dylan rollicking, and realized he might have made a mistake as to what was really going on.

Because Kellan and Neil was constantly rump riding each other, Seth was annoyed at himself for jumping to the conclusion they were doing that at a time they should be concerned about more important things. He held up the two cups of coffee he'd brought with him and asked, "Am I interrupting something?"

"No" — Kellan arched one eyebrow when he glanced at Neil — "but if you had shown up last night, I'd have said yes."

Mortified, Neil lifted a hand over his eyes while mumbling, "What's wrong with you?"

"What? It's no secret we're fucking, and he certainly knows we're doing it. He isn't stupid when it comes to couples in love, and it's a relief to finally be able to tell somebody I actually got laid and it was by my best man." Kellan bumped Neil with his shoulder, and wrapped a wing around his back to pull him closer to his side.

"Yeah, but... he doesn't need to hear about what we do." Neil lightly back-fisted Kellan's shoulder and then reached down to hold his hand. "And how can you make fun at a time like this. Don't you know what's at stake for you right now?"

Seth's posture shifted, pleased to have heard Neil's concern about Kellan. He held back saying anything, just handed them the coffee instead.

Kellan closed the front door. "Have a seat and fill us in with what's going on."

Seth first mentioned they had less than an hour, so he needed to be quick. He spoke to Kellan but swept his gaze to include Neil. "The priority of the mission is high, Kellan. One the military figures you can pull off successfully."

"I expected that. What is it?"

"It's what we spoke about before. They can't seem to locate the Seeker you ran up against in Michigan a few days ago, and they require the skills you have to find it. They believe you'll be able to lead it back to AZ better than a chopper team could."

"What's in it for us if I do this?"

"I had mentioned again about you and Neil living together in a secure location, but the NSA Director of Operations was in the conference, who I didn't know or was expecting, and he looked as though he wasn't willing to accept all of what I was proposing."

"This is a bunch of crap. It's either all or nothing, no half measures, and certainly don't tell me I'll be getting paid and then never fork over the funds after I've done the work." Kellan stood up, almost knocking a lamp over with his angry wings, and before it toppled to the floor, Neil reacted instantly and stopped it.

With an ominous tone, Kellan said, "You see that? I can't live without him. What's he supposed to do while I'm held in a birdcage? Only see me every few days for a conjugal visit? Fuck that shit and screw them. They can go find their own damned monster, because the way I see it, their promises don't mean shit."

"You and I know it doesn't work like that when everyone seems to think of you as a machine. Nobody in that conference knew this, but when I talked with Colonel Riley afterwards, he led me to believe it wasn't as bad as it sounded. I got the feeling he was on your side, and that we don't have to worry about anything if you help them out with this one mission."

Kellan found it strangely amusing that the military looked at him as a machine more than a living creature, and that they only wanted him for battles and fixing what they lost control of.

Neil moved out from behind the table after securing the rocking lamp and asked, "Did you discuss Kaleb at all?"

"Very briefly with Colonel Riley," Seth responded. "I didn't feel the time was right to bring up any more deals, so I tried keeping Kaleb out of the conversation as much as possible. I only casually mentioned him and asked if he knew where he was."

"Did he tell you?" Neil asked.

"No, he didn't. He brilliantly skated around giving me an answer. I wanted to throw the question out there again, but I couldn't seem to find the right moment to work it in."

Kellan interrupted, "Here's a thought. We could trade the Seeker for Kaleb."

"That would be a good plan if there's any hint they might go back on what they said. While I continue looking through Kaleb's files, I'll try to find more negotiating leverage before you return with the Seeker."

"I can't see that working at all," Neil argued. "And Seth... had you ever given any thought that the government already assumes one of the reasons Kellan so willingly returned was to find Kaleb? They must know you've been snooping around in the files, and had been feeding what you've found to Kellan."

Kellan drew his wings in. "It was just a thought. I'm grasping at any available straw I can now that it's crunch time. What's the time? Are they coming to get me or do I just fly out the window and follow that hummingbird?" Kellan pointed and then mumbled, "What the heck?" He was surprised he mentioned the bird because there it was, hanging out at the window.

"Incredible," Neil said. "What is up with that busy bird?"

Seth reacted in a way that made Kellan and Neil turn toward him.

"What is it, Seth? You know something about that bird, don't you?" Kellan asked. "It's been following me around since I left TC. Almost like it's keeping an eye on my ass. What is that thing? Is it even a real bird?"

Seth took a deep breath, almost sighing, and instead of delving into an explanation just then, he simply said, "There's my tiny friend."

"What do you mean by that?" Neil flared up.

"That hummingbird is another TC experiment. One of the good ones. It's trainable and follows commands like a porpoise."

"What? You're crazy," Kellan yelped. "How the heck did that place train a tiny hummingbird?"

Seth set his coffee cup down and stood up. "I know it sounds unbelievable, but it's true. That bird was the smallest tracker we could come up with that could move as fast as the subjects we needed it to follow."

"So you sent it out to follow me?" Kellan asked.

"Actually the military did, but I had known about it. They're always several steps ahead of everybody. They figured we'd be in the predicament of possibly losing you. And guess what? We did. Sure the military has chips and tracking devices that can be implanted or worn, but they know it can always be removed or deactivated if somebody knows what they're doing. Look at the Seeker; there's solid proof that could happen."

"I can't believe this shit. You're not on their side now, are you?" Kellan stood stiffly, his chest jutting forward, resembling a steel shield of armor. He looked impressive, like the winged warrior he was built to be.

Seth quickly responded. "God, no. Not at all. The hummingbird was sent out to make sure you were safe the entire time you were away. It was my idea and the only way the military and I would know you were okay. I was concerned for your wellbeing; they were concerned about the millions of dollars they had spent on you."

Neil stood quietly, trying to absorb all of the hidden shit that had come out of TC. It was truly amazing and almost unbelievable. He looked out the window and saw the hummingbird still hovering there, looking inside the room, watching them.

"Let me guess. The next thing you're going to tell us is that it's equipped with a camera and everything it's seeing right now is being fed to somebody in this building, aren't you?" Kellan asked.

In silent agreement, Seth looked straight into Kellan's eyes and curled the corner of his mouth. "With that said, we better get moving because they're probably wondering what we're talking about and why we keep looking at the hummingbird."

"Ears—does it have ears?" Kellan turned to look at the bird in the window, examining it, searching to find where a microphone could possibly be stashed on such a small animal.

In an instant, the room became quiet. They glanced at each other and then at the hummingbird. Neil was the only one who stirred, turning his back on their new feathered friend who was looking in. Neil moved across the room to hide as best he could behind Kellan's wings.

After Kellan and Neil reacted to the bird having mechanical ears, Seth replied, "This one doesn't. Just a pair of eyes that transmit the images it looks at back to base."

Neil squawked, "This one? What the hell? Does that mean there are more of these things flying around?"

Being truthful, Seth told them there were many more. But only a few had been released. Seth walked to the window and opened it. The bird didn't move, just hovered like a tiny helicopter looking back at him. Seth figured they were being watched, and because of that, he held up ten fingers in front of the bird, letting whoever was watching, if they were, know they were on the way in that many minutes.

Neil had mentioned before in a private conversation with Kellan how remarkable everything seemed to be that came out of

TC and AZ. He'd repeated a few times that it was as if he'd fallen into a science fiction film, one only a select few would ever see, the kind where learning secrets could be lethal. Without mistake, this could be another time to bring it up again.

Neil watched the bird land on the outside window sill where it stayed, just perched there. Neil blinked and asked, "I presume I'll be waiting behind, right?"

Seth put a hand on Neil's shoulder and explained, "That's the best plan. Just stick around here with Dylan and the little bird."

"I thought as much, but it doesn't hurt to ask. Just make sure Kellan will be coming back here when he's given them what they need."

"That's all been set up. This is the only place for him now," Seth said. He took a few steps closer to the door and reached for the knob. "The clock is ticking, Kellan. We need to get going."

Neil raised his voice, "Wait a minute. This place? It sounds to me you know something you're not telling us? Are they going to hold him in captivity at *"this place"* when this is over, or let him live peacefully with me in that secluded location you mentioned? Somebody's giving us a load of bullshit and as far as I know it's coming from you, Seth."

Placing a tighter grip on the doorknob, Seth turned his head back and said, "There's no reason for me to keep secrets from either of you, and I'm telling you everything the way I heard it. I stand by the feeling I got from Colonel Riley when he said this all seemed worse than the way it appeared. I don't believe he was lying, they're probably just not telling us everything until they are secure enough with the outcome of this operation. I know this is upsetting to hear, Neil. It is for all of us, but that's how the military operates, and it's all we've got right now."

Neil pressed his closed fists to his temples. "Dammit... I didn't mean to snap, but I can't lose him now. If they don't let us be together, how am I supposed to adjust to life without him?"

Kellan moved in front of Neil and took hold of his hands. He started to say, "It'll be all right", but Neil interrupted by taking Kellan's mouth in a punishing kiss that drove away all thoughts about Seth and missions and mechanical watchdogs. The kiss lingered for several minutes, as if one soul was pleading for the other not to disconnect.

Neil slowly pulled back and whispered into Kellan's ear, "I love you, Kell. I'll be waiting here for you. Then we can go get Kaleb." He crossed his arms and turned away.

Kellan recognized Neil was troubled, and asked, "Neil, What is it?"

"What if this is it? What if I never see you again?" Neil hesitated. "Will you ever forget me?"

Kellan looked into space to stop the tears forming in his eyes. "Only when I don't know how to breathe. But we don't have to worry about that now, do we. I love you, Neil, and I'll see you soon," he optimistically said. When he turned to walk away, his wingtips brushed Neil's neck and traveled down his spine. He knew he was going to a war he might not win, and the possibility of that moment being the last time he'd touch Neil was breaking his heart.

Seth finally opened the front door and waited for Kellan to follow him out.

Chapter 27

Reaching the situation room, there was an MP at the door who was meant to block anybody from entering until probed and searched. The MP first waved a scanner wand up and down Seth's body, and when the MP was done with him, turned it on Kellan.

After a few minutes of probing for items not allowed in the situation room, Kellan and Seth were let through the door. The first person they came to was the Colonel who stood staring at Kellan as if he'd never seen him before. It was a while, so presumably the gawking was within reason. A few moments passed before the Colonel's eyes shifted to Seth.

The Colonel said, "Please. Come in and take a seat."

Seth thanked the Colonel then headed for a chair to sit down. But Kellan stood, and by the way his eyes traveled from one person to the other, it was noticeable he was keeping a close watch on everybody in the room.

Colonel Riley took a seat across from them and as he sipped the remainder of the coffee from his paper cup, looked at Seth and

Kellan with an intimidating glare. He reminded them that Kellan had always been and would always be an asset the government owns, and because of that, Kellan was required to follow orders given if it sat well with him or not.

There was no reason to tiptoe around the subject they were all there for. Holding back was never in the nature of the military. The Colonel got to the point straightaway and spoke about the military's intentions to use Kellan as an instrument to strike at one of the primary uses for Seekers—their ability to fly. The Colonel wasn't about to go into great detail, but if Kellan was going to be successful at detaining a Seeker on the loose, he needed to know what they might be capable of if he hadn't already figured that out. In so many words, the Colonel mentioned the Seekers had shown signs of learning and thinking on their own. Those things evolving beyond the design parameters hadn't been part of the plan. But their small brains found a way of developing, and they could very well continue enhancing the terrorist-like skills they'd been programed with.

The military's intentions were never to let the Seeker's out in the first place, but Kellan's escape had set in motion a chain of events that required him as part of the solution to reacquire control over the properties.

Colonel Riley then said to Kellan, sweeping his gaze over at Seth a few times as a way of including him in the conversation, "The Seekers, as you've found out first hand, are killing machines with the strength of a gorilla that's able to fly. The bad news is, that particular Seeker hasn't had any contact with our team for several days, and according to what Seth had told us, it had come in contact with you recently and then gone rogue. We need to get that one back under our control before anything disastrous takes place and puts the world in a chaotic tailspin. For that reason, Kellan, you've been called to duty. You have what it takes to find it quicker than any military machine can." Then he went on to tell Kellan what he already knew. "You can easily see through the darkness, you have hawk-like flying skills, strength, and an unparalleled sense of smell. We are counting on you to assist with immobilizing it."

"Whoa. Wait a second here," Kellan barked, his tone sounding like a protest. "Are you saying you want me to kill it?"

"Let me rephrase that." The Colonel took his reading glasses off and set them on the table. "What we want is for you to find the Seeker and lead it back here where we will then step in."

"Fine. That I'll do. But killing it will be your job." Kellan remained firm.

"That's the plan, Kellan. Our problem is trying to locate the Seeker, and because those models have been programmed to hunt you, you're our best chance to get the mission underway."

Kellan started walking toward the door.

"Where are you going?" Colonel Riley asked Kellan.

"To get this bat hunt off the ground. I know what needs to be done, so just make sure you're ready when I get back." At the door, Kellan faced off with the MP who looked determined not to let him pass. When Kellan took another step, the MP gripped the gun at his hip, preparing to use it.

The Colonel stood up and advised the soldier, "It's all right. At ease, soldier. The angel is on our side."

"Let's get this over and done with so I can get back to Neil," Kellan said, cautiously stepping back as he kept an eye on pistol Pete and his magic scanning wand.

In the split second Kellan moved backward, he felt a stinging bite at his shoulder. Another second passed and he went down.

Chapter 28

When Kellan finally surfaced from his drug-induced state and slowly opened his eyes, he didn't recognize anything around him. He was sweating and panicky, his heart racing faster than it usually did when he was upset, his body filled with emptiness, and his soul weeping as if in denial.

It only took Kellan a few minutes after waking up to regain his senses, and when he felt more like himself, he remembered the mission he had agreed to be a part of.

"What the fuck?" rolled off Kellan's tongue. He sounded groggy, even to himself. Kellan prodded at a sore spot on his shoulder. He recalled the prick but nothing after that until waking up here, wherever here was. Blinking the blur in his eyes away, he glanced around and discovered he was in an empty barn. As for where the barn was located was anybody's guess. Straight ahead, and unusual for a barn, was a large leaded window that let the glow of the silvery moon inside. He could tell by how dark it was outside that the entire day had come and gone without him.

Kellan had always known the darkest hours were better than daylight for him, which helped prevent him from being seen. What he didn't understand was why the military sedated him and transported him to a place in the middle of nowhere. Why not let him spend the day at AZ with Neil until nightfall, and then let him loose?

Kellan stood and shook the loose straw from his wings, brushing some from his pants while wondering where on earth he really was and if he was alone.

Bringing his wings back down from over his head, Kellan went to the door and opened it to see what he was dealing with outside. When he looked out, there was no mistaking he wasn't in Phoenix anymore. The darkness, the cold, and the stink made him feel like he was standing in the land of evil, and he couldn't seem to shake the horror of being in a dream. There were several pines swaying creepily to fit the mood. They were the type that grew in the cooler regions of North America. Mist and fog moved eerily at the base of the mountains in the distance, giving the woods along the river the feeling of being a haunted forest. With all that he saw in front of him, and because the Seeker was last known to be following the path he'd taken to Arizona, Kellan figured someplace in Colorado was where they had put him. Everything around him pretty much felt like it was. A chill raced up his spine and pricked at his brain. It wasn't because he was in a colder state than the one he just left, but because there were so many miles between him and the one he loved.

It was a bitter time for Kellan. He would have preferred to be digging a ditch in the quarry with his bare hands than to be drawn deeper into a dark mission so far away from Neil, not knowing if he was or wasn't being taken care of. Kellan didn't smile much at the moment, and did his best to banish any upsetting thoughts he had of Neil being caged the same way he was the last time he'd been in the government's custody. He hoped Seth would be there for Neil in his place.

Kellan took a deep breath, trying to shake off his annoyance at his situation. Whispers of horror and dread fueled his imagination, ramping it to the point it burned hot. He knew, beyond a shadow of a doubt, what he faced was dangerous, and although he'd gone up against Seekers before, this time the risks, and the stakes, seemed higher.

Kellan never considered himself as having a tremendous amount of courage, even though everyone else he knew seemed to think so, yet he was sustained by a powerful inner conviction. Even with the terror that lay before him, he was determined to survive it. He had to—for his sake and Neil's. Kellan wasn't going to allow himself to be afraid.

If Kellan closed his eyes and really concentrated, he could almost see, or at least pretend that his existence was a prelude to something much more important. Nothing bad could last forever, though he had no proof to that effect, just hope and a belief in himself and Neil. The thought of his lover was the one thing that helped make him stronger.

"What next?" he wondered. Should he go out and look for the Seeker, or just hang tight and wait for it to come to him? The military was convinced the monster would sniff him out, chase him, and try to kill him. That's what it was bred to do, designed in case Kellan realized how powerful he was and discovered he was able to survive on his own.

For the time being, Kellan thought only of going outside to have a look around, maybe take to the sky for a brief, rejuvenating flight that would get the oxygen moving through his veins. While flying, he could view the lay of the land, perhaps try to pinpoint where he truly was.

Cautiously stepping further outside the empty barn, Kellan was forced to jump out of the way when the wind grabbed the doors and slammed them shut behind him. A brewing thunderstorm was the cause of that, and showed signs of imminent arrival by the way the dark clouds rolled across the sky. After the startling barn door bang, Kellan shot straight into the sky with one sweep of his open wings. As he flew, he dodged scant raindrops and lightning flashes that were bounced from cloud to cloud.

ᴄ꙰ ᴆ

That same evening when the sun had set and darkness had fallen like a shroud over AZ, Seth joined Colonel Riley in a small room where they could view Kellan's movements on screen, and monitor the signal from the tracker they'd implanted in his shoulder that morning before transporting him to the vacant barn in Colorado.

As soon as they entered the dark room, the sensors detected them and the lights went on. They settled in front of the monitor that displayed a road map image much like Google Earth, only this one showed a red light flashing wherever Kellan was currently located. From what they saw at that moment, it was holding steady.

Colonel Riley seemed to be more composed than Seth, but it was evident he was impatient by the way he was tapping his forefinger repeatedly on the keyboard.

Seeing Riley's tension made Seth restless. Huffing, because nothing was happening on the screen, he stood up and whirled behind his chair where he leaned into it, crimping the back rest with a tight-fingered grip.

Riley then practically did the same, but circled the chair completely and sat back down. He leaned in, propping his elbows on each knee.

Seth settled in his seat again, but only for a few seconds. Then got back up, returned to the same place he just left, but this time drummed his fingers against the leather back of the chair. Then his toe started nervously tapping the floor as he stared at the screen. "Why isn't he moving yet? Is he all right?"

"He's fine. You need to settle down. If this doesn't pan out the way we're expecting, we have helicopters about one-quarter mile away that can be there within minutes."

"All right, all right." Seth tapped the end of an ink pen again and again on the palm of his hand and then chattered, "Why hasn't he moved yet?"

"Seth. At ease. Please. The tranquilizer we gave him was a twelve-hour dose. He'll be mobile soon," Colonel Riley assured Seth.

Within a few seconds of Riley raising his voice to Seth, they saw the red light flicker and then move from the position it had been in. It didn't go very far, but at least it moved. A good sign. When that happened, Seth felt a hint of relief because Kellan being awake meant they'd be making progress toward their goal.

Knowing Kellan was alive and kicking but not convinced

about a positive outcome, Seth still smiled for the first time that night, and the worry lines in his forehead began to fade. Then he turned to Colonel Riley—who had already rolled his chair closer to the screen to get a better look and to confirm the red dot actually moved—and asked, "What next?"

"We wait. Any sudden or erratic movements from that red light will most likely mean he's found the Seeker and is probably involved in a chase or a battle."

"I know Kellan is capable of taking care of himself, but what if he needs help? Is everybody prepared to reach him in time?"

The Colonel clicked the mouse a few times, zooming away from Kellan's red light, and showing an expanded view of the mapped area. "You see those two blue lights right there?" He pointed. "Those are the choppers I had told you about. They're waiting to move in as soon as Kellan gets the Seeker out in the open. If at any time Kellan is at risk, they've been instructed to paralyze or kill it. They're ready."

After hearing that, Seth just gave the Colonel a sketchy nod.

It was already eleven-thirty and nothing other than watching the red light move slowly around the screen in small circles had occurred—no long distance covered or any erratic movements.

They agreed Seth would wait around for another hour, maybe two, and if there were no changes to Kellan's position, then he'd leave for home and come back in the morning. Even though Seth should be exhausted and the screen had been unchanged, he remained glued to the monitor, completely engrossed. The whole thing made Seth feel as though he was involved with some kind of FBI manhunt, and a big part of him was getting a thrill out of it to the point he couldn't sit still. He had to move around again before his fast pumping heart exploded. While doing that, he viewed his cell phone display to see if Neil had sent him a, 'what the hell is going on', message. Surprisingly, there was nothing, and understanding the way they had left him earlier, Neil was probably going apeshit crazy with worry. Accomplishing the mission meant Kellan's return allowed them to move on to the really important things... finding and uniting with Kaleb.

Seth went back to his chair, and after sitting for what seemed like five minutes, he flinched when voices outside the door pulled his attention away from the screen.

Colonel Riley and Seth turned toward the door at the same time and saw two bulky men standing there. Seth had no idea who they were, nor had he ever seen them before, but the way the Colonel was acting, he seemed to.

The Colonel leaned into Seth and whispered, "Our relief team."

Seth watched the two men approach, tilting his head to one side when he heard them talking. He couldn't tell what they were saying, but it didn't really matter to him as long as they got the job done and made sure Kellan was kept out of danger.

The Colonel stood up and said, "Good to see you. So far there's been little movement with Kellan, but that could quickly change. He's red, the choppers are blue. If anything happens, call me straightaway. You know the drill."

Seth followed Colonel Riley out the door where they split up. Seth made his way to the lift and the Colonel walked down the hall in the opposite direction until he disappeared around the first corner he came to.

Chapter 29

Back in the dark skies of Colorado, circling the clouds, Kellan pushed through the headwinds, surging gusts skimming every feather.

The winds increased in strength, and the forces battered Kellan as he searched the sky for his enemy. As befitted his situation, a crack of thunder shook the air around him, and lightning lit the sky as if the sun quickly came and went. It was an all-out storm now, with powerful winds, rain, lightning and cracking thunder.

Kellan gazed at the churning weather above him, and shot upward with powerful thrusts of his wings now turning gray as dark clouds masked the brilliant white. He climbed higher and higher to outwit and put the storm below him.

On his way up, he gasped when something hidden in the dark clouds grabbed his ankle and viciously yanked him downward. He lashed out blindly, kicking at whatever had a hold on him, breaking its grip for only a second.

The wind howled and the rain was coming down in sheets, like the sky was falling, snuffing out Kellan's ability to fly. Then he saw it, flying erratically and screeching, mad as hellfire. It was black as the night sky. It was the Seeker and it was coming straight at him.

Kellan cursed under his breath as the demon approached him full force.

The Seeker was relentless. It dove beneath Kellan, then spiraled over top of him and grabbed him from behind. It squeezed Kellan, pinning his arms and wings against his body. The breath of the Seeker smelled of blood and decay, so rank that Kellan wanted to gag.

Kellan strained to free himself, but the Seeker was remarkably strong. The storm winds jostled them, blowing their bodies around, from left to right, and up and down, like two message bottles caught in a rapid river current.

Kellan growled in a keening of rage that amazingly topped the vocal screeches coming from the Seeker. Tapping into his primal emotions, Kellan thrashed his head back into the Seekers face with a brutal knock, bashing skull against brow.

The blow was enough to loosen the Seekers grip, permitting Kellan to spin in its arms. Kellan looked into his attacker's face, into its bottomless black eyes where he saw the limitless depths of death. Every fiber of Kellan's being screamed to get away, all the while growling and baring teeth.

Thunder cracked, and the shock of it loosened the Seeker's grasp even more, giving Kellan the chance to break free. As a quick defense, Kellan raked a clawed hand down the Seeker's face, scraping across the cornea, gouging and poking its deep black eye.

Shrieking, its cry mournful, the Seeker recoiled and grabbed its damaged face. Blood trickled and drowned its eye, shutting down its ability to see.

At that moment, the Seeker was defenseless, Kellan's strength intensified, pure adrenaline coursing through his body. He pushed away from his attacker and spun with incredible swiftness, looking back as the Seeker dropped away from his grip.

As if the heavens were on Kellan's side, lightning zigzagged from the sky and the bolt of electricity clipped the Seeker, flipping it into a downward tumble, head over heels, faster and faster. The sound of the strike resembled the crack of an enormous whip when it made contact.

Kellan spun in the air, turning away as the luminescent beam snuffed the Seeker out.

The storm raged harder and Kellan struggled to steady his flight. Fighting the wind, rain and thunder, he flexed his wings, thrashing beat after beat to lift himself higher, taking himself above the clouds and away from the storm and the falling beast.

ك ڀ

In the interim, Colonel Riley felt like he had just laid his head on the pillow when his phone rang. Glancing at it with one eyelid still squeezed shut, he noticed the call coming over at two in the morning was from the security office he had recently left. He hardly expected to be called back so quickly, but hearing the tone of the request for his return told him the Seeker and Kellan might be on the move.

As soon as Colonel Riley stepped through the office door, and before he sat down, the monitors told him that Kellan's red light had been exhibiting an erratic flight pattern. The crazy path of Kellan's light gave reason to believe he could be in battle with the Seeker.

With evidence on the screen showing Kellan's movements becoming ever more irregular, the Colonel immediately radioed the choppers, ordering them to close in on his location and report back with what they saw.

The pilots answered, "Roger that."

Chapter 30

After the battle with the Seeker, Kellan cocooned himself in his own wings, spiraled downward toward earth in the shape of a torpedo, looking to find where the Seeker might have landed, if it had actually hit the ground.

As minutes passed, the thunderstorm eased up a little, but not enough to make it any easier for Kellan to fly. The wind and rain beat against him as if it was trying to knock him from the sky. He straightened out and wove his way between the tall pine tree tops, scanning every bit of earth for the missing Seeker.

There it was, in the middle of a wide-open spot on the ground as if all the trees, plants, and undergrowth had been blown clear when it landed. Its twisted form lay still like a lump of dirt. One black wing stretched flat across the ground above its head, the other looked like crumpled paper over top of it, covering half its face.

Cautiously floating closer to the smoldering Seeker, Kellan back flapped until his toes tapped lightly across the ground, each step matching a wing beat, keeping his feet from completely touching down. He stopped and stood at the Seeker's feet and observed it. There was no movement. It didn't appear to be breathing either, and the earth around it seemed to be hissing.

Kellan looked around, expecting immediate action once the Seeker was down. Maybe a helicopter with a net, or perhaps another Seeker. He felt a sudden coldness in his chest, uncertain whether the Seeker was dead or alive. His senses sharpened, becoming more aware of everything around him as he kept half an eye on the body on the ground. His heartbeat was strong, even, and steady. But he hated those tense feelings, as if something was about to happen. It happened in combat, especially when things seemed as though they were going wrong. He was tempted to slit the Seekers throat to make sure it was done with this time, but he couldn't. He wasn't a killer.

"Where the fuck is the military," he complained.

As if by his command, the thumps of the chopper blades rose over the trees and bright lights suddenly flooded the place, illuminating Kellan and the downed Seeker.

Kellan turned toward the thwacking blades and bright lights, throwing his hand in front of his eyes to quickly block the beam. He flipped a wing from around his back as if pulling a vampire cape over his shoulder, spun in the dirt and then flew away. About fifty feet from where he had left, he whirled in midflight to face the choppers and hovered there with slow, steady wing beats in the dark, damp sky. With knowledge they were there for the Seeker, not him, he watched and waited.

Suddenly, as if the noise of the chopper had woken it, the Seeker twitched.

"Dammit. Couldn't that fucking bat wait two more minutes?" Kellan thought.

The thumps of the chopper blades must have been what pulled the Seeker out of its lightning-induced coma. With an unexpected snap, it shot to the sky like a stray missile, drawing the chopper's lights with it.

Kellan's gaze followed the Seeker as it climbed and flew toward him at an awkward angle, its flight path smoothing out, steadying as though it had not been struck by lightning. Moving way, Kellan pulled his wings in, letting himself drop.

Ignoring the helicopters as though they weren't there, the Seeker brazenly gained speed and went after Kellan. Its core was rotten, programed to find, fight, and disable its target. Chasing Kellan, the Seeker rolled midflight, each beat of its leathery wings cracked as if bones were breaking.

Within a split second, as Kellan spun to locate how close the Seeker was, the beast rammed him in the ribs, pushing him backward. Its chilling shrieks exploded in Kellan's ears, the high pitched sounds battering Kellan's wits like a drill to the skull. Before too much distance got between them, Kellan's wings came around and folded over the Seeker, wrapping them in a gray feathered cocoon. Without beating wings to hold them up, they dropped, gravity pulling them down. As quickly as Kellan's wings bent around the Seeker's body, they uncoiled. He flapped them hard, gaining altitude that kept them from hitting the ground.

Clinging to Kellan with clawed fingers, the Seeker growled in his face. Its rancid breath smelled of decay and rot. The stench was so strong it took Kellan's breath away.

Strength grew in Kellan as his anger intensified. He growled through gritted teeth, gripping the Seeker by the throat, removing blood flow and oxygen to its brain. He could see the Seeker's dark eyes rolling back, its lids fluttering and then dropping shut. Without a second thought, Kellan squeezed harder, pressing each thumb into its throbbing larynx, shutting off all passages at the throat. With accelerated energy, Kellan yanked the Seeker's head into his, cracking it hard, skull against skull. The shocking blow forced the Seeker's grip to loosen on Kellan. Its mouth gaped open as if trying to draw in a breath. Dazed for a moment, it came back quickly, the Seeker swinging a fist upward into Kellan's jaw. The strength behind the impact pushed them apart.

At the instant Kellan's head snapped back and his feet lifted up in front of him, the Seeker reacted and broke free. It snapped its wings, banked left, and then shot straight up.

Reversing his momentum, Kellan back flapped, putting himself upright. He angrily beat his wings and took off after the Seeker, leaving a misty trail of water cascading off his wingtips. When he caught the Seeker, he grabbed its leg and yanked it down. Then with boundless energy, Kellan swooped in front of it and swung a fist that connected with the Seeker's jaw, its wingtip clipping Kellan's shoulder as it spun.

At that moment, a chopper's spotlight pinged them, the beam so bright it was blinding. Kellan looked over his shoulder into the shining light behind him, slowed his wing beats and hung there. His breathing steadied as he analyzed his surroundings, one chopper to his left, and the other at his back. They were still at a fair distance away, but the wind they were generating made them feel closer.

Before the Seeker regained its wits and figured out it was still in battle, Kellan dipped his shoulder and angled to the right. Then he flew upward away from the spinning blades and the Seeker he had stunned with a sidewinder's punch.

The Seeker snapped out of its daze and flew after Kellan again, baring its jagged teeth, screaming as if it had never been stunned by a blow to the jaw.

Following the Seeker, the chopper stopped within thirty yards from them, its high-tech firearms ready to shoot.

Escaping the Seeker's fury, Kellan quickly banked behind the chopper, staying clear of the feather jarring vortex being generated by the rear blade.

The Seeker headed for Kellan, almost senseless with blood lust, its urge to kill increasing. As it approached, Kellan broke to the right and dove at the same moment the chopper spun to face them.

Watching the Seeker relentlessly coming for him, Kellan snapped his wings downward, which pushed him into a twisting backflip to get away. Beating his wings harder, he flew in a wide arc until he reached the front side of the helicopter where he hovered at a safe distance, looking face to face with the chopper's pilot. He glanced a few times at the second chopper hovering across the way and keeping a safe distance from the commotion, as if waiting for orders to attack. Each time its nose lifted and lowered, it appeared to Kellan as though it was breathing.

Without thought of being knocked around, the Seeker flew under the chopper to sneakily get to Kellan. The wind current pushed it toward the ground in an unstable tumble, flipping it several times before it regained its balance and continued flying.

With forward thrusts of each wing above his head, Kellan

pulled himself further away from the whirlwind developing at the front of the helicopter. The laser-like light from the chopper's nose pierced his eyes, bringing out sparks that matched the shimmer in his wings. Tainted by dark energy all around, Kellan extended his arms at his sides and balled his hands into tight fists, ready for whatever happened next. Blinded by the light, he waited, whispering to the Seeker if it was nearby and listening. "Come get me you fucker — and make it snappy." He lifted his arm across his brow to block the beam.

No sooner had he said that, the Seeker approached from the rear and latched onto Kellan's back. Its rotting breath singed his neck.

Aiming to get the Seeker without injury to Kellan, the chopper backed away. As it went up and then back down in a smooth wave, its lights swept across the clouds and lit up the scattered raindrops falling from the sky. Regaining its position at a distance, it held the nose light on the two creatures in battle.

In spite of the attack from the rear, Kellan buckled forward, flipping the Seeker over his shoulder, putting it head down in front of him. As the Seeker tumbled heels-over-head, Kellan caught it by the ankles. Quickly heaving the Seeker upright, Kellan pulled its back against his own chest and held it tightly. As they plummeted, Kellan snapped his wings out to level their flight above ground, and before he knew it, they were headed straight for the barn he had awakened in.

Locked together, they crashed through the weathered barn door, breaking it down, wood splinters shooting inward with them. When they landed, they tumbled head over feet, one over top of the other. With a sudden thwump, Kellan stopped and stood as the Seeker kept going, ending its rolling a few feet ahead.

Swiftly the Seeker stood and looked at Kellan, its head tilted at a curious angle as it crept toward him, teeth exposed, saliva dripping like acid rain.

Keeping the Seeker in his sight, Kellan took off and snatched a chain he'd seen coiled on the ground. He angrily whipped it over his head, bringing it around front and snagging the Seeker around the wrist as it leapt from the ground to fly.

"This shit has got to end." Kellan dug his feet into the ground as the chain snapped taut, bringing the Seeker's ascension to an immediate stop. As the Seeker jerked backward, Kellan jumped over top of it and started flying. He sharply banked to the right at an increasing speed that hurled the Seeker into a wing over wing log roll across the ground. Keeping his forward momentum, Kellan pulled his wings in, and spun head first through the large glass window, towing the Seeker with him at the end of the chain. Glass fragments spiraled away from Kellan's spinning body as if they were water crystals being shaken from the coat of a dog.

As Kellan flew, the Seeker bounced behind him across the ground, and before it had any chance to recover, Kellan turned toward the hovering choppers at the open field. When Kellan noticed the Seeker wasn't resisting, he landed and quickly wrapped it with the chain to restrain it.

Kellan held the chain-bound Seeker tightly against his chest, lifted off, and flew to the open field at the same time the two choppers came around at sharp angles and faced them. Nearly exhausted, Kellan put the Seeker between him and the helicopters, letting them see he had it. Lazily staring into space, the Seeker bared its jagged teeth as if trying to roar, but only saliva and blood emerged.

One chopper dropped back, took a wide arc out over the trees, and then positioned itself a short distance behind them, keeping watch.

Still holding the Seeker, Kellan nodded to the pilot up ahead, and then slowly looked over his shoulder at the chopper thumping behind them. He was sure they couldn't hear him, but he still hollered, "Take this mother fucker out."

At that moment, the chopper in front of them began to wind down. The engine thumped as the feet touched ground, pegging Kellan and the Seeker with the bright white light. The side door of that chopper opened, and clinging to the frame was a sniper with a rifle — one shot and the Seeker would sleep.

As Kellan dangled the Seeker under him, two pops sounded from the gun. Two darts hit the Seeker's left thigh, one immediately following the other.

As the Seeker lost consciousness, Kellan gently lowered its limp body to the ground in a respectful way, satisfied to see the ugly monster out of commission.

Soon after, the other chopper set down, and when the door on that one opened, two large men with high-and-tight haircuts came running out. They carried a case that was similar to body bags—a seven-foot-long black vinyl zippered bag—but with one difference... a ventilation screen was sewn at one end.

As they stuffed the Seeker inside the black sack and zipped it up, Kellan reacted as if he was witnessing somebody close to him being put away. Despite his success in fulfilling his mission, gloom settled on his shoulders, a heavy weight difficult to explain. He tried to shake it, but because of his sympathetic soul, the remorse he felt for the bad guy persisted. He quickly blessed the miserable Seeker that just tried to kill him, and watched the men complete their task.

Kellan brought his wings up and then down, gathering wind that lifted him backward and out of the way. The Seeker was then quickly carried to the chopper, one man at the head, one at its feet, and two others on each side at the middle.

While all the commotion went on around the Seeker, Kellan glanced at every inch of his body, looking for scrapes and bruises that might need to be cleaned or possibly sutured. Being strong and thick skinned, he didn't find anything life threatening, and seemed to have walked out of the battle without major injuries.

Before the helicopters headed back to AZ with the sleeping Seeker, the lieutenant from chopper one offered him a choice—a ride back to headquarters or getting there under his own power if he felt up to it. Whichever it was, he told him he was expected back by morning.

Kellan had no reason to go against the orders of returning to AZ by the time he was told. No qualms at all with that. In fact he wanted to go back. The military had something he wanted as well as the man he was in love with. For those reasons, Kellan was eager to return, get his life back, one that would allow him to make a family with Neil, Dylan and Kaleb, and hopefully not one with probing doctors and gray-green institutional walls.

Before Kellan left, he needed to confirm there was no further reason to be concerned about Seekers pulling him from the clouds, or trying to drown him in a nearby lake.

The lieutenant confirmed all was good before jumping into the chopper and moving out.

After the choppers lifted off, Kellan crouched down, sprang from the ground and took flight. He stayed low at first and then quickly banked off to the left before shooting straight up to the clouds in a twisting spin.

By himself and feeling content for the first time in days, Kellan was determined to take advantage of the joy he had for flying. By quickly back flapping, he teased the headwinds and dropped backward, did a few somersaults, flipping head over heels and spinning several times as he flew. He was a master flyer and anybody watching would have thought the same.

Off in the distance, someplace further ahead of him, Kellan could hear the blades of the two choppers banging in the wind, dispersing thumps that were fading as he dropped further behind them.

While soaring alone, putting the job he was on out of his mind, Kellan thought about Neil and Kaleb again. There was no stopping the effects it had on him while he let the memories of TC wash away. His main man Neil gave him a rock-hard erection and his unknown angel child made him grin. Those were definitely his happy thoughts and he was holding on to them. The two images together gave Kellan the hope he needed for whatever he was about to face when he got back to AZ. The zipper on his jeans went taut and the corners of his mouth lifted, creasing his cheeks.

Flying fast because he couldn't wait to get back to the place called AZ.

Chapter 31

As Kellan flew, he maintained the sense of comfort he recently acquired from knowing the Seeker was out of the sky, and that he was much closer to seeing his boy, Kaleb. The thoughts he had were pleasing ones, but he also knew it wouldn't take much to turn his world upside down all over again. Remembering he was a mutant freak, he realized it was just the way it was, and was probably going to be like that for the rest of his life.

As he continued flying, he found himself over what appeared to be a desolate street somewhere near Phoenix. He figured he might only be a few miles east of AZ by the bright lights he spotted ahead of him in the distance. While looking down at the forsaken town and hoping nothing would rise from it and be one of those upside down moments that would ruin his flight of contentment, he spotted what might have been cheesy-looking bars and hotels, greasy food shops, and a one-pump fuel station. To him, the district looked to have once been a place where anyone could get laid for a few bucks and some change. He wasn't sure about that, but by the way it looked now, it might have been one of those places unfortunately turned to a darker side during the last years of its existence. Kellan thought, *"Man, oh man,"* and was thankful as all get out he still had some miles to go, and the dust covered road below him wasn't his designated landing strip.

Right on time and before the sun came up, Kellan flapped his last wing beat and landed in the courtyard at the center of AZ, smack dab in the middle where every high concrete wall of the hexagonal building surrounded him as if he was caged again. He would rather have touched down in the secluded back yard where Dylan and Neil were, but he wasn't certain where it was in the cluster of buildings at the large military compound. The campus layout where he stood reminded him of the Pentagon in DC. He'd never been there before, didn't really know what the Pentagon looked like in the middle, but from photos he'd seen, the DC structure was the first place that came to mind. The second vision was a prison. That was evident by the high concrete walls with windows so small, an escape by anybody was near impossible, and if they were successful, the barbed wire security fencing that circled the place would catch them for good.

Kellan glanced at just about everything, even looked to the sky, and as soon as he brought his gaze back down from above, he saw a pack of men coming out a door from the west side. The expression on Kellan's face got brighter when he saw Seth walking toward him beside Colonel Riley. Behind them were two large men. At first he thought they were the high-and-tight soldiers that took the Seeker away in the body bag, but if his memory served him well, they weren't. They were taller and quite a bit more fit.

Kellan understood the Colonel and Seth were on his side to protect and assist, but there was always that small percentage of apprehension that caused him to keep an eye open for any foul play.

Kellan swiftly made his way toward them at the same measured pace they were coming at him, seeming relentless, unstoppable, and as stubborn as mountain rams. He was sure they were as eager as he was to get his life back on track, finish what had been started so the whole Seeker versus Angel could be put to rest. He was so ready to see Neil, and if not known by them already, he wanted to get to know Kaleb.

"Welcome back, Kellan." Seth stopped directly in front of him and then stepped aside so Colonel Riley could welcome him home, too.

Just like before, the Colonel was stiff and military-like, shaking the angel's hand sternly and then saying, "Good morning, Kellan. Please follow us."

Kellan really wanted to see Neil, but protocol came first, so he went with them as the Colonel had instructed. They brought him back to the same room where they originally started the mission, only this time he was a little more alert, protecting himself from anything similar to that unexpected shock to the shoulder blade he got the last time that had him waking up someplace he didn't recognize.

Settling in, Kellan sat on a high stool that allowed his wings to dangle toward the floor without the discomfort of dragging on the floor. Seth was next to him, with the Colonel on the other side of the table facing them. The guard he had dubbed Pistol Pete stood stiffly at the door, guarding the room as well as the entryway.

Kellan listened carefully to Colonel Riley. Kellan appreciated the man's expressions of gratitude for a job well done, especially since he'd avoided serious injury either to himself or the Seeker. That the man worded it as an achievement was enough to ruffle his feathers and make him feel hopeful that what he'd been promised might actually happen.

When the Colonel switched to the topic of Kellan's future, the details were still sparse. Although the man assured him that he'd be taken care of in that secluded location, there was a lot left unsaid. Unfortunately, before he could question the man, he was dismissed and escorted to his apartment.

Chapter 32

Excited to see Kellan again, Neil greeted him with misty eyes. When he blinked, a tear trickled down his cheek. Kellan brushed it away while Neil let him know he worried throughout the night and hadn't gotten any sleep because of it.

"It's all fine, Hun. The Seeker's where it belongs and this warrior is here with you now."

Neil looked at Kellan's scrapes, fingered the small bandages sticking to a few spots on his body, and asked, "Are you okay? I mean... are there any major injuries I'm not able to see?"

Kellan kissed Neil's forehead and said, "I'm perfect. Just these few scratches."

Before Kellan had a chance to back away, Neil whispered, "Make love to me, soldier man." He wanted nothing other than to have Kellan take him to bed straightaway.

Kellan's actions right then told Neil his angel couldn't wait to get him there. Instead of taking him to the bed, Kellan ripped both their clothes off like there was no tomorrow and laid Neil back on the dining table. They mashed their stubbled faces together in scratchy, hungry kisses, as if making up for lost time.

At times, some more than others, Neil never minded how eager Kellan was to climb on top of him and just get to it. He also gave in and found it erotically nasty whenever Kellan's open hand smacked his ass cheek while penetrating him from behind on all fours. Moving in slow motion wasn't always what made the connection a perfect one. Getting off by way of a quickie put Neil in a happy place.

Neil's body vibrated as Kellan explored it, touching him everywhere — kissing him everywhere. Everything Kellan was doing seemed right and perfect to him. He gasped for air as he took every inch of Kellan's thick erection to the hilt.

Enthused by what was happening to him, Neil's ass sucked Kellan right in. His body arched upward, and Kellan's pressed down, and within a matter of minutes, he took Kellan's eruption inside his ass as his own ejaculation splashed their chests and marbled the dining table all around him.

"Holy fuck!" — Kellan puffed — "Sorry about the quickie" — his body twitched — "but your ass was so damned tight and hot, I couldn't hold back another second. My sperm wanted inside you as badly as my dick did."

Astonished as well by the sudden surge, Neil exhaled as he said, "It seems... I was as worked up as you were." Neil recognized the connection they just had was a profound way of communicating their love for one another beyond what any words could express. This time, his release had come quickly, as if the comfort of having Kellan back in his arms safe and sound had a lot to do with it. He inhaled and looked up at his angel, then grunted when he pushed himself forward against Kellan's chest in order to sit up.

"What's happening?" Kellan asked as he stood and stumbled backward a few steps, his wings coming around and tapping Neil's shoulders.

"I'm not done." Neil took hold of Kellan's wingtips, spun him around and pushed him wings down across the table. "How about this, soldier?" He climbed up and took a seat over top of Kellan, pressing back until Kellan's stone hard cock sank all the way inside his ass again. As Kellan pushed his hips upward, Neil closed his eyes and hummed, "Ho fuck, that's good."

They moved together, slowly at first. Then faster. And faster still. Neil rose and fell hard on Kellan, liking the rough ride, and by the way Kellan was reacting, he did too. Each time Neil bounced, Kellan's wings thwacked noisily in the semen that had already been splattered across the table top. The wild assault on Neil's prostate quickly drove the semen inside of him, out. Streaks splashed across Kellan's torso.

Kellan clenched his teeth, and growled, "That's my man. Take my cum into that sweet ass." He pushed his hips into Neil and held them there.

After feeling what Neil thought to be the final spurt from Kellan's dick, he collapsed from the intensity of it all, looked into Kellan's eyes and confessed, "Not bad for a dining room screw." He rolled off his angel and snuggled closely at his side, lying on his wing like it was a favored feather bed.

They cuddled for a short time before putting their pants on and going to the kitchen shirtless to clean the semen from their bodies with the towel hanging on the oven door handle. After the speedy wipe down, Neil attempted to grab the towel in midair that Kellan was caught tossing into the sink. Neil immediately said, "Whoa. If we're going to be roomies, you need to know a peeve of mine that involves kitchen towels."

"What's that?"

"When you remove a towel from the rod, please replace it with a clean one," Neil ordered. "One thing that drives me bloody nuts is when I wash my hands in the kitchen sink and then wander around with drippy fingers because the towel I was expecting to be there is missing. The same goes for the toilet paper. Please dear God, do not leave that holder empty."

Kellan laughed. "Yes, boss. I can live with those two rules."

Neil pointed a scolding finger. "There's more, but you'll learn those as we go along."

In less time than it took to blink, Neil's head was cradled in Kellan's hands, his fingers weaving through hair at the back of his skull, and before Neil spoke another rule, his mouth was covered with a kiss.

Pulling back, Kellan confessed, "Hot damn, I love you. From the deepest part of my heart, I love you. Quirky ways and all."

Chapter 33

"Kaleb. Come here and sit down. I have some good news I'd like to tell you," Mister Trotsky said as he watched the kid pushing his hand inside a large foam fan finger that showed he was the number one fan of the Miami Dolphins.

The littlest angel known to man galloped across the classroom, one foot being dragged behind the other in some sort of a hop and a skip. He concentrated more on the big foam hand he was wearing than anything around him. As he ran down the center of the classroom, Kaleb bumped into every chair, ricocheting off one in the very last row that almost sent his little body to the floor. Quickly thinking, Kaleb beat his little wings and broke his fall. He smartly flew to a chair next to the teacher and stood on the seat.

"Look Mister Trobsky, I'm as tall as you." He bobbed up and down, poking the teacher's head with the large foam finger. He laughed.

While taking the abuse from the ten-year-old angel who had

the energy level of a wild humming bird, Trotsky said, "I'm glad you're here, Kaleb. But I need you to stand still now." He leaned away from the finger bouncing off the side of his head before it found his glasses and jostled them off the bridge of his nose.

Kaleb screamed and then laughed when Mister Trotsky lifted him from the chair and lowered him to the floor. The ruckus out of Kaleb was because he thought the teacher was trying to tickle him. When he laughed, it always made Mister Trotsky chuckle too, and the unmistakable look on Trotsky's face made it clear to Kaleb he was trying to hold back laughter. If Mister Trotsky made any kind of noise that hinted he was about to laugh, Kaleb would know he'd gotten away with something, which to Kaleb, meant he could do it again.

As soon as Kaleb's feet touched the floor, he stretched his arms out in front of him and acted like he was flying, skipping a few feet forward and then making a U-turn back to where he started. He held his wings against his back because the rule was: *No flying indoors.*

Skidding across the floor in stocking feet, Kaleb banged into the chair he was standing on earlier and then removed the big foam finger from his hand. He stood behind the chair, gripped the back of it with wiggling fingers while he watched Mister Trotsky's face peer at him with pursed lips. With his chin resting on antsy fingers, Kaleb waited impatiently for the teacher to say something. But without a word, and the same way a dodgeball would be palmed, Mister Trotsky placed a hand on Kaleb's head to move him around the chair, and motioned for him to take a seat on the stool next to it.

When working with Kaleb, Mister Trotsky had always mumbled the same thing, *"Must have patience."* He then sat across the desk from Kaleb and faced him.

"Did I do something bad, Mister Trobsky?" Kaleb asked, forgetting Trotsky mentioned he had good news, or Kaleb never heard those words because he himself seemed to suffer from Attention deficit hyperactivity disorder. At AZ it was documented in his file as ADHD.

"No, Kaleb. You did not." Talking to a ten-year-old was not the same as speaking to an adult since they didn't process information quite the same way. Too often kids reacted in totally surprising ways.

"Then why aren't we at the park?" Kaleb stuck a finger in his nose.

Trotsky handed Kaleb a paper tissue. "We can go to the park soon. But for now I have good news I think you're going to like."

Kaleb rotated his finger inside his nostril.

"Use the tissue, Kaleb, not your finger." Mister Trotsky held back his laughter.

Kaleb finally sat still and listened to what Mister Trotsky had to say. Kaleb heard he'd soon be graduating from his classes at AZ and moving to a house. Kaleb nodded that he understood and seemed to be happy with having his own bedroom, bathroom, kitchen, and living room. Kaleb saw getting away from the school would be like being on a summer break. What worried him most was who would be helping him learn new things every day. Kaleb fidgeted a little, almost looking sad. "Will you be coming with me, Mister Trobsky?"

"In the beginning, I'll be there with you. And you know what, Kaleb? If everything goes well, I might be able to stay." Trotsky kept most of what he'd been told from Kaleb, in case any of what he said made the kid feel afraid and alone.

"Does it have a park like the one here so I can fly?" Kaleb wondered.

"I would imagine there will be many places for you to fly. Maybe a bigger park than what you have here."

"You promise?" Kaleb grunted when he bent down to pick up the spongy finger that had fallen to the floor earlier.

"I can't promise you that, Kaleb, but I am sure the new house will have many of the same things you have here."

"Are they moving me away because I did something wrong?"

Trotsky stood up and walked over to Kaleb's side of the table, pulled a chair up in front of him so he was closer to his level. "No, Kaleb. You've done nothing wrong. It's part of growing up and is the next step in your schooling. It's time for you to be in a home environment and learn to live like a family would. It'll be nice. You'll be in a nice house with a yard and maybe a pet."

Kaleb repeatedly tapped the foam finger on the desktop. "You mean with other angels like me? And when will I be sent away?"

Trotsky didn't have all the facts, which made it difficult for him to answer Kaleb's questions. He'd probably already said too much, possibly given out incorrect information even. He changed the subject. "Let's do this. Put your shoes on and we'll go to the park right now."

"Only if you promise you will go with me when I'm sent away." Kaleb rubbed his eye with a balled fist.

That was the only answer Trotsky knew for sure, it's what Colonel Riley had already told him would happen. "I promise. Let's get to the park so you can fly."

Chapter 34

On the opposite side of AZ from where Kaleb and Mister Trotsky were, Kellan and Neil had been going over the plans with Seth and Colonel Riley for the trip to the secluded mini-mansion in southern Colorado. It was the safe house Seth had mentioned and where the military had decided would be the place for them to live. Kellan had no choice other than to go with that because of who and what he was.

The home came with an abundant amount of land that would give Kellan the space he would need to fly without being seen, even during the daylight hours. However, there were a few rules, but nothing like what he was used to when he lived at TC.

It was a lakefront house that sat in the middle of fifty acres of vacant land, seeming to be in a world of its own with nothing nearby for miles. The place could be overwhelming, but as long as the boys didn't mind living where nobody else did, it was a suitable place for a gay angel and his family. For Neil, the waterfront property would feel like home.

211

Every aspect of their move was in place, and if desired, they could take to the sky by chopper that same day.

Before anybody left the office, Kellan asked, "When can we meet Kaleb?" As soon as Kaleb's name was mentioned, he noticed Neil immediately perked up and glanced across the table at Colonel Riley.

The Colonel lowered his head, looking at them over the top of his reading spectacles and told them they would meet him at the house in Colorado. Kaleb would be flown out separately with Mister Trotsky, his mentor and teacher. Having Trotsky with Kaleb during the transition would be much less stressful on the little angel.

"Does he know about me? I mean us?" Kellan brought a finger to his chest and then relocated it toward Neil.

"Not yet. We've decided to wait until he gets to the house. We'll have a better idea what to tell him then," the Colonel said. "Kaleb *has* been told he will be moving from where he is to a new house, and according to his mentor, he seemed to handle that part of it okay."

Knowing he'd be meeting his cloned son soon brought tears to Kellan's eyes. He could hardly believe there was another angel on the planet, and to know the little angel was his child, punched a hole in his heart that left him with a welling ache inside. He was anxious, he wanted to see him, and didn't want another day standing in the way of being able to hold his kid and tell him they were of the same blood.

Colonel Riley stood, directing his words to Kellan. "Right now Kaleb thinks he's the only angel in the world, and he's never known any different, just like you while growing up." Riley stopped speaking a moment. "Put yourself in the mind of a ten-year-old boy and double or even triple the punch. Think about how you reacted when you found out Kaleb existed. It was probably heart-stopping news to you. That's what we are concerned about. Information like this could be difficult to assimilate. We know his mind is strong, like yours, but we need to go at it with great caution."

Kellan blinked about twenty times in less than a minute. He understood the Colonel, but found it difficult to contain his excitement. Reluctantly he said, "I've been without him this long, so I suppose one or two more days won't matter that much."

There was no mistaking the government had withheld a lot of information from Kellan all those years, so doing the same to Kaleb was a no-brainer. As much as Kellan wanted to see Kaleb, he had no other choice but to do what they said. He had no idea where Kaleb was held, which meant he had to rely on the military to take him and Neil to his child at their new home. Anticipation set in, making Kellan antsy, and some of his anxiety transferred to Neil, as if they were connected.

During the time they were discussing what was going to happen, when and where, Kellan took a moment and observed Neil. He noticed his posture had changed from when he first sat down, sinking deeper into his chair and locking his arms together across his chest. To Kellan, body language told the story, and from what he saw, Neil seemed far away, almost as if he was sitting alone. Then when he saw Neil's eyes slowly shift from one corner to the other, he wondered if it might have anything to do with all that had recently taken place and what was to come of the rest of his life.

Kellan had concerns of his own, and his thoughts at the moment were that Neil could be thinking the same things. Kellan was troubled about how having Kaleb in their lives would change his relationship with Neil, or the other way around, Neil's with his. A developing courtship came with a massive amount of passion, and Kellan knew there'd be no more sex on a whim because the needs of a kid would come first, and he'd be surprised if Neil hadn't thought about that, too. All this time, Neil had been passively going along with just about everything, and because their relationship was still so new, Kellan worried Neil wouldn't be able to make any more life altering adjustments. He remembered Neil mentioning that he'd gotten past all the outrageousness of living in an unbelievable world, but that moment when Kellan watched him, realized that Neil might not have.

Setting his thoughts aside, Kellan remained quiet and allowed the plans to fall into place as they had been decided. He knew if he wanted to be with Neil, it was essential that he follow along and submit to the rules as laid out. After that, they could focus on family life.

He and Neil briefly spoke about settling in as a family earlier, not in depth, but they had. They played with the idea that Neil would take the role as daddy, doing the cooking, home upkeep, and nurturing, while Kellan did all the fun stuff that a dad would do, like play ball and teaching the kid how to ride a bike. Kellan knew everything about the situation would be borderline frightening, and at times exciting. It was hugely life changing for him as well as Neil, and something like that would take time to absorb.

Only a few days ago, it was just Neil and Dylan living alone. Neil had been working as a medical nurse while Dylan guarded the lake house and played with stuffed toys all day long. That was all going to change very soon. They were only hours away from being parents of a little angel, which they were thrilled about, as well as nervous. Kellan recognized that taking care of a child was a big undertaking for Neil, and that the angel factor was over the top. One thing Neil had said to him was that he'd be caring for someone he'd fallen in love with, an incredibly amazing creature that fell from the sky and into his life, the attractive angel who instantly became his loving boyfriend and the one he wanted to be with for the rest of his life.

During the next twenty minutes it took to explain where they were going, showing pictures of Kaleb and giving them an estimated time the little guy would be at the house, head of security charged the door as if a fire was coming up behind him. Realizing the ruckus he made, he excused his actions and said, "Pardon my intrusion, sir. I didn't mean to startle anybody. The chopper is prepped and ready to take them to the plane, sir. The pilots are standing by, sir." He was very formal, standing stiffly and looking up into the ceiling lights the entire time he addressed the Colonel.

"A few more minutes and we'll be ready," Colonel Riley assured him.

When hearing that, the MP withdrew to wait outside the door for further instructions.

Keeping on topic, the Colonel established that Kellan was content with his new living arrangements at the mini-mansion and assured him there was no need to leave this time. There would be everything he and Neil required to live comfortably, and if they found a need for anything more, all they had to do was make the staff aware of it.

Only a few short hours were in the way of Kellan meeting with his offspring, the child he'd yet to meet but deep down already loved.

Chapter 35

Choppers of any kind had recently become a non-festive event for Neil and certainly wasn't a thrill ride for Kellan. Both preferred those menacing whirlybirds with the thumping blades to be out of their sight forever. It seemed that whenever a helicopter was around them, bad shit hovered right there next to it. After the last few trips in the military chopper, Kellan hoped he'd never have to step foot inside another one again. He had his own wings and could fly, so he didn't see the point. One winged bird inside another — it seemed out of sorts if he thought about it logically.

The flight from AZ to the house had been planned for early that morning. The chopper had been warming its engine on the helideck, waiting for Kellan and Neil to board. Even with the intended destination in Colorado being a short jaunt from where they were, there were two helicopters and a jet scheduled that would get them there, bunny hopping from one aircraft to the other.

On the way to the chopper, Kellan pondered with the idea of avoiding another ride in it, thinking perhaps he'd try one last time to convince the military to let him fly to the home with Neil in his arms. But as he understood earlier, that would be a battle he wouldn't win, so keeping that idea to himself was a wise decision. It was probably for the best anyway, figuring the original plan would get him to Kaleb without having to do the work at keeping everybody in the sky.

What seemed like only minutes after lifting off, the helicopter landed at the first stop where a private jet was waiting to fly them to the foothills of Colorado.

Stepping from the helicopter after everyone else got out, Kellan concentrated on his wings, making sure to keep them low and tight. The moment he was well clear of the spinning blades and the vortex they generated, his feathery plumages went up, out to his sides, and then back again.

Like any person who required high security, they moved from one aircraft to the other in less than a minute. Within the next couple of minutes, the jet was racing down the runway and airborne the minute after that. It was as if they were in a high speed chase and they were the prey, trying to get away from whatever was on their tail in three minutes flat. The experience was almost like being on a thrill ride, exhilarating as well as nerve wracking.

They spent a little more than an hour on the plane. Kellan probably could have flown faster, but protocol was in order and there was Seth, Neil, Dylan and a few good men to carry as well. That would have been murder on Kellan's wings by the time they made it to Colorado.

It was rather cramped inside the plane for Kellan. The fuselage wasn't designed for a passenger like him who carried a set of wings on his back. In fact, the world wasn't either. For obvious reasons, it was never easy for him to sit in a chair that had a back on it, and because of that, he stood most of the way, hanging onto the back of Neil's seat with one hand and his other locking fingers with Neil's. The only time he actually sat, uncomfortably, was at take-off and then would do so again when they landed.

Feeling the same way he did when trapped in the chopper,

Kellan couldn't wait to get out of the jet. Once they landed, and as soon as he helped Neil from his seat, he practically pushed everybody who was in the way out the door. Dylan and Seth pranced behind. They too seemed antsy to be debarking and setting foot on solid ground.

The flights weren't over yet. There was one more chopper ride before they were at their new home. Thankfully, that flight was only about fifteen minutes from one place to another.

While airborne on the final leg, Kellan and Neil observed the grounds below as the aircraft approached the house. There were MP's outfitted in camouflage uniforms all over the grounds. Some of the men stationed along the twenty-foot-high barbed wire perimeter had body armor on. From above, it looked like a war zone until they got closer to the house. With all those armed men strategically placed, the property appeared more secure than the White House, which deterred attempted invasions of unwelcomed guests.

As predicted, the house looked deserted. The windows were dark as expected during mid-day, and even though the siding was probably weather sealed, it held all the run down attributes of a scary dwelling that the walking dead wouldn't even want to visit. The side yard was littered with two junked vehicles from the nineteen-fifties, a midsized sedan and a pickup truck; both were totally rusted to the point you couldn't tell what color they once had been. A little further back, near what appeared to be a dilapidated carriage house, were broken down horse buggies. They were sitting lopsided, with some parts broken away, and revealing spots that looked burnt.

There were other areas around the property that had a lot of spare parts for appliances, like stoves and refrigerators. By the looks of everything scattered around, it seemed upgrades had been done to the inside of the house throughout the years, and nobody bothered to discard the junk the way they should have. Perhaps it was a way to make the home uninviting. Everything had flowery weeds and scant brush coming up around it, looking overgrown and unkempt.

The house, however, had one thing going for it in regards to the exterior. The lakeside was tidy and had minimal appeal. A few hundred yards from the house, there was an area for the chopper to land without clipping a pile of rubble or chopping down any trees. It was a large empty spot shaped like a crop circle that made a suitable landing pad for a helicopter. There were no actual roads or pathways leading to the property, leaving the only way to it by means of the sky. Any other way, such as by ground transport, would be challenged by security.

Neil stood next to Kellan outside the chopper and whispered, "Are we supposed to live in that monstrosity?"

Neil's comment was overheard by Seth, and to assure them, he said, "The house is still in the process of being renovated. Ignore what you see and follow me."

There was no turning back now. All seven thousand square feet of their happy ending was staring them in the face. It was going to be their Home-Sweet-Home with a lakefront view.

Chapter 36

The stairway creaked as they went up to the front door, the way an old cranky house would. If Neil wanted out, the time was then to speak up before going any further. But he loved Kellan too much to do that, so he would stick it out and do his best to adjust.

When the MP at the door stepped aside, that allowed Seth to open up the double doors. Kellan and Neil were pleasantly surprised by what they saw inside. Even if it was less homey than what they would have liked, it was a far cry from how it was first presented to them on the outside. The phrase, "don't judge a book by its cover" was clearly the case with that house.

Seth led them through the foyer and into the parlor. To their left was a grand staircase that resembled the one on the movie set 'Gone with the Wind'. It was massive, like a royal court. From what they were able to see at that point, the place was magnificent, full of grandeur, more than they would ever need. Beyond the parlor on the main floor, there were more rooms, big and spacious, all appearing to have twelve foot ceilings or higher.

The best part of the house was the all-season solarium on the lake side. Plenty of light entered the house there, and if Kellan wanted to, there seemed to be enough open space for him and Kaleb to fly at the same time.

"If you'd like, I can show you to your room. It's on this side of the house, second floor, facing the lake." Seth led them to the stairway at the back of the house.

Taking it all in, Neil asked, "What do you mean this side of the house?"

Seth answered, "The house is divided into sections, like a duplex. This side is the residential living space, and the other side, which is a bit smaller, is for the staff. When this place was an actual home, that side housed the servants, but now it's for the doctors, nurses and maintenance staff. They'll be here around the clock so you won't have to even pick up a dish if you don't want to. It's all set up. You guys are going to live like royals."

Neil wrung his hands a few times while they climbed the stairs. "I'm not comfortable having people waiting on me like that. Sure, once in a while would be nice, but every day would be strange."

Kellan put a hand over Neil's mouth. "Hush. You'll get used to it, and you need to be taken care of like the prince you are." Kellan removed his hand and kissed Neil.

Seth huffed when they finally made it to the second floor landing, like he'd just run a marathon. "You can do what you want, Neil. As much or a little. My guess is that you'll try to tackle the entire place, but always know that the staff is here to help you. Look how much it took out of me just climbing these stairs."

They turned into the main bedroom assigned to Kellan and Neil. The space was more than either of them could have imagined, one that would be suitable for a palace prince.

Neil glanced around the large bedroom, almost tripping over Dylan who darted in front of his feet to get inside. The room was for the two of them and Dylan, but could easily handle six more. The place combined a vintage color palette with modern décor, the result cozy and welcoming even in bright light.

Kellan let go of Neil's hand and headed for the fireplace along the wall facing the foot of the bed. It was mammoth in size and he could actually stand in it if he wanted to, but seeing the fire burning inside it gave him good reason not to test his guess on the measurements.

Attracted to the crackling flame and how it made Kellan glow, Neil walked around the bed placed in the center of the room and stood next to his shining angel, sweetly kissing him on the cheek in front of the fire.

Seth faced them and said, "As you can tell, this is your sleeping quarters. Around the corner over there is the en suite bathroom. It's meant more for relaxation than freshening up. The shower's even large enough for Kellan. You should check it out."

Kellan made his way to the bathroom, and while standing in the shower he approved of, his voice echoed when he asked, "When do we get to see Kaleb?"

"Soon," Seth hollered back. "For now, why don't I show you his bedroom down the hall?"

Neil's stomach grumbled.

"You hungry, Neil?" Seth asked.

"No, not hungry. The thought of being face to face with Kaleb has me a little tense."

As they walked to Kaleb's room, Seth mentioned that he didn't have all day to show them every room in the house, and that he'd leave it up to them to finish the tour on their own. It was their home, so roaming it freely was up to them if they wanted.

Stepping up to Kaleb's room where the door had been left open, and feeling a bit anxious as if Kaleb was inside waiting for them, Kellan took Neil's hand before entering the bedroom. Everything inside was so much smaller than what they were used to, and clearly designed for small children. It was organized very neatly with minimal items strategically placed for a kid with wings. Whoever decorated the place had thought it through carefully. Unlike the expected powder blue room that would typically be for a boy, this one had every color of the rainbow. It wasn't princess bright with a ton of sparkle but rather displayed calming tones that were soft and powdery. To Kellan, the room was the sweetest he'd ever seen, and he liked that it wasn't in any way gender specific. At least that's the way he saw it. If a boy was partial to pinks and yellows, Kellan was completely okay with that, and if a boy was attracted to blue and brown tones, that was okay too.

Briefly glancing around while repositioning a stuffed black bear sitting on one of the two twin beds in the room, Seth pointed out the intercom system hanging on the wall beside the door. "Every room in the house is equipped with a smart automation tablet. They control everything inside and outside the house. The master and utility room are the main dashboards and can put the whole house on lockdown, whereas Kaleb's can only make and receive calls as well as do video face-time. You know kids—give 'em a ladder, they'll use it to get on the roof. To prevent those kid-like attempts, limited features were programed into their tablets, but, you're welcome to add and delete whatever you like. I haven't met Kaleb yet, but I'm sure he's like most other kids when it comes to mischief. Anyway, when you need to get hold of somebody, just enter a location or a person you'd like to connect with and then tap send. It's that simple, works the same way a smart phone does. The face-time is optional and can be activated by simply tapping the pictogram of the little camera in the corner."

Totally fascinated with electronics and what the devices were able to do, Kellan swiped a finger over the screen a few times and found the tablets contact list. There were locations around the home as well as individual names of people he presumed were going to be staying someplace in the house. Eager to see if his and Neil's names had already been programmed, he scrolled to 'Master bedroom' and selected it. When it populated, he saw both their names were linked to it. He smiled and then swiped again, moving quickly to Neil's name where it didn't come up as his alone, but displayed as Neil & Kellan, and the same when he looked at Kellan & Neil. Seeing that made Kellan realize the military recognized them as a couple, not just individuals. It finally felt like a family life was coming together as it should. Above his name was Kaleb's, and that's when the reality of it all hit him. He was a dad, and was about to see his kid for the first time. That thought made him wonder what Kaleb was going to be like. Was the kid really a spitting image of himself, like having similar characteristics and wings he was able to change from light to dark? When they had seen him in the recorded videos, there was mention that he resembled Kellan, and could clearly identify Kaleb as his offspring.

Upon leaving Kaleb's room, Seth told them he needed to get settled in himself, explaining that he had his own apartment in another part of the house where the medical staff was set up to live. That part had private entries from the outside, making the residence seem more like personal condo's than being part of the mini mansion. Kellan was delighted to hear Seth was going to have the same responsibilities he had when at TC—his caretaker and friend. Seth also informed them he'd be taking on a few additional challenges that had not been disclosed to him just yet. He'd find that out in the morning, and hoped the assignments wouldn't be too much of a shock to his system.

Not much longer after Seth mentioned he needed to split, Kellan sensed in him that he was beginning to withdraw. The man's mouth had opened and shut a few times and nothing came out.

Seth shook his head as if he was trying to keep himself awake, and said, "I think I've reached my limit for the day. Everything else in here is standard stuff, spread wide because the house is so big, so are you guy's fine with finishing the tour on your own so I can hightail it out of here and get my own shit done?"

Without protest, Kellan agreed for both him and Neil. Shoulder to shoulder, the three of them filled the corridor on the way to the main entrance, casually checking every doorway they passed. Kellan's wings dragged along the walls as if he were dusting them clean.

At the door, Kellan gave Seth a grateful smile for all he'd shown them so far, and then he was out, out, out.

Chapter 37

As soon as Seth left the house, Kellan and Neil went into a family-style room next to the kitchen. It was a room that seemed cozier than the rest of the house because of its lower ceiling and smaller floor space. The television and comfy furnishings added to that relaxed feeling as well as the natural light filling the room through the large windows.

From what Kellan recollected in the Kaleb files he'd viewed a few days earlier, he recognized the room and seemed to remember images of him sitting on that sofa playing a video game in front of that television screen. He could picture him sitting on the sofa with his bright blue eyes, blond wispy hair, fair skin and big wings. When he looked at Neil, he wondered if he was thinking the same thing. Was that the room in the files or was there a duplicate house like the one they were standing in, and that was the place Kaleb was at the time of the recording? Maybe the military was already planning his move, and getting him accustomed to living outside of AZ. If that wasn't it, then what was it, because his understanding was Kaleb had never been to the house before?

Before they settled or did anything else, they heard a knock at the front door.

Dylan switched to protective mode and immediately ran to the foyer barking like it was already his house. He was good for that, but only when he wasn't alone. Otherwise he'd be like, *"no way in hell I'm answering that door if I don't know who's there."*

Neil stepped around Dylan and opened the door. Standing with Seth was the smallest angel they'd ever seen. There he was, the sweet little soul they'd wanted to meet, and like Kellan, the boy was wearing no shirt because his wings made it difficult to wear.

Dylan calmed down and let out tiny whimpers, and Neil whispered, "Oh, sweet Lord Almighty."

Standing with Neil and also staring, Kellan's eyes instantly glazed over when he met the most amazing pair of blue eyes surrounded by the longest lashes he'd ever seen. He moved his gaze to the tiny boy's shaggy blond hair and then to his wings. Kellan didn't know what to say to the most beautiful boy in the world who immediately mesmerized him. The young boy's beauty and the shock of finally seeing him had Kellan immediately tongue-tied, unable to utter a word as he and his son stared at each other. Kellan's heart sped up. The thumping jumped into his throat, beating so hard he felt the adrenaline flood his tongue with a bitter taste. He swallowed to get rid of it. His hand lifted to his chin. One finger brushing lightly over his lips.

ೞ ౠ

The winged child gave Kellan a funny look, like there was something wrong with the gigantic angel standing there looking down on him. Obviously, Kaleb had never seen another person with wings before, and for that reason, he appeared dazed. Kaleb shyly giggled and then moved closer to Seth's side.

All his life, Kaleb had understood himself to be the only angel alive, at least that's what he was led to believe. If he had questioned it, which he never thought to, perhaps he would have been told.

Kaleb stood still as Kellan knelt down in front of the fragile looking angel. Looking directly at Kaleb's face, Kellan saw his own image right there with him, as though he'd shifted back in time.

"Are you my dad?" The question immediately sealed a precious bond when Kaleb whispered those words.

Kaleb's voice caused Kellan's chest to flutter and his breath to catch. At that moment, Kellan looked to the floor. A tear came out of nowhere and fell to the floor. Returning his gaze to Kaleb, Kellan whispered, "Yes, Kaleb. I'm your dad."

Kaleb wrinkled his little nose, and dimples formed in his cheeks when he smiled. "That's what they told me, but I thought I better ask." His head tilted and his lips pursed smartly.

Kellan and Neil were speechless after hearing how intelligent the boy's vocabulary appeared to be.

Pointing at Neil, Kaleb asked. "Who's that? Is he mine, too?"

Smiling at Kaleb's claim to the human, Kellan answered, "This is Neil. He's mine, but I will certainly share him with you." He reached up and took Neil's hand.

Walking behind Neil and lifting the back of his shirt, Kaleb peeked under it before quickly skipping back to the same place he started. "Where are your wings, Mr. Neil?"

Kaleb had asked the question so seriously, that Neil seemed to have been caught off guard, and that left Kaleb without an answer.

Being familiar with some of the innocent questions Kellan had asked while growing up, Seth answered for Neil. "Neil is like me, Kaleb. He was born without wings. He's special in many other ways."

Kaleb wrinkled his nose and then questioned, "But when my dad wants to fly, how can Neil go with him if he doesn't have any wings?"

Kellan curled his arm, making a muscle with his bicep that looked like a football to Kaleb. "Your dad is very strong, Kaleb. I can carry Neil very easily in my arms when I fly. Why don't we go out in the sunshine and I can show you."

Having no fear, Kaleb tucked in his wings and gladly took Kellan's hand. "Will I be big and strong like you some day?"

"I'm sure you will be," Kellan answered.

Hand in hand, Kaleb and Kellan headed out the front entry before Seth and Neil had, and when they all made it to a wide open area outdoors, Kellan let go of Kaleb's small hand and spread his wings. His feathers wavered when the wind blew over them. Watching Kaleb, Kellan asked, "Are you ready to see your dad fly?"

Kaleb nodded, his mouth hanging open when he saw how large Kellan's wings were. Before Kaleb could say anything, Kellan took off running and jumped into the wind, snapping his wings out and pushing them down hard. Upward he surged, rising higher. Banking, Kellan dove toward the ground, added a sharp twist to the left and scooping Neil into his arms.

It wasn't difficult for Kaleb to be astonished by how effortlessly Kellan coasted in and scooped Neil into his arms. He grinned as Kellan smiled back.

After a few wide circles, Kaleb studied Kellan's fancy maneuvering as he ascended, and admired his smooth forward wing beats that brought them to a hover. Afraid to blink, Kaleb watched Kellan gently set Neil on the ground next to Dylan.

"That's how we carry the wingless, young man," Kellan said.

In a rush, Kellan spun and forced his wings into a hard downbeat that pushed him straight up into the sky. He added a few twists, spins and crazy dives that helped release all the energy and excitement from meeting his son for the first time.

Unable to contain his excitement alongside Dylan who was yipping, Kaleb hopped up and down while clapping his hands. Before he knew it, his wings started beating and his feet lifted off the ground. He went with it, took charge of the wind and flew.

Simultaneously, Neil and Seth brought their hands to their mouths, covering them while looking up at the two angels in the sky. Their expressions clearly displayed they were amazed with what they were looking at.

Kaleb went up fast, as if the headwinds carried him away, meeting Kellan in the sky before spiraling ahead of him. Kaleb banked left, then right. He went up and then down, playfully flying beside his winged dad. They were high, and the land below looked so far away. With them, birds flew—a falcon or a hawk. It looked to Kaleb as if they were checking them out, probably thinking, *Man, those are some goofy looking birds.*

After showing off his instinctive skills, Kaleb steadied his flight and soared at his father's side. Their wingtips brushed one another as if they were reaching for the other's touch. Suddenly, Kaleb dipped away, soaring lower in a wide open circle. As he descended, Kaleb noticed Kellan had stopped, high above, hovering.

Kaleb crazily spun even further. "Down here, Dad," he shouted and waved, making sure his father knew where he was. Then he flew slower, eager to have Kellan closer to him. As though Kellan had sensed Kaleb's wish, he dropped like an arrow, piercing the air feet first. He caught wind with open wings when he came upon Kaleb's side. While hovering with slow beating wings, Kellan reached out to Kaleb, pulling his boy against his chest and hugging him for all he was worth. Tightly. Holding him. Adoring him.

Despite his growing anxiety to be flying beside his dad, Kaleb treasured the hold Kellan had on him, and as the embrace got tighter, he sensed Kellan didn't want to let him go.

Kellan whispered, "I've missed you, and I'm sorry I wasn't with you all this time." There was an unconditional bond taking place at that moment, one that neither could keep from happening. Kellan's wings began to slow their tempo even more, and they gently spun toward the ground.

Kaleb focused on Seth and Neil looking at them as Kellan set his feet on the ground. There was evidence on Neil's and Seth's faces that seemed as though the proof of God had landed right there in front of them, being blessed to witness such a beautiful image.

Several moments had passed, and Kellan was on his knees still hugging Kaleb. With a quivering tone, he said, "Oh my God, I love you, Kaleb." Then he kissed the little angel's cheek, holding the connection for several moments to make sure the love was absorbed.

While making noises because of the tight embrace Kellan had on him, Kaleb squeezed out a grumble, "Da-aad, you're embarrassing me."

Kaleb's funny words made Kellan smile and a joyful tear escape his eye. He chuckled and said, "From now on, no hugs *or* kisses in public." As difficult as it was, Kellan eased Kaleb out of the hug with a gentle hold on each skinny arm.

The separation didn't last long. Kaleb lunged back into Kellan, wrapped his arms around his neck and squeezed. "It's okay, Dad. It's just us." He gave Kellan a sloppy kiss on the cheek the way kids do and then blew into it, making a noise that sounded like gas was being passed. All so quickly and full of energy, Kaleb pulled back, laughing, raced from Kellan to Neil, where he leaned against him. Then he swiftly bent over to pet Dylan, paying close attention to the spots behind his ears.

Kellan mumbled, "And so it begins."

Chapter 38

After their flight in the open field, they approached the mansion at the waterside and sat on the porch to enjoy the sun going down on the other side of the lake.

Like many ten-year-old children, Kaleb was full of questions, and as he asked each one of them, he moved around the deck between Seth, Neil and Kellan. A few times, he petted Dylan on the head as he passed by him.

On one round, Kaleb stopped to press his face against the glass doors that led to the inside of the house, framing his face with his hands to ward away any glare. "Whoa! This place is huger than I thought, and that's the biggest TV screen I've ever seen. Awesomeness."

Kaleb's enthusiastic outburst was a surprise to Neil and Kellan, and their eyes met, each mirroring the same question. They'd understood from the recorded video feeds that Kaleb had been there before, sitting on the sofa while learning to fly a plane on that TV screen he'd seemingly never seen before. Perhaps

Kaleb wasn't recognizing the inside because he was looking at it from the outside. Keeping that in mind and knowing kid's rarely pay attention to details when they aren't interested, Kellan and Neil shrugged it off as no big deal.

As soon as Kaleb pulled away from the plate glass door, the first question he asked Kellan was where Mister Trotsky was. After that, and practically within the same sentence, he asked where his school was and if Trotsky might be there.

Kellan didn't answer either question, but instead insisted that Seth explain to Kaleb that Mister Trotsky might still be at the school in Arizona. It was important to Kellan that Kaleb be given honest information about what was going on, and that everything would be okay with his new classes at the mansion.

"Who will be my teacher if Mister Trotsky won't be?" Kaleb asked, his face looking worried. "I remember Mister Trotsky saying he would be here."

Kellan reached out for Kaleb, taking him by the hand. It was so small compared to his own, almost half the size. "It'll be okay, Kaleb. I heard you were going to have one of the best teachers on the planet." That comment made Seth smile.

So he could look Kaleb eye to eye, Kellan lifted him up onto the rail of the porch, setting him there and letting his wings dangle to the ground behind him. "Didn't you say you wanted to grow up just like me? Big and strong."

Kaleb shyly nodded.

"Well, this is your chance. You're going to have the same teacher I had when I was growing up..." Kellan glanced at Seth, "...and he's looking forward to teaching you everything he taught me."

There was that funny look again where Kaleb might be thinking there was something wrong with Kellan. Every part of his little face squeezed together into a knot and his head tilted with it.

"Let's play a game. Why don't you guess who your teacher might be?" Kellan said.

Kaleb first pointed straight ahead, poking Kellan in the chest, and then hollered, "You!"

Kellan shook his head. "No silly. Guess again."

Laughing, Kaleb then pointed to Dylan.

"He'd be perfect if you wanted to learn how to fetch sticks, bark the alphabet and wag your tail." Kellan shook head again. "Good guess, but you're not quite there yet."

That's when Kaleb got it right. He pointed at Seth and said, "It's him, right?"

"You guessed it. Seth will be your teacher and I bet you'll turn out just like your dad." Kellan wrangled his fingers through Kaleb's mop-top head of hair.

Kaleb asked if the school was nearby and when would he be able to see it. But before anybody could answer him, he rolled right into his next question. "Are we living here, Dad?"

Kellan loved hearing Kaleb call him dad, and seeing Neil's expression just then, he did too. After processing the questions without giving answers, Kellan lifted Kaleb from the rail and set him down on the porch floor.

Kaleb shook his wings and he walked over to Neil, laying a gentle hand on his knee and asked, "Are you going to live with us too, Mister Neil? You can if you want. I'm pretty sure my dad would really like it if you would."

Neil was spotted pulling his lips into his mouth, pinching the top and bottom between his teeth. That motion indicating he might be trying to hold back a chuckle or prevent any mention of how connected to Kellan he already was. The predicament Neil was in made him blush.

Kellan and Seth glanced at each other, exchanging a look of understanding that it was a good time as any to reveal who Neil was.

Moving quickly, Kellan stood behind Neil and said, "Neil is already part of our family, Kaleb." He reached down and held Neil's hand. "I love Neil and he loves me."

Kaleb pursed his lips and scratched his nose. One little finger slipped into a nostril. "So that means Neil is going to be my daddy?"

There was no further explanation needed, and by Kaleb's response, he might have already been introduced to the situation before he got there. Kellan lifted Neil's hand and kissed it. "Yes, Kaleb, Neil is your daddy."

They weren't expecting what came next.

Kaleb raised his arms above his head and hooted. "That's

awesome... so totally awesome. I have a dad, a daddy... and a dog." He hopped on both feet around the porch, his wings flopping against his back, insistent on taking flight.

"Whew! That went well," Neil sputtered.

Still excited, Kaleb took off running toward the stairway, leaped from the top step and into the air. He flew, doing loop-de-loops and midflight summersaults.

"I can see that kid's talent of flying was passed on from his father." Neil stood and faced Kellan. "Are you going to go get your son, dad?"

Kellan grinned from ear to ear. "No, daddy. I think we should just let our boy fly freely."

Kellan recalled that only a short time before Kaleb took off, the family was just himself and Neil. Now they were dad, daddy, dog *and* son. As Kaleb had said earlier, "How awesome is that?"

Chapter 39

They waited for Kaleb to get back from his blissful flight after he'd heard the news about having a family. When he finally returned, Kaleb looked as though he landed a bit hard and had to run really fast to keep from doing a total face plant in the dirt. He seemed to still be that excited. He pulled his wings in, folding them into a tight accordion against his back and started walking toward the house.

The four of them were still on the porch when Kaleb rounded the corner of the house. He had a look on his face that seemed to be thinking that exploring would be better than just sitting where they were.

Instead of waiting for the sun to go down, Kellan preferred to see the school Kaleb would be attending on the lower level of the mini-mansion. He more or less wanted to become familiar with where it was and how to get to it. He was committed now, and that was his duties as a dad kicking in. As soon as Kaleb made it to the top step, Kellan asked, "How'd you like to see your new classroom, Kaleb?"

The kid was like a rubber ball when something motivated him, and within seconds of being asked, he started jumping up and down on the tips of his toes. Due to the excitement, his wings expanded and started beating, putting him airborne after the first few hops. There it was—the Attention Deficit Hyperactivity Disorder kicked right in.

Neil laughed and so did Kellan, both guessing that the display of excitement meant Kaleb wanted to see the classroom.

To settle the hopper down, Kellan reached for one of Kaleb's hands and motioned for Neil to take the other, putting the bouncing bugger between them.

Instead of taking a route through the house, Kellan decided it would be a better idea to walk outside and go through the main entry to the school on the lower level. He preferred to keep the main house feeling like a home and not associate it too closely with medical and school visits. "Follow Seth. He'll show us the way."

When they reached the front entry of the school, Kellan stepped aside to let Seth open the door and lead them through the hallways to the classroom. Once they got there, it looked to only have enough space for three or four students, and it would be a bit crowded if there were any more than that.

Kellan heard Kaleb singing, thought it was cute the way his soft cherubic voice reverberated acoustically off the tiled walls. He turned toward Kaleb and asked, "What's that song you're singing, Kaleb?"

"Oun't know, just a song. But it's a good one, huh?" Kaleb answered.

Kellan and Neil let go of Kaleb's hands at the same time and watched him take off for the book shelf at the back of the room, his wings banging into everything as if he forgot he had them. He went straight for one that had super heroes, hollering he wanted to be one someday, but mentioned he'd wait until he was about fourteen and a half when he'd have all the muscles needed to save the world.

Seth and Neil entered the room after Kaleb, and then Kellan followed, but was forced to stay at the door because of the limited space inside. Behind them, the door's spring-forced hinges automatically pulled it closed.

Kellan hunched over what looked like a laboratory table at the front of the room and watched Kaleb run a finger over the binding of each book on the shelf. When Kaleb lifted the super hero book and sniffed the pages, Kellan was certain the kid liked to read. Kellan knew right then that Christmas and birthdays were going to be easy.

At that moment, there was activity coming from the hallway outside the classroom door. They heard relaxed voices, and then the sound of the doorknob being turned.

The door was pulled opened by a heavy set clinician, and in front of him, a small skinny figure emerged through the entrance. The small boy was wearing flowery Hawaiian-style shorts, no shirt, and he was carrying the stuffed black bear from the bed they'd seen in Kaleb's room. The boy was clearly startled by the sight of strangers, including two angels, and his eyes reflected his disbelief.

Straightening up, Kellan turned when he heard a small voice resonate behind him that rattled out questions. "Who are you? Are you my new teacher? And why is there another bed in my bedroom upstairs?" Kellan's heart rate kicked into high gear.

At first, Kellan's brain couldn't grasp what his eyes were showing him. Thinking it was some kind of magic trick, he shifted his gaze across the room at Kaleb and then back at the thin figure in the doorway.

For the second time that day, Kellan met the most amazing pair of blue eyes framed by the same long lashes he'd seen on Kaleb. He gazed at the tiny angel's shaggy hair, blond too, like Kaleb's. He leant forward and fingered the boy's white-blond feathers. There was no doubt, he was there, and his wings were real. The little angel was a spitting image of himself and a copy of Kaleb.

Kellan stared at Seth, Neil and Kaleb in turn. Each one wore the same baffled expression, reflecting Kellan's own question: could it be possible?

Believing the angel was another child of his, Kellan felt his eyes mist over. He couldn't seem to control it. During the years of his being at the TC lab, Kellan had never been aware a single child of his existed, much less two. He was amazed that TC was able to keep such a major secret from him, even the files with the information were hidden well. Kellan swallowed anxiously and then asked him his name.

The clinician still standing behind the small angel answered, "His name is Kieran. And as I'm sure you're all wondering... yes, he's Kaleb's brother." He hesitated a few seconds before adding, "This is Kaleb's twin brother."

Kellan glanced at Seth and mouthed, "Did you know?" Before Seth had a chance to reply, Kellan turned his attention back to Kieran. He felt blindsided once more, a feeling clearly reflected by most of the people in the room.

With all that was going on, Kellan hadn't noticed that Kaleb moved from the bookshelf to his side until he felt the little body press up against him and grab two of his fingers with his tiny hand. Feeling the firm grip gave Kellan the idea that Kaleb was trying to show the new angel that the big man with large wings was his dad. Kaleb reached up with his other hand, locking Kellan's between his two small ones as best he could. Along with the possessive grip, there was a look on Kaleb's face that was recognizably one of wonder, one that seemed he was trying to figure out what he was supposed to say to his mirrored image looking back at him.

Deciding to let Kaleb take the first step and introduce himself to Kieran, Kellan nudged him until he released the hold on his hand.

Kaleb told Kieran his name and then asked, "So... you're my brother?"

Kellan observed the interaction between the two of them, and the way it appeared, Kieran seemed quieter than Kaleb. It was noticeable by the way Kieran held is gaze on the floor most of the time and occasionally turned back toward the clinician as if looking for reassurance that it was okay to give an answer. As Kieran snuck a few peeks at Kaleb, his little hand was twisting and tugging on the teddy bear's ear, and that gave Kellan the impression that Kieran had become tense.

There was no answer from Kieran right away, yet when he did nod, everyone knew it would be yes. Kaleb smiled and told Kieran, "This is my dad, and him over there is my daddy. If you want, I will share." Kellan grinned, because he thought the way

Kaleb staked claim to him and Neil came off as being cute. The entire room had gone silent while waiting for some type of response from Kieran regarding Kaleb's offer, but the only thing the little angel did was tug on that poor bear's ear even harder than he had been. Before the pause stretched out to the point of being any more uncomfortable, Kellan quickly shifted the attention away from Kieran by introducing Seth.

Feeling a bit overwhelmed with everything at that point, Kellan was determined to get a handle on the situation and adjust to having another kid added to his fast growing family, if the cards were planned to be dealt that way. Presuming so, he would make it work, however, the person he was more concerned about adjusting was Neil, wondering if he'd be okay with raising two little angels instead of one.

Kellan's gaze shifted back to Kieran and Kaleb, who within a short period of time had wandered to one of the desks, found paper and pencils, and were drawing pictures of superheroes and strange creatures. While observing their behavior, Kellan realized these two kids weren't identical after all, but close enough that their minor differences hadn't been noticed until they sat down next to one another. He nudged Neil and remarked, "Check out their hands."

Neil remarked, "A lefty and a righty. I wonder if that was done deliberately?"

"I'm not sure, but, that'll make it easier for us to tell them apart."

With his eyes fixed on the two little angels, Kellan couldn't believe how amazing they were, and how the appearance of two individuals could be so similar. With Kieran now in the picture, a few things that confused Kellan were making better sense — the reason for two "twin" beds in Kaleb's room and why Kaleb didn't recognize the family room when he pressed his nose against the window earlier. All this time, Kaleb was the who Kellan thought was on the video feed, because he was the only small angel he'd known about, when actually, it was Kieran learning to fly that plane on the television screen. Aside from Kellan's intense fascination with his kids, all the adults were just as rooted in place as he was, mesmerized by the young angels, and as it seemed, if anybody made a move, the incredible image just might disappear.

With the conditions of the crowded room becoming warmer very quickly, Seth suggested the four of them move to the living area to get more acquainted with the newest member of their family.

Chapter 40

Once they gathered in the mansion's great room on the main level, there was no time wasted getting locked into a family embrace with Kieran and Kaleb caught in the middle. Kieran interlocked with his brother Kaleb like they'd always been together. The boys were acting as if the normal bond between twins had emerged seamlessly.

Kellan held on to everybody tightly, being in no hurry to let any of them go. He heard a few sniffles, understanding they were having trouble keeping their emotions in check. He had mist in his own eyes as well, however, he fought them back believing dads were supposed to b the protectors of the brood.

It took some time, but eventually, the family broke apart from the group hug in the middle of the room. Kaleb and Kieran stayed linked by holding hands like they were the best of friends. Because the kids were doing it, Kellan grabbed Neil's hand and did the same, but snuck in a chaste kiss that expressed his love, the sweet kind parents do in front of the children. He pulled back and laughed when he saw Kieran pointing a finger at them and heard him thundering, "Ew."

The entire experience that had recently taken place didn't seem real to Kellan, maybe because it came at him in one fell swoop. With that, it caused many different emotions within him to surface.

Kellan kept in mind that people always needed to be part in something. He wanted to, but maybe didn't really know how to go about it at the time. He'd never really, really loved anybody until Neil had come along. He was thankful that Neil was with him, and even with the blissful feeling of being blessed by that, he was also scared half to death about being a father to two youngsters. Neil's kiss, and all the love it conveyed, went a long way in alleviating his fears.

Because Kellan had always been a lone bird, something he's been wanting for a very long time was to be a part of a family. He felt strongly about that—everybody deserved one, and nobody should be denied one. As luck would have it, that something he himself needed to be part of came true the day Kaleb stood on the mansion's doorstep in front of him and Neil, and then again when Kieran asked who they all were when the little guy came across them in the small classroom.

As far as Kellan knew, he and probably Neil too, understood their life ahead would be the most amazing thing they'd ever have the pleasure of experiencing, during the smooth times and the rough. Neil had told him that it wouldn't be the same without the love of his life, his friend and companion to be there with him through it all—Kellan, his knight with wings. Kellan himself thought that nothing would be able to top that feeling—that it could only look up from that day forward.

"Can I have one more kiss before we start rearing these children?" Neil pleaded.

That's when laughter echoed from the ceiling. A sure sign some ruckus had started, distracting Neil's pleasant thoughts and causing Kellan to stop kissing him.

Neil and Kellan looked up.

"Hey guys. Didn't I hear your Daddy mention there was to be no flying in the house?"

"Yes dad," two little angel voices said.

Epilogue

The four of them, plus Dylan were finally at home, living peacefully in a place that felt far, far away. Wasn't that something?

After getting a sense of how quiet the place was, Kellan established the house was truly secluded the way they needed it to be, deep in a valley overlooking their own private lake and high mountain peaks. There were also the trees he liked so much, especially the ones that waved in the breeze as if trying to get his attention. That was the life. The twins and Neil seemed to love it as well. Dylan... his contented disposition gave the impression he could take it or leave it.

Kellan and Neil were learning honest-to-God patience for the first time in their lives. Raising two rambunctious ten year old twins with wings, when knowing nothing about child rearing, was proving to be quite the challenge. Many times Kellan thought those two would never grow up. But he'd rather they stay as they were — cute, lovable, and sort of cuddly.

243

Late one evening in September, Kellan was enjoying his time with Neil in front of the fireplace. Across the room, Kaleb and Kieran were standing on the sofa playing a video game on the sixty-five inch Samsung. The one that Kaleb thought was so awesome. The gaming images were incredibly lifelike, and by the looks of it, they were making a couple of hockey teams trash each other on an ice rink. The boys were controlling everything, and seemed to enjoy having the players beat the crap out of each other more than scoring points. It was, however, better to see the bloody mess on the big screen than to see the stains on the kids' clothes and wings. They were typical boys after all, which fighting matches were in the cards, and would probably continue until they realized knocking fists and feathers wouldn't get them anything other than a few bumps and bruises. Kellan pointed out those brawls as moments of brotherly love and mentioned that two dads were better than one when it came to splitting up fights between boys. Whenever the little whippersnappers tried to get away with a quickie, Kellan thought it was funny the way Neil kept after them with his, "I said no's." The tricky part for Neil was that the little angels could fly, and he couldn't.

Disciplining boys that age had its ups and downs, but they needed to know what was right from wrong. It was becoming part of the daily routine, but Kellan as well as Neil vowed to do whatever was necessary to make sure the angels grew into well-rounded young men who would value life the same way they did.

Kellan and Neil were committed to Kieran and Kaleb, putting the kids' wants and needs ahead of their own, which meant the things they enjoyed were purely becoming extinct. By the time evening arrived each night, they found themselves on the verge of exhausting, and their ritual of sticking their dicks into one another was becoming more and more trying. They were still completely captivated by the early stages of their love affair that sharing their bodies with each other was a total must. Even if it meant penetration only and falling asleep like that. With kids in the house, their daily passion was kept on the down-low, leaving the hollering, screaming, and dirty words a thing of the past, or when the boys were at school.

Between raising children with Neil, Kellan was troubled about how the government was planning to use the three of them in the future. More than himself, he was terrified as to what would come of the boys. They were his, and like most fathers, he'd do whatever it took to protect and keep them safe. Kellan did what he could to forget about what might happen; like using their DNA to perform genetic manipulations that would create new life forms. He struggled with the idea they'd be trained for some kind of ultimate battle, and the most frightening thought was they'd be taken away to military camps overseas. Double the scare, was them never coming back. They were all beautiful creatures created by the government, and it was important to Kellan to make them aware of how valuable the three of them were. His priority was to convince the military they were no different from any normal person, and that they weren't expendable, but loving beings who deserved to live and thrive like any human did. The wings were what made them seem like freaks, nothing else. With all the concerns Kellan had about the young angels, he did the best he could to keep his anxieties to himself so *his* worries weren't anybody else's.

Consequently, distractions from scientific experimentation on his children were essential. To make that happen, Kellan took his family on many outings, like a recent walk together in the gardens growing along the side of the house. All of them, including Dylan. It so happened to be early evening and the pinpoints of light were just beginning to flare in the sky, bringing out the stars that twinkled down on them. Crickets chirped a medley that quickly became a melody. Further ahead of their Dad and Daddy, Kieran and Kaleb ran together, occasionally flapping their wings that lifted them off the ground and back down again. From afar, they appeared to be birds picking at worms.

Holding Kellan's hand, Neil asked, "What's on your mind, Kellan?"

Lowering the phone after snapping pictures, Kellan told Neil he was extremely happy, had everything he wanted, and never wanted any of it to change. Ever. He kissed Neil, and added, "I love the freedom, our winged kids, and you. Believe it or not, this place. I'm glad I've been given the chance to pass on the enormous amount of love I have for you, give you my total heart. This is the life, Neil. This is what it's all about."

Taking a deep breath, Neil kissed his angel back. Holding it with gentle passion.

Breaking the lovebirds apart, Kieran and Kaleb sneakily flew in and screeched, one echoing the other, "Ew. Daddy is kissing Dad again. Ew. Germs." Then they sang, "Dad and Daddy sitting in a tree. K-I-S-S-I-N-G. First comes love. Then comes marriage. Then comes an angel in a baby carriage." They laughed hysterically, and as quickly as they zoomed in, they flew away.

Kellan grinned hugely when he heard the song the boys selected, and he felt Neil smiling just as big against his lips. Kellan raised a brow and said, "Marriage?"

ଓ ୬ଠ

Kellan was sitting up in bed with the back of Neil's head cradled in his lap looking up at him, giving him a ghost of a smile when he said, "We survived another day." His voice wispy. His face emotionless. He as well as Kellan knew, Kaleb and Kieran were handfuls. Chasing them, feeding them, and watching them grow, were the tasks that always put both of them into survival mode.

Holding the phone in his hand, Kellan opened a photograph he'd taken earlier that day. It was becoming one of his favorites. They were all in it. Smiling. Kellan was standing tall and majestic in the back, Neil in his arm at his left, and Kieran and Kaleb kneeling in the front row with Dylan. He positioned the picture in front of Neil, and heard him sweetly coo when he saw it.

Kellan remembered that moment. It made him smile, and then the thought hit him: He was at peace for the first time in years. Maybe ever. Hopefully it would continue for the rest of his life. However long that might be.

ABOUT THE AUTHOR

Gregory Jonathan Scott was born and raised in Grand Rapids, Michigan where he met Scott just out of high school and started a life with him before relocating to South Florida.

As a child, Gregory was always told he had a creative imagination and the artistic ability to transform a blank canvas into an eye catching work of art. Shortly after high school graduation, and together with his true love Scott, discovered the thrill of pottery and ceramic art. There was where the two of them opened a business for ceramists that rapidly became the first choice for any hobbyist, storefront and scholastic industry looking for supplies related to ceramics and pottery. During that time, Gregory was approached by art magazines to write short articles and educational columns pertaining to the ceramic artistry. Captivating readers by his writing style quickly grew, which ignited his desire to express himself further. Finding a love for writing, alongside his artistic hand, gave him inspiration to design and write M/M romance Novels.

Gregory and Scott are still together and are currently enjoying home life in South Florida with their lovable Shetland sheepdog and a sweet stray cat that showed up one day and decided to make their house her home.

Gregory Jonathan Scott

OTHER WORKS BY
Gregory Jonathan Scott

TAKE TO THE SKY SERIES
INTO THE HEADWINDS – 2ND BOOK
TAKE TO THE SKY – 1ST BOOK

PLUS

ENCOURAGED BY SPARKS
CRASHING INTO LOVE
THE PLANTATION AFFAIR
HEARTBREAK BEAT

Gregory Jonathan Scott

www.ingramcontent.com/pod-product-compliance
Lightning Source LLC
Chambersburg PA
CBHW031312170626
46807CB00001B/395